GW00371129

JULIET DYMOKE

Bend Sinister

London

DENNIS DOBSON

First published in Great Britain in 1962
by Jarrolds Publishers (London) Ltd
This edition published in Great Britain in 1975
by Dobson Books Ltd, 80 Kensington Church Street,
London W8
Printed in Great Britain by
Whitstable Litho Ltd, Whitstable, Kent

ISBN 0 234 77350 2

For my daughter
PATRICIA

Contents

'O lovely Monmouth, glory of our land,
Who for God's word did like a pillar stand.
Methought all joy would vanish from the earth
And pleasantness would stop with Monmouth's breath.'

Western Martyrology

Bend Sinister

PROLOGUE

Holland—July, 1685

IN THE slanting sunlight of a hot July afternoon Kit van Wyngarde stood on the steps of the house that had once been his home and stared up at the shuttered windows.

The façade rose high above him, grey and forbidding. It seemed to frown down upon him with eyeless disapproval, a deserted tomb from the long dead past. He felt its weight upon him and then, thankful that after today his responsibility for it would be over, he braced his shoulders and went up the steps. His fingers fumbled with the stiff lock before the door swung back to reveal the hall.

It was grey with neglect. Dust lay everywhere, thick on the solid Dutch furniture and hanging heavily in the long shafts of sunlight which poured in from the high windows of the gallery. Despite the warmth outside, he shivered.

Crossing the hall, he began to mount the stairs, one hand on the banister, glancing as he went at the portraits on the wall. Many of them were unmistakably van Wyngardes, with the high forehead and broad splayed nose that distinguished the family, and they seemed to stare disdainfully down upon him as if he was an intruder—as indeed he was.

He turned the corner and went quickly along the gallery to his grandmother's rooms. She was long since dead but her embroidery box stood as it had always done on a stool by her winged chair which was drawn close to the empty hearth as though expecting her.

He leaned against the door, the past flooding in on him, more real than this lonely present, for it was here, twenty-four years ago, when he was a mere boy of fifteen, that he had met the man who was to change his destiny and set the course of his life.

Now he was returned, alone and penniless, without hope, without anything except his memories. He pressed his head against the door and closed his eyes. How was he to bear it? How could any man live with the memories he had? Still as the silent house itself, he did not move for a long time.

At last, however, the sound of his name being called roused him and returning to the gallery he leaned over the balustrade to see his servant in the hall below.

'What is it, Jerry?'

'Why, sir, you told me to wait outside for a few minutes and it's been more than an hour!'

'I'm sorry, Jerry, I'm afraid I forgot you. I had other things on my mind.'

Jeremy's round red face softened instantly. 'I know, sir. What do you wish me to do now?'

Kit hesitated, a heavy frown on his face. There were indeed things that had to be done and he shrank momentarily from facing them. But there was no escape and bracing his shoulders he said, 'I must go to Gouda so you had better fetch fresh horses.' He added involuntarily: 'It was good of you to come with me, Jerry. I seem to need you.'

Hodge's face grew even rosier. 'There weren't no question of it, sir,' he answered gruffly, and stumped away down the hall.

Kit withdrew from the banister, a faint weary smile on his face, and went slowly to the spiral stair at the end of the gallery, climbing to the room at the top.

It had been his when he was a boy. The old globe from which he had learned his geography still lay on the desk, and as he put out a finger and set it revolving it moved wheezily, cobwebs trailing behind it. He turned away and caught sight of himself in the large mirror that hung on the opposite wall. When he had last looked into it he had seen the laughing carefree face of a boy; now, almost with a shock, he saw a man older than his years. His long fair hair was streaked with grey at the temples, his eyes lined and sunk with grief, and it was as if in that transition he saw the whole of his life written in the square of glass. Not wanting to look any more, he sat down on the window-seat, flinging wide the casement. The sun was sinking but it was still warm and the evening breeze felt pleasant against his face, yet even the familiarity of this place meant nothing to him now.

Aware of a need to blot out the present by turning to the past, he began thinking of that afternoon so long ago when a strange fortune had seized him, tossing him into a new world, a world that had given him everything a man could want, before it had crumbled, flinging him back homeless and nameless into the place of his childhood.

At first only jumbled recollections filled his mind—memories of the magnificent Rupert of the Rhine, of Harry Richmond, of the King he had never understood, of Bab May and Mark Rainsford and the 'mad' Earl of Rochester, of good-natured Tom Bruce and above all of Jamie. All the memories led to Jamie.

There had been women too and their images came before him— Ann with her voluptuous body and sensual mind who had debauched his boyhood and cheated him of his dreams; Cathy who had given him her love freely and whom he had hurt so deeply; and Elizabeth whom he had allowed to give him nothing until it was too late. But he dared not think of her. She was no more than five miles away, yet he could not, must not, go to her except to take his final leave.

To avoid thinking of her he tried to order his thoughts, to see the pageant clearly from the beginning, from that afternoon when Harry Richmond had come to fetch him. He remembered he had gone into the main square of The Hague to watch a parade of the Holland regiment and imagined himself a soldier.

.   .   .   .   .   .

A little later Jeremy Hodge opened the door softly. He had been searching the house for his master and when he saw him sitting there so still, with his eyes closed and that strange desperate look on his face, Jeremy turned with sudden decision and tiptoed out, unheard.

BOOK ONE

The Young Hectors 1661-1665

HE WAS going to be late for dinner and that, as far as his grand-mother was concerned, was one of the unforgivable sins. Racing down the wide street that led from the Binnenhof, embattled place of the House of Orange-Nassau at The Hague, he ran however less because he was late than because he was young and strong and delighted in the swiftness of his body, and when he reached the iron gates of his home he leapt up the steps two at a time. The door, massive and studded with square-headed nails, swung back before he could lift the knocker.

'Master Christian!' The anxious face of old Hans the steward appeared. 'It is past the dinner hour and Mevrouw——'

'I know,' he laughed, 'I know, she will scold me. But I forgot the time. I'll go up at once.'

'Wait, young master. You'd best change your coat, for Mevrouw has a——'

But he was gone, up the stairs and along the gallery to his grandmother's apartments. He opened the door of the little sitting-room after the briefest of knocks and went straight in.

'I am sorry I am late, madame, but there was a troop of——' He broke off abruptly, for he saw then that she was not alone.

She sat as usual in her winged chair, her claw-like hands clasped over her ebony stick; to the boy she had always been so old that she seemed ageless, but neither her tongue nor her wit had grown weary with the years, and he stood, now, glancing awkwardly, first at her and then at the stranger who leaned against the chimney-piece.

Kit had never seen him before. He was perhaps in his late thirties, a man of medium height and sturdy build, and his trim figure suggested the bearing of one trained in the military life and

17

physically disciplined. He was standing easily, one arm along the shelf, the other smoothing the curls of his brown periwig, but he was looking at Kit with peculiar intensity, his grey eyes fixed on the boy's face.

Kit stood still by the door. 'I beg your pardon, madame. I did not know——'

'Obviously you did not know I had a guest,' his grandmother interrupted sharply, 'otherwise you would have presented yourself in a more seemly manner.' She looked him up and down. 'You have not changed your dress.'

He flushed, the colour rising easily under his fair skin. 'No, madame, I was late.'

She turned to their visitor and said coldly in English: 'I must apologize for my grandson. His manners are usually rather better.'

The man by the hearth was smiling. 'When I was a boy,' he said in a pleasant conversational tone, 'I must admit the sight of a regiment on the march could make me lose count of time too. My father always said I would be a soldier.'

'And are you, sir?' Kit asked in his careful English, grateful for the stranger's understanding.

'I had the honour to serve in the French army with the Duke of York and before that I fought for his late Majesty in our unhappy civil wars. Now that King Charles is restored to his throne I command a troop of his guard.'

The old lady tapped her stick impatiently on the floor. 'Christian, you have not been properly presented. This is your mother's cousin, Colonel Richmond. He has come to ask my permission to take you into England with him. He offers to complete your education and obtain for you a place at court.'

For a moment Kit stared from one to the other, dumbfounded. Was it possible that he had heard aright, possible that this unknown cousin should be offering him a chance to move out of the narrow world that had already begun to irk him?

Since his father's death, nearly two years ago, this great house had become too quiet, too dominated by his grandmother. The only other occupant was his snappish aunt Sophia, widow of the old lady's second son, Dirk, and she, to his relief, was more often than not away visiting. There was no man in the family to guide or secure his way in life, and at a time when many boys were entering the houses of great men as pages or clerks, or leaving with other companions on a grand tour of Europe, he had stayed on at home.

Now, astonishingly and out of the blue, this chance had come to him—and to go to England, to the splendid court of the restoration, was beyond his wildest hopes. He became aware that the Colonel was speaking.

'Your father, Christian, once told me that should anything befall him he wished me to interest myself in you, especially as I have no son of my own. But when he died I was in Spain, and in no position to do anything for anyone. Now that the King is restored, and with him my fortune, it is very different.' And then, as if sensing the conflicting thoughts that must be running in the boy's head, he went on smoothly: 'It is a good thing for a young man to travel, to visit countries other than his own, and a new era is beginning now in England. There will be great opportunities for men with ambition.'

A flicker of excitement ran through Kit, but for all the new world the Colonel's words opened up before him, for all the golden promise that he had never been able to see in his own dominated country, an inherent loyalty, a tradition of caution, bred in him since babyhood, made him hesitate.

'I had thought,' he said, and wished his voice did not sound so uncertain, 'to serve the Orange.'

A faint smile crossed the old lady's face and she gave Richmond a look that was distinctly malicious.

'Naturally,' he answered, ignoring the glance. 'You are a van Wyngarde. But the Prince is only a child, is he not? He cannot yet be twelve years old and is a virtual prisoner as well.'

'That's true, sir,' Kit agreed, gravely, 'but I do my studies with him. We are both students at Leyden University.'

'The Grand Pensionary is well aware that he must educate the Prince so that he may one day occupy his position as Stadtholder in a fitting manner,' Mevrouw van Wyngarde put in. 'We may at this moment be a republic in name, but the nobles of this country still have some influence.'

'They can surely do little while the Prince is still a child,' her guest pointed out. He looked across at the tense eager boy opposite him. 'Your loyalty does you credit, but this is not the time for it. Let me remind you that King Charles is the Prince's uncle and will be anxious to see his nephew occupy his rightful place when he is of an age to do so. There may come a time when you can be of service to more than one Stuart. It is possible, you know.'

A silence fell, and years after Kit was to hear an echo of these words, and know that a man cannot serve two masters. Now, however, he saw nothing but the future that lay before him, the chance to go out into the world of men. He glanced uncertainly at his grandmother.

She reached out and took his hand in hers. 'The Colonel is right. It is an opportunity we ought not to miss. You will return well equipped when the time comes for you to give your service to the Orange.'

Kit returned her look steadily, the last shreds of dull duty falling away. 'Do you really wish me to go, madame?'

'I can see you wish to go and I would not stand in your way.' She gave his hand a quick pressure and turned back to their guest. 'Then it is settled. When do you wish to leave, Colonel?'

'In three days' time if Christian can be ready. I am instructed to join the Queen-Mother at Beauvais and accompany her and the King's son to London.'

Mevrouw sat up sharply. 'The King's son? You cannot mean James Walter or Barlow or however he is called?'

'I do, madame. The King wishes him to reside at Whitehall.'

Kit leaned forward eagerly. 'But he used to live near here, sir.' He shot his grandmother a quick look and added cautiously, 'I knew him a little.'

The old lady snorted. 'Not with my approval. The son of a trull who has had more lovers than she can number! Why, the King cannot even be sure the child is his.'

For the first time Richmond lost his tactful manner. 'Madame, I assure you he does not doubt it, and indeed——'

She shrugged her shoulders, interrupting without ceremony. 'Well, I suppose he is not the first monarch to honour a by-blow. Let us hope he begets an heir with equal ease. Christian!' She turned sharply on her grandson. 'You will be late for your studies. If you should see Mynheer de Witt at the palace pray tell him I will send a letter tomorrow, informing him of our plans for you.' She looked him up and down for a moment. 'In a week,' she said at last, and in a curiously harsh voice, 'in a week you will be at Whitehall.'

'*Serviat aeternai quia parvo nesciat uti.*' The boy at the big desk stared at the words, his forehead creased with anxiety. He was alone in the large, sombrely furnished room, and once or twice he stared longingly out of the window to the sunshine beyond.

'. . . *parvo nesciat uti,*' he repeated, and chewed at the end of his pen. Then, as the door opened, he turned round expectantly. 'Ah, van Wyngarde. I cannot do my Horace. Be so kind as to assist me.'

He spoke in a grave adult manner, quite unlike that of a boy of eleven, but William of Orange had not had a normal childhood and he was not a normal boy. He never addressed even his friends informally and he behaved as he had been taught that a great-grandson of William the Silent should behave.

'It is a difficult passage,' he added, defensively, 'and my head aches today.'

Kit came over to the desk and leaned over his shoulder. 'Let me see. Yes, you have "he will be a slave for ever" correctly, but then comes "because he does not know how, *uti* to use, *parvo* small means".'

The Prince's brow cleared. 'I see. Thank you, van Wyngarde.' He wrote the words in a clear bold hand and then sat back, looking at them thoughtfully. 'It is a very apt sentence, is it not?'

Kit glanced at him. 'Your Highness refers it to yourself?'

William leaned his elbows on the desk, his large eyes brooding and dark with suppressed feeling. He had been pushed from pillar to post ever since his birth, shortly after his father's death; he had been squabbled over by his mother, Mary Stuart, and his grand-mother; adopted by the State; guarded and educated by the Re-publican, John de Witt, and he had learned early the solitary nature of his position. He was William, by the grace of God Prince of Orange and hereditary Stadtholder of the United Provinces, and yet—he was nothing.

He clenched his fist. 'I will not always be a child or a slave, van Wyngarde, and when I am grown I will learn how to use any means, small or large, to gain my way. You will see.'

'I believe it,' Kit said simply. However strong a hold the de Witt brothers had on Holland now, he was sure that when William was a man the Orange party would put him in his rightful place. He was quite used to the Prince's outbursts, for William had few friends he could trust; then, unable to keep his own news to himself, he told William of the unknown cousin he had found waiting for him at home this morning.

William listened in silence and when Kit had finished regarded him with his large hazel eyes. 'You are fortunate,' he said, and got down from his chair. He was a slight thin boy, troubled always with asthma, and his face had a permanent pallor. 'I shall be sorry to see you go, but I wish you well at my uncle's court.'

'Did you ever meet him?'

'Once. He came to see my mother.' William's eyes shadowed, for that mother had been dead less than a year. 'He is tall and black. I remember he made us all laugh and——' He did not finish the sentence, for at that moment the door opened and the Grand Pensionary himself came in.

'Well, sirs, is your Latin finished?' Tall and well built and now in his middle fifties, the Pensionary had the air of a man sober and wise and well versed in dealing with other men and other nations as well as the constant dangers that threatened his country. He glanced from Kit, his eyes taking in the defiant Orange ribbons that decorated his hat, to William who still stood by the window. 'You do not seem to be at work.'

William spoke stiffly. 'Van Wyngarde has been telling me, sir, that he is leaving us to travel into England.'

The Pensionary turned expectantly to Kit who explained, sensing as he did so the disapproval with which his words were received.

'I see.' There was a heavy frown on de Witt's face. 'It seems to me a pity that so many sons of our noble houses should be so eager to hasten away. There is much for you to learn here.' He became aware that both boys were staring at him in awkward silence and sighed a little. 'Well, I'll say no more. Pray continue your studies, gentlemen.'

When he had gone William said, 'He knows well enough where you will give your loyalty when the time comes.' He looked at Kit with a solemn expression in his large eyes. 'I trust you not to forget that, van Wyngarde—nor that you are a Dutchman. You will come back, will you not?'

'Of course,' Kit said, but William's intensity embarrassed him. He wanted to serve the Orange, but when they were men, not boys in this arid, half-prisoned existence. As soon as he could he

took leave of William and went out into the courtyard—conscious
that he was also going out into a new freedom.

.   .   .   .   .

Three days later he set off for England with the Colonel, glad
when the farewells were over and the coach, piled high with
baggage, was rolling away over the cobbles. He leaned out for one
last glimpse of the turret where he had always slept and, aware of
the enormity of leaving home, closed his eyes. When he opened
them the Huis van Wyngarde was gone behind the trees.

Unknown to him, Colonel Richmond was studying his young
companion. He saw a face framed in long fair hair that fell straight
to his shoulders, only a few strands cut short to lie on a broad forehead; his brows and lashes were much darker and his eyes, long and
grey, held a strangely grave look for one so young, but there was
intelligence in the thin face and despite the gravity a hint of humour.
Richmond liked what he saw.

'You were very interested in my soldier's talk,' he remarked at
last. 'Had you ever thought to enter an army?'

'I used to think I would like it, but I fear I have not the stomach
for it.'

Richmond smiled. 'Oh? What makes you say that?'

'I don't know—well, perhaps because I once saw a man run
down by a carriage. His brains were splashed all over the cobbles.'
He added, thoughtfully, 'I was sick.'

Richmond's smile grew. 'A man does not have to like such a
sight to make him a good soldier.' This boy beside him might be
sensitive but he had not, Richmond thought, the look of a coward,
either moral or physical.

At noon they stopped for a meal, and Richmond questioned him
about his friendship with the King's son.

'We used to play together until he went away,' Kit explained.
'His mother was pretty and very kind to me, but I am afraid my
grandmother did not like me to visit her house.'

Richmond suppressed a smile, for Lucy Walter could hardly be
called respectable. 'Perhaps not. Anyway, his Majesty wishes the
past forgotten. He is to be Lord Crofts' ward, as you are now mine.'

'Why, sir? I mean, why should Jamie be Lord Crofts' ward
and not just the King's son?'

'Because,' Richmond said carefully, 'although he is the King's son, you probably know he was not born in wedlock, and there are those who will be jealous of the King's love for him. It is best that his origins should be forgotten.'

Kit's brow creased. 'I see. I am glad I am not a King's bastard,' he added philosophically, and the Colonel was forced to hide his mouth behind his napkin.

At Beauvais they found the Queen-Mother and her train lodged in the house of a French nobleman and there Richmond paid his respects to her and presented his ward.

Kit answered her questions politely, a little in awe of this thin wrinkled lady whose regal hauteur, for so long her only weapon against the world, was somewhat overpowering.

Then the door burst open and a light-footed figure came flying across the room, brown curls blown and brown eyes bright with eagerness. Kit stood still, aware of acute embarrassment as the newcomer caught his hands.

'Christian van Wyngarde, you remember me, do you not? I have not forgotten you. Grandmère,' he turned to Henrietta Maria with a graceful bow, 'Grandmère, will you give us leave to go into the garden?'

His manner was naïve and charming and even the Queen-Mother's severe expression softened a little as she gave her consent. He seized Kit's arm then and hurried him away out of the formal gathering of adults into the garden beyond, where he sat himself down on the terrace steps, his long legs in their blue satin breeches stretched out in front of him. He was two years younger than his companion but quite as tall.

''Pon my soul, it's good to see you again. There are no other boys here and it's mighty dull. Do you recall how we used to meet in the square and the Binnenhof guards would not let me sail my boat on the lake? Do you still live in the big house with the iron gates?'

Kit found it almost impossible to recognize the little dark boy he had once played with in this lively youth with the dazzling smile and astonishing beauty of person. He thought of William and his gravity and then, glancing again at the King's son, felt himself respond overwhelmingly to the eagerly proferred friendship.

'I'm glad to see you too, Jamie—and that we're going to London together.'

'Yes. But I've been there before, with my mother.' For a

moment a graver look came into the brown eyes. 'They took me away from her, you know. I'm not sure why. Now they say she is dead.' He paused, and a momentary desolate child-like grief crossed his face. Then it vanished as quickly as any unpleasant thought from his quicksilver mind. 'But I don't want to think of the past. We are going to Whitehall and it is a splendid palace. We shall have banquets every night, and masques and dancing.' He clapped Kit on the shoulder, his eyes sparkling. 'We shall enjoy ourselves, you and I —and I cannot call you anything so solemn and so Dutch as Christian. I shall call you Kit.'

So Kit he was, from then on, not only to Jamie but to everyone else, and Jamie's warm welcome overcame the worst of his shyness.

On the voyage across the Channel next day they stood side by side on the deck, revelling in the high seas that sent the Queen-Mother and her ladies scurrying below.

When at last the storm abated a little, Colonel Richmond took the two boys to the rail that they might see the cliffs of England and the King's barge as it came to meet them. Jamie chattered excitedly but Kit stood silent.

An unaccountable feeling had seized him. It was like a call of the blood, a recognition that he was returning home, to the place where his roots lay—yet he was more than half Dutch and he had never known his English mother, nor left Holland before. He stared in utter bewilderment at the rising cliffs, at the woods beyond the grey solidity of Dover Castle. What was it about this greenness of hills, this whiteness of cliffs that drew him, claimed him?

He was so absorbed that he was taken unawares when, barely ten yards from where he was standing, King Charles stepped aboard to greet his mother. Then he turned and hugged his son with a boyish laugh, all his delight in him showing in his face. Very tall and slim and dressed in sable black, Charles's body was loose-limbed and graceful and Kit became aware at once of the fascination of his personality, of the dark, vivid, saturnine face redeemed by a brilliant smile.

More gentlemen came aboard and Richmond pointed them out.

'There's the Duke of York, his Majesty's brother, and that's Prince Rupert, his cousin. There's his Grace of Buckingham in the silver and pink coat, and Baptist May, groom of the bedchamber to the King. That's Mr. Secretary Nicholas, and Ned Hyde behind him; Ned's Earl of Clarendon now, and Lord Chancellor too, and well he deserves his honours.'

Kit listened to the flow of names and descriptions, but he had not been able to take his eyes off his Highness Prince Rupert of the Rhine. He had heard tales of this cavalier prince, of his astonishing military feats, of his sea voyages, of his temper, and above all of his ability as a swordsman, a horseman and a leader of men. Rupert, he thought, was quite the tallest man he had ever seen, and broad-shouldered too; a long periwig hung in curls about his shoulders and he was magnificently dressed in scarlet and black—his favourite colours, as Kit was later to learn—but it was his face that was wholly compelling. A long aquiline nose jutted forward between strongly marked brows, while his chin proclaimed a stubborn will, and his dark snapping eyes missed nothing. He held himself aloof from the laughing concourse—dignified, silent, a little arrogant.

Kit felt bewildered, overawed by the brilliantly dressed men and women crowding the deck, by the talk and the laughter, the extravagant wit and flowing compliments. It was a strange alien world, and he wondered if he would ever learn to live in it. He was even more discomposed when a few minutes later Richmond, standing now by Rupert's side, beckoned him to join them.

'So,' Rupert said in his distinctive voice, 'this is the boy, Harry?' He stared so long into Kit's face that the latter felt a hot painful colour flood into it. He had not expected at this early stage to meet royalty, least of all this overpowering prince.

'Well, boy?' Rupert queried abruptly. 'I stand in need of a page. Will you serve me?'

Sheer astonishment robbed Kit of speech. He had thought he might enter some nobleman's household where, in comparative obscurity, he could learn to know this new world, but he had never, even in his wildest imaginings, thought he would be employed by a prince of the blood. He recalled with a feeling akin to horror that Rupert had once been nick-named 'the devil prince'—yet there was something in the strong face that drew him as surely as the white cliffs had done a few moments ago.

He answered involuntarily. 'If—if your Highness thinks I would be of use to you. . . .'

He saw the Prince exchange a curious glance with the Colonel, a glance that held amusement and something else that was hard to define.

'You will be more than that,' Rupert said.

2

For more than two years Kit's life was ruled by the sound of Rupert's voice. Harsh and resonant and still retaining its German accent, it called for him a dozen times a day and he scampered to obey, knowing it did not pay to keep his autocratic master waiting.

It took him a long time to get used to London, longer still to Whitehall.

He had ridden into the city with Colonel Richmond and was astonished at the sprawling, colourful, dirty maze that it was. In The Hague the streets were clean and tree-lined, swept by boys and washed regularly, but here in London no one seemed to care for cleanliness at all. The kennels that ran down the centre of the streets and were supposed to carry away rubbish were choked with filth of all kinds from kitchen litter to excrement, and the stench was something that even after long years at Whitehall he was to find hard to bear. But there was a virile life in this city that was quite unlike the sedate mannerliness of The Hague.

If London was a robust lecherous giant of a city, Whitehall, he soon learned, was no more than its cultured master, bearing the same attributes with a veneer of courtliness and luxury.

Prince Rupert had lodgings in the Stone Gallery above the Privy Gardens and Kit himself was allotted a room, though it was little more than a cupboard, which he was to share with another page, Tom Spinney.

His first encounter with the Prince was somewhat unnerving. On the morning of his arrival, Spinney, a cheerful friendly youth, had taken him into the reception chamber and was instructing him in his duties when their master stalked in, immense in riding-clothes and scarlet cloak, his face dark with anger.

'Have either of you,' he demanded, 'seen the yellow bitch?'

Dumbfounded, Kit gazed at the furious Palatine. He had not the slightest idea to what or whom Rupert referred, and wondered in horror if it could be to an errant mistress, though he had heard the Prince was abstemious in such matters.

Rupert turned to Tom. 'Did you let her out this morning?'

Spinney had gone scarlet with mortification. 'Y-yes, sir. She whined to go into the garden before your Highness was awake, so I——'

'Fool! Dolt!' Rupert roared. 'Don't you know by now that the palace teems with thieving knaves? They're eager to get their hands on any dog of mine or his Majesty's because they know we'll pay a reward to get it back.'

By this time, having tumbled to the nature of the lost object, Kit recovered himself sufficiently to address his master.

'If it please your Highness, I saw a yellow-coloured greyhound among the bushes in the garden not half an hour since.'

Rupert swung round. 'Did you, by gad! Then go and fetch her.'

So his first task was to crawl on hands and knees in the bushes of the King's garden and retrieve a snappish and unwilling animal that appeared to desire nothing more than to take a piece out of his leg.

Rupert was pleased. His piercing eyes bored into Kit's flushed face. 'Thank you, Christian. I think you and I will do very well together.'

His pages were part of his 'family' and he treated them, Kit discovered, with a mixture of fatherly care and military discipline. He was hot-tempered, demanding, energetic, and whether he was in attendance at Whitehall, in council at the Admiralty or working in his laboratory, he expected them to be within call so that one bellow would bring them running. It was, to say the least, daunting to a shy half-foreign boy, but the Prince saw that they had free time for sport and exercise and he lectured them frequently, warning them against over-indulgence in wine, too much interest in the petticoats and too much attention to gossip.

'Moderation,' he told them, 'that is the key to a man being master of himself. Allow yourselves no excesses and then nothing will master you.'

Permitting himself little relaxation or latitude, he spoke with feeling, and Kit, seeing the gay easy-going King imparting free manners and sexual laxity to the court, was secretly relieved that Rupert did not participate in the things which shocked his calvinistic upbringing. Painfully conscious of his awkward English, his stiff manners and plain clothes—for his grandmother did not believe in rich dress for youths—he tried to overcome these things, but he felt he cut a poor figure as he hurried about doing Rupert's bidding.

He was frequently lost in the maze of houses and courts, passages and alleys, coalyards and butteries, and at times his head whirled with the very size of it all, with the pageantry, the throngs of people who were allowed to wander freely in the public galleries, with the vast entertainments, the numberless courtiers and hangers-on.

But life teemed here, ran wild in the twisting alleys, crowded in the ramble of lodgings; it surged in the great halls and galleries, echoed in a drunken snatch of song, in a strain of music borne on the hot summer air, in the smothered laugh from a darkened chamber. It was vivid, engrossing, wholly demanding.

It captured Kit and held him prisoner, a bondage that was to last for more then twenty years.

.   .   .   .   .

But just now he was a page and Jamie was the King's son, and in a disappointment that grew daily he saw little likelihood that they would ever spend much time together.

When Jamie was married in the spring to Anna Scott, who was only twelve but Countess of Buccleuch in her own right, and at the same time created Duke of Monmouth and Buccleuch, Earl of Doncaster, Baron Scott of Tyndale and installed as a Knight of the Garter, he seemed to have moved into a world far beyond Kit's penetrating.

They snatched an hour together when they might, but for the most part Kit spent his free time in the more lowly company of other pages and he did not always keep free of trouble. One morning when he had been at Whitehall nearly eighteen months he came upon Tom Spinney talking with another page, a dark-haired boy whom he knew to be newly in attendance on the Duke of York. The Duchess, it seemed, was in the throes of giving birth to her second child and the dark boy was recounting the confusion prevailing in the ducal lodgings.

'You may thank your stars your master is unwed,' he was saying with feeling. 'I tell you, the scenes that go on in my master's apartments are beyond belief, what with his Highness flaunting his latest mistress and my lady Duchess having hysterics enough to

bring on a miscarriage!' He glanced at his companion. 'But no
doubt your prince leads you a dance?'

Spinney shrugged. 'No more than most, except that he commands us as if we were an army.'

The dark boy grinned. 'That must be why he is unwed. Can't
you imagine how he would treat a wife? "My lady, come forward,
right turn, to bed, quick march! Prepare for battle, ma'am!" ' He
mimicked the heavy German voice in a staccato fashion. 'Would
any lady take that lying down?' Collapsing with laughter at his
own joke, he added, 'At least my master is more of a man in his
amours than yours.'

Kit felt the hot blood rush to his face and without pausing to
think fell on the startled page. 'You lying dog, don't you dare open
your mouth to slander so great a prince. You bastard, you . . .' He
had his hands on the boy's shoulders, shaking him so violently that
the mocker, losing his balance from sheer surprise, fell over back-
wards. They rolled across the floor, grappling together to the
delighted and encouraging shouts of Spinney.

Still blind with anger and his desire to defend Rupert, Kit did
not hear a door open nor Spinney's hissed warning. Then the
familiar voice bellowed out.

'If you wish to brawl and make a fool of yourself, Christian,
you may do so at your pleasure, but not outside my lodgings.' And
with one deft movement Rupert seized his errant page by the collar.

Kit felt himself swung round in an iron grip and then the sting
of Rupert's cane on his behind as if he were a schoolboy. For a
moment he wriggled wildly but there was no escaping that grip.

The Prince shook him angrily and then released him. 'So you've
a temper!' he said, ironically. 'You must learn to master it, for I've
one too that will not tolerate such an exhibition of yours. Now go
and clean my boots. If I can't see my face in them when you've
done I'll thrash you again. And the rest of you, about your business
at once.'

They went, sheepishly, Kit with his face crimson with humiliation. He bore the Prince no resentment for this, for by this time
Rupert could do no wrong. All his boyish idealistic admiration for a
man who was every inch a man was laid at Rupert's feet.

The next day the dark page sought him out when he was
fetching some fresh linen from the laundress.

He came straight up to Kit and said bluntly: 'Spinney tells me you would not explain to the Prince why we were fighting. I honour you for that and would tell you that I meant nothing by what I said. It was idle talk, that's all.'

He held out his hand in so open a manner that Kit could not refuse his own, and they walked back to the royal apartments together. The boy told him his name was Mark Rainsford and that his father was Baron Rainsford of Westfield which bordered on Tolbrooke, Colonel Richmond's property.

'I am going home for Christmas,' he concluded. 'Will you be going to Tolbrooke with the Colonel?'

'I don't know,' Kit said, 'I should like it.' He eyed the thin wiry figure beside him, glancing at the lively intelligent face. He decided he also liked Mark Rainsford and approached the Colonel on the matter the next day. Richmond welcomed the idea, Rupert's permission was gained and on Christmas Eve, towards dusk, Richmond's carriage turned into the wide drive that led to his home.

He glanced at his young cousin. 'Well, Christian, it is a fine house, is it not?'

Kit leaned forward as the carriage circled the approach to the steps of the terrace. The house rose tall in the dusk of a winter afternoon, gabled and mullioned and built of warm red brick. Lights glowed and the door had been opened by the steward, on watch for his master's arrival.

'It is a very big house,' Kit said. 'But what has happened to that wing on the left?'

'It was destroyed during the late wars when we were under siege. General Fairfax offered me honourable surrender terms and I accepted them to save the rest of the house.' He glanced at his ward and smiled a little. 'Some of my friends thought I should have fought to the end—indeed a rumour did get about that the house had been destroyed and all of us in it slain.' There was a curious edge to his voice.

Kit stared up at the façade. 'I would not have wanted to see it burned. It would have served no purpose, surely?'

'That is what I thought,' Richmond agreed. 'It is no part of a soldier's duty to indulge in useless heroics.'

He looked pleased as he leaned forward to open the door.

On Christmas night, sitting on the stairs with Mark Rainsford and listening to the waits, Kit said: 'I like your English Christmas.

We were never quite so gay at home. Is your mother come? I met your father after church.'

Mark shook his head. 'No, did I not tell you? She was brought to bed only last night. I wanted a brother—I had four, you know, but they all died before they were breeched, poor little brats, and now the new baby is a girl!' He snorted in disgust.

Kit laughed. 'How is she named?'

'Elizabeth,' Mark told him indifferently, and went on to talk of the hunting they were to have the next day.

.   .   .   .   .

From that time on Kit spent most of his leisure hours with Mark. They began to discover London together, visiting the taverns and the new coffee-houses in Palace Yard or Spring Gardens. They went to St. Paul's, where they joined the throngs parading the aisles, spending rashly, as young men will, on new clothes in order to cut a dash among the other blades. At the theatre, the King's or the Duke of York's, they cheered or jeered the play from the cheapest seats in the house, and on one occasion got wildly drunk, an experience which Kit did not enjoy, for it only made him sick.

In the second spring he went home for a brief visit, and entertained his grandmother with a graphic account of his life at Whitehall.

'You're growing up, Christian,' she said, and her hand reached out for his in a familiar gesture. 'It seems it was a fortunate day when Colonel Richmond came.'

'I think so,' he said honestly. He had expected more caustic comments and he thought she looked older and more shrivelled. He felt sorry for her, sorry that his visit could be no more than two weeks, but somehow, after a re-acquaintance with Dutch austerity, he was glad to return to Whitehall.

On the first evening he went to supper at Hercules Pillars with Mark and Tom Spinney. Their pleasures were becoming a little more adult and they sat talking and drinking themselves into a state of mild inebriation until the landlord finally ejected them.

'Plague take the fellow,' Mark said truculently. 'I've no mind for bed yet, at least not my own. Let's see what Mother Creswold can offer us.'

Tom giggled. 'Last time I had a silly wench with spots.'

'Then try your luck again, my boy. Come, it's not yet midnight and we'll be there before the noble gallants can skim the cream. Are you coming, Kit?'

Aware of irritating nerves, Kit said with as much ease as he could that he was weary from his journey and would go home. He had crossed the courtyard below the Stone Gallery, wondering why he felt so desperately shy in the company of women, and in a spurt of annoyance, directed against himself, was running up the stairs two at a time when he cannoned straight into the Palatine Prince.

Rupert took him by the shoulders and swung him round so that he might see his face in the candlelight. 'Well, Christian, have you forgotten all my teaching in a week? Do I have to remind you again that no attendant should run in the palace? Pray walk, lest you should meet his Majesty.' He looked searchingly at his page. 'You are a little drunk, Christian. Well, no matter, you are not the fellow to over-indulge that way. Is Tom returned with you?' And then as Kit shook his head, flushing a little, he laughed. 'As I thought—I'm glad wenching is not to your taste. Self-discipline is more important.' He gave Kit's shoulder a quick squeeze and leaving him astonished by his apparent omniscience strode off down the dark passage.

Kit went away to his own room, oddly comforted, but there were times when he envied Mark's sophistication, Tom's blundering acquisitive search for knowledge, and most of all the new Duke of Monmouth's pleasing manner.

'I wish I could be as easy with people as you are,' he remarked once to the latter when they were coming from a game of tennis.

Monmouth glanced at him. 'My poor sobersides, are you wanting to be the courtier? I had much rather you were yourself.'

'That's not what I mean. Jamie, do you like dancing attendance on court ladies and paying them compliments?'

The Duke burst out laughing. 'Why, it means nothing. It is all part of a game. You must not take it so seriously.'

'It seems nothing is taken seriously at court,' Kit said, and then, aware that he had sounded priggish, added lamely, 'Well, a page does not have time for frivolity.'

Monmouth, he thought, had too much. The young Duke's life was all gaiety, dancing, playing cards, attending the theatre or racing his fine horses in the park or at Newmarket. His pockets were well filled and nothing out of his reach. Small wonder that a crowd of the wildest rakes in town attached themselves to him, knowing his father's love would protect him and them from any consequences of their folly.

It worried Kit, who saw no need to flout the law and convention in order to enjoy oneself. There seemed to be nothing, however, that he could do about it, until one evening, suddenly and dramatically, the gulf between his world and that of the King's son was bridged once and for all.

He had taken a letter from Rupert to Robert Boyle, the scientist, and was returning through Covent Garden when he heard a commotion on the other side of the square.

Outside a tavern a group of young gallants were gathered, shouting and laughing and apparently cheering on one of their company who was facing a stout and enraged watchman.

'Pray go home, sirs,' the latter was bawling, and at the same time brandishing his staff of office. 'You are become a great nuisance to soberer citizens. Now go home or I'll clap the lot of you in jail.'

'What, all by yourself?' queried a voice from the group, and the others shouted with laughter while the young man in front flourished his sword and ordered the watchman out of his path.

'Have at him, your Grace,' one of his companions called encouragingly. 'Send the fellow packing and show yourself fit for more than playing cards with the Queen's ladies.'

'Now then, young sir——' The watchman stepped forward and at the same time someone held high a lantern. In its light Kit saw embodied the voice he had recognized, saw Monmouth swaying unsteadily, his face flushed, his sword gripped in his hand. Behind him the faces of young Kit Monk and the seventeen-year-old Earl of Rochester betrayed their drunken state, while the lantern was held, somewhat precariously, by Baptist May. Leaning against the hitching rail, and urging on the infuriated young man, was the Duke of Buckingham.

All this Kit saw in one glance, but before he could decide whether to speak to Monmouth the latter took a step forward, shouting again to the watchman to give way.

The poor man, alone and uncertain what to do, seemed nevertheless determined to do what he considered his duty and rather foolishly came forward, waving his staff in an effort to make the Duke put up his sword.

Monmouth, beside himself with annoyance, part drunk and goaded on by Buckingham's lazy insinuations, tried to match his blade with the staff. After a moment's angry breathless struggle the watchman's boots seemed to slip on the cobbles and he fell heavily forward.

There was a gasp from the onlookers. The man had reeled sideways into the gutter, clutched at his stomach and then rolled over on to his back where he lay staring sightlessly up at the darkened sky.

'Oh God!' It was Monmouth who broke the silence. He stood trembling, his eyes, wide and fearful, fixed on the sword still in his hand but reddened in the lantern light. 'Oh God, is he dead?'

Without pausing to think, Kit ran full tilt across the square and, pushing the shaking young man aside, bent over the watchman.

Seeing who it was, Monmouth clutched at his arm in both relief and appeal. 'Kit! I never meant to do it, I swear I would never——'

'I know,' Kit said shortly, and put his hand over the man's heart, though he knew the truth already.

Bab May stepped forward and held the lantern over the up-turned face, repeating Monmouth's question.

'Aye, he's dead.' Kit glanced up and then at Buckingham. 'And for no more than doing his duty.'

Rochester yawned. 'He was a stupid fellow. We all saw how he rushed on my lord Monmouth's sword.'

Monmouth licked his lips. 'But I killed the man. What—what must I do?'

'Nothing,' Buckingham said tersely. 'You are the King's son.' He looked bored now with the whole incident. 'We all saw it was an accident and will bear you out.'

Kit stood up with sudden resolution. 'I saw it too, your Grace, and it was indeed an accident, but one that would not have happened but for your urging.'

A silence fell on the little group. Bab, still grasping the lantern, looked across at Kit in considerable surprise, while Rochester rocked back and forth on his heels, a faint smile twisting his mouth. Monk looked down at the dead man, saw the wound in his stomach, and clapping a hand over his mouth disappeared down an alley.

Buckingham's face went slowly red. 'Who the devil are you that you dare take me to task?' And when Kit, outwardly cool, informed him he added angrily, 'Then by God I'll see Prince Rupert dismisses you for your impertinence.'

'That, your Grace, will be as his Highness wishes. I spoke only the truth and,' Kit glanced down at the corpse at his feet, 'I think your Grace is aware of that.'

'Kit! Don't say any more.' Monmouth came forward and put a tentative hand on Buckingham's satin sleeve. In the light of the lantern it was plain he was near to tears. He looked down at the corpse and shivered. 'My lord, what should we do with him?'

'Good God,' Buckingham snapped irritably, 'what a pother about an obnoxious fellow who asked for what he got.'

Seeing a hackney carriage approach, he flicked his fingers at the driver and opened the door. 'Come, your Grace, you had best accompany me home to your father before there is more trouble.'

Something in his tone reached through the younger Duke's anxiety. He flushed. 'I will go home with Mr. van Wyngarde,' he said with dignity, and turned his back on Buckingham.

The latter shrugged and climbed into the coach. Rochester followed him in with a wry smile but Bab paused to touch Kit lightly on the arm.

'You're a level-headed fellow, whatever-your-name-is, and perhaps the best company for his Grace. If you will see him safe home I'll arrange for the man to be taken away. Good night to you both.' He climbed in and the carriage was driven away.

Monmouth shivered again. 'Let's go home, Kit. I—I can't bear to look at him any more. I never meant to harm the poor fellow.'

'I know.' Kit took his arm. 'But you are foolish, Jamie, to go out with men who have the advantage of you in years and experience and hard heads. Wait awhile, and beat them at the things you can do, racing, wrestling, riding. . . .'

He talked on, piloting the Duke back to Whitehall through the dark streets. He had forgotten he had been rude to a powerful nobleman. It was enough that he had been there when Jamie needed him.

.   .   .   .   .

In the morning he went to find Rupert, only to discover that his Highness had posted off at dawn to Chatham where the navy was refitting, preparing for the inevitable scrap at sea with their hereditary enemies, the Dutch. So instead Kit sought out Colonel Richmond, knowing he had easy access to the King.

Richmond listened in silence. Then he said: 'It was folly, Christian, and Buckingham ought to have known better, but it was no more than an unhappy accident. I'll see that his Majesty knows the truth.'

Kit heard no more and saw nothing of Monmouth for a week, as the King took him off racing to Newmarket.

Rupert rode back to London a few days afterwards and within an hour of his return had a public brawl with Buckingham. The latter, it appeared, had stabled his horses in that part of the mews which Rupert considered his and, when asked by the irate Prince what the devil he meant by it, replied that as his horses were superior in quality he considered them entitled to the best quarters. Whereat Rupert, in one of his rages, pulled Buckingham off his horse. The Duke lost his periwig and his dignity, and the affair would have ended with swords out had the King not fortunately been on hand to intervene.

Kit, delighted that Rupert had trounced Buckingham, nevertheless answered his master's summons on the following day with some trepidation. Rupert seldom sent formally for his pages, his custom being merely to bawl for them.

'Well, Christian,' he stood straddling the hearth, 'it seems I must part with you.'

Taken completely by surprise, Kit stared at him. 'I must leave your Highness?' He passed his tongue between lips gone dry. 'Sir, has his Grace . . .'

Rupert gave him a sharp look. 'I'm not sure which Duke you are referring to, but it is his Grace of Monmouth who is to rob me. He appears to have need of your sobering influence—or so his Majesty thinks. That affair a week back has been hushed up but he wants no repetition of such incidents.'

So great was his relief that Kit could say nothing and merely let out an involuntary sigh. Rupert smiled a little.

'Are you so pleased to leave me, then?'

The familiar hot flush that he could never quite control crept into Kit's cheeks. 'Sir! You know I did not mean . . .'

Rupert smiled. When he was in a good mood it was an extraordinarily sweet smile. 'I know you did not. But your time with me was coming to an end anyway—you were eighteen recently, were you not? It is time you moved on to another post.' He saw the slight apprehension in his page's face and went on: 'I am to tell you that his Majesty has been pleased to appoint you clerk to Sir Henry Lightfoot who is to be comptroller to the Duke and Duchess of Monmouth. Now that they are to have their own household, and no doubt their own debts, the King thinks it better that the disbursing of their monies should be in other hands than those of the Duchess's mother. Young Monmouth is vain and silly and wild but not I think either cruel or licentious, though he is easy imposed on. He appears to have a fondness for you and the King believes you may keep him from too much folly.'

Kit had listened to this speech in growing astonishment. Awed by this sign of the King's notice of him, he was aware that it was rather more of a responsibility than he had bargained for. But he was to go to Monmouth as he had always wished and that in itself was worth any difficulties he might encounter. How far and how deep they were to go he could not guess.

Rupert came across to him and laid both hands on his shoulders. 'I think you will do well enough in your new post, my boy—you're a good hand with figures and diligent too. As for the rest, I would warn you of one thing. I have not had you under my roof for more than two years without coming to know you well and I see that you are too filled with ideals, too ready to believe all men to be good. Indeed, you think me all kinds of things I am not.'

At once Kit would have demurred, but Rupert held up his hand. 'You see! You would defend me even against myself. Don't put your whole trust in princes, least of all a Stuart prince. If you do you will get hurt, for we are none of us heroes—neither my illustrious cousin, nor myself, and certainly not young Monmouth.' He gave a faint sigh. 'I wish I had had him in my service for a year or two. I would have taught him to be a man and hold his own with the rakes and hell-raisers.'

Kit smiled. 'I wish you had, sir. He would have benefited—as I have.'

Rupert looked straight at him. 'Have you, Christian? Yes, I think you have. I have shouted at you, beaten you, run you off your feet, but you have borne it well. You will not suffer others to turn you against your own good judgement. If nothing else I have taught you——'

'Moderation!' Confident enough now to tease Rupert a little Kit finished the sentence for him, and the Palatine's sardonic grin spread over his face.

'Oh, I know you young rascals think me an old kill-joy who has forgotten that hot blood runs in a young man's veins, but it is not so, by God!'

The Prince paused, his eyes fixed broodingly on the window, his thick brows meeting over the bridge of his jutting nose, and Kit guessed he had gone back to the days of his youth when he had fought his way through the civil wars and conquered his own violent nature even if he had not conquered his enemies.

Abruptly Rupert brought his gaze back to his page. 'Well, go to Monmouth, boy, and God speed you. But remember what I have said. Don't expose yourself by over-confidence in any man— or woman either. And come and see me sometimes.'

'I will,' Kit said warmly. 'And for what your Highness has done for me I can never thank you enough.'

Rupert gave his shoulder a shake. 'No more of that! God's death, is that the hour? I've to be at an Admiralty meeting in ten minutes.' He looked down at Kit, the smile gone from his face. 'I shall miss you, boy,' he said briefly, and stalked out of the room.

3

'Harry! I had hoped to see you this morning. Come, match your stride with my long legs and we'll out-distance these importunate fellows.'

Used to the King's method of getting rid of the perpetual crowd of petitioners who surrounded him whenever he walked in the park, Colonel Richmond smiled a little at these low-spoken words and walked smartly beside Charles in the direction of the lake.

'That's better,' Charles said, and thrust his arm through Richmond's. 'Odds life, I love my subjects but there are times when I prefer to love them from a distance. There's not a fellow there but claims he served either my father or myself. I sometimes wonder that Cromwell had any followers at all!'

Richmond laughed. 'There are always those that must run with the hare and hunt with the hounds. Well, sir, how may I serve you?

Or do you just want me in order that you can tell someone what you think of your more trying citizens?'

Charles rubbed his chin amusedly. 'No, Harry, I don't need a whipping-boy today. I want to talk to you—about your ward.'

'Kit? I trust he has not incurred your displeasure?'

'On the contrary. He is proving himself extremely reliable and old Lightfoot gives me an excellent report of him, but it is not in that capacity that I need him. I want to send him to Holland.'

Richmond would have paused in his surprise, but was borne on by the King. 'Oh, only for a short while—a week or two at the most. The truth is I have had disturbing news out of Holland.'

Richmond glanced sharply at him. 'I hope your nephew is not ill. Kit says he suffers poor health.'

'No, he is not ill, but in a sad case. The Orangist party grows stronger, and now that their hereditary prince is near man's estate they would see him accorded his rights. The result of this is that de Witt has taken alarm. He will never willingly allow William to assume the office of Stadtholder, and he has dismissed every one of the boy's English servants, men I could trust. Now there is no one who has access to the palace who can keep me in touch with my nephew. And there may come a time when this is essential.'

Richmond was startled for the second time. 'But he's little more than a child.'

The King paused and leaned against a tree, his arms folded across his chest. 'No, Harry, he is on the verge of manhood, and from what I hear, a purposeful youth only too eager to try his fortune. With my help, what might he not achieve?'

'Wonders, no doubt,' Richmond murmured drily and Charles shook a finger at him.

'I'll not have you tease me. When I was William's age I had been sent from pillar to post, seen battles and sieges and bloody warfare. William has not had an easy life either. We may make a good bargain—freedom for him, a subsidy for me.'

'So that's it. It smacks of bribery.'

Charles laughed, a hard cynical laugh born of his penurious years and seldom heard in public. 'Oddsfish, what are all politics but bribery of some sort or another? Look at my cousin Louis on the French throne—the man who tried to deal honestly with him would get a very poor recompense.'

'Perhaps. And where does Kit come in?' But already Richmond knew the answer and his face was troubled.

'Harry, I must have someone who can gain access to William, and who better than a Dutch lad who was educated with my nephew and who has always been admitted to the palace? He would be above suspicion.'

Richmond's expression was grim now. 'You want him to play the spy?'

'Spy is an ugly word. He will be a link between William and myself, that is all. But I see you do not like it.'

The Colonel turned away, plucking at the leaves of a lilac bush. 'I fear it is Kit who will not like it.'

'Why? Has he strong feelings about this war we wage?'

'Only that it is being waged against de Witt, not against the Prince.'

'Well, then, there is nothing to worry about. He need know nothing but that I want to help my nephew.' Charles took Richmond's arm again and began to walk him up and down. 'You must understand that Louis is beginning to exert more and more pressure on me. He is restless, eager for power—his eyes are on the Netherlands, and who knows, on England too. I need weapons to fight him. William will be one, and that will benefit us both.'

Richmond laughed. 'Very neat! Do your ministers know anything of this? Lord Clarendon, for instance?'

'Hardly—I've no mind to be lectured. No, this is my own idea, not yet ready for the council chamber.'

'I see.' Richmond was silent for a moment, struggling to reconcile his private dislike of it with his unquestioning devotion to the man beside him.

The King seemed to sense his thoughts. 'Harry, you are a soldier and soldiers tend to simplify everything. Leave this business to me and I will endeavour to conduct it without offence.' He laughed suddenly. 'You need not fear I will corrupt your ward's principles. As for his morals, if they are corrupted it will be Jamie's fault.'

Richmond smiled a little, knowing himself defeated, and for the rest of their walk listened to the King discussing Lady Castlemaine's plan for a river picnic at Greenwich.

The same subject was occupying young Monmouth at that moment. He was sitting on the side of Kit's desk engaged in making paper darts and sending them sailing across the room.

'Jamie, do stop,' Kit said absently, his mind intent on his ledger. 'Forty-five pounds to Mr. Watts for a new saddle and trappings! Surely you cannot need——'

'Need—what is need? Why, needs must, of course!' Monmouth threw back his head and laughed. 'And don't start telling me how extravagant I am.'

'The household expenses are far too high this month. And was it really necessary to fit the staff out in new livery?'

'I'd a mind to yellow.' Monmouth leaned over and wrested the quill from Kit's hand. 'Now forget the bills for a while. We are to have a picnic on the river and you must come with us.'

'But with Sir Henry sick of a fever and Mr. Ross away at Windsor, there's more than usual to do.'

'That may be, but you are coming out today. It is an order, sobersides,' he added laughingly, and Kit made a resigned gesture.

'Very well. If you will go away, and leave me in peace for an hour, I'll come.'

Having gained his point Monmouth departed whistling and leaving behind him a confusion of paper darts which Kit, with the air of one used to such nonsense, retrieved and smoothed out for further use.

Living in Monmouth's house in Hedge Lane had changed many things for him. He was so much less the servant than the friend. Sir Henry, the comptroller, fussed in and out but his health was poor, and it was on Kit and Jamie's old tutor, Tom Ross, that the affairs of the household descended. Consequently, he found his position of more importance than he had expected. Men who had been no more than names to him came in and out of the ducal apartments and treated him civilly. Monmouth's particular friends clapped him on the back and called him 'Kit'. A few tried, through him, to insinuate themselves into the Duke's favour but he soon sent them packing—and Monmouth preferred to have no favourites. He was rather, Kit told Richmond, friend to all the world.

Tall, elegant, already known as the handsomest man in England, the young Duke was ready to take life with both hands and if he shocked the moralists by his wildness, his flirtations, his noisy escapades, he won them back with his charm. It was, Kit thought, his greatest asset.

In the circle surrounding him, soon nicknamed 'the young Hectors', Kit had himself found kindred spirits: Rochester, when he was the poet and not the drunkard, and Bab May, with his lean intelligent face and shrewd understanding of his fellows. They were wild, profligate, seldom sober, but they were men for all that and Kit, though he doubted he had the makings of a rake himself, enjoyed their company.

These last eighteen months in Monmouth's service had been the happiest in his life—so happy that he had not been home since he had left Rupert. He felt a little guilty about this, but caught up as he was in the pace of Monmouth's life there seemed to be no time for anything else. Nor did he want to go home just now, for the long-pursued sea feud between the English and the Dutch had burst into serious war, and at the Admiralty the Duke of York, Prince Rupert and the indefatigable Mr. Pepys worked to fit out a fleet to meet the enemy.

Kit suffered some doubts over his own position, but unwilling to relinquish his post immersed himself in his work and ignored the talk of war.

He was engaged now in assessing the household expenses and sighing over the bills for the Duchess's dresses when Anna herself came in.

'Mr. van Wyngarde, be so kind as to unlock my chest. I fear I must have another twenty pounds for the tables tonight.'

He got up reluctantly. 'Your Grace is not fortunate at cards. If you could be a little more careful—at least until your Scottish rents come in.'

Anna sat down on the window-seat and watched him turn the heavy key in the lock of the iron-studded chest. 'Perhaps my luck will change tonight. Are you coming to our picnic?'

He smiled a little, counting the money into her purse. 'Yes, madame. I tried to persuade the Duke that I had work to do, but I'm afraid he won the day.'

She shrugged her shoulders. 'He always gets his way.' There was a sharp note in her voice, and when she had gone it occurred to Kit that she was the only person on whom Monmouth seldom bothered to exercise his charm.

Two hours later he was aboard the royal barge and headed in the direction of Greenwich Palace. The sun was warmer than was usual in May and he sat back on the cushioned seat with the other attendants, prepared to enjoy himself.

They picnicked in Greenwich Park on the hill above the river and having eaten his fill Kit lay under the shade of a tree and watched the King, who had ordered a competition among the ladies as to who could make the best daisy-chain. Charles was laughing at the Queen's efforts and teasing her so that she blushed with pleasure at his attention while Lady Castlemaine, flourishing a long chain, was exchanging some whispered gossip with her cousin Buckingham. Sir Charles Sedley was playing 'she loves me, she loves me not' with Frances Stuart's daisies, and even the serious Duke of York—who seldom unbent enough to be frivolous—was showing Lady Denham, with more proximity than was necessary, how to slit the daisy stalks without tearing them.

Kit was thinking how odd it was that the highest in the land could disport themselves like children freed from the schoolroom, when a voice close beside him said:

'Our sovereign makes a pretty picture, doesn't he?'

He sat up and saw a girl spreading her skirts beside him. She was tall and buxom and her hair, a rich golden brown, was dressed in the newest fashion, the curls looped to frame her face. She was smiling, and her warm brown eyes looked into his with undisguised interest.

'It would be delightful if Master Wright could paint him thus instead of in all his fine robes, would it not?' she went on. 'Perhaps he could call the picture "Old Rowley at play".'

He knew his face must have betrayed his reaction to this for she laughed at once.

'Have I shocked you, sir? I assure you it is not only the gentlemen at court who bandy about that nickname for his Majesty—though perhaps it is better suited to the stable.'

Recovering himself, Kit smiled a little. 'I ought to know by now that nothing is secret at Whitehall.'

'Should you? Have you been here so long?'

He explained how he had passed his four years in England and in return she told him that her name was Ann Ratcliffe and she had recently been appointed maid of honour to the Queen.

For the rest of the afternoon they sat under their tree talking of Whitehall and the people they knew. He learned that her father, who had died fighting for the King at Worcester, had been acquainted with Colonel Richmond.

'The Colonel was in my father's troop then,' she said, 'and a mighty wild troop they were, from all my brothers told me.

Ralph and Michael were no more than boys then, but they went to fight with my father. It made men of them when they ought to have been at their lessons—why, Ralph fathered a bastard before he was sixteen!'

She chattered on, giving him a brief glimpse of a chaotic home life with raffish brothers and an easy-going mother who let her children run wild. It sounded wholly alien to his own quiet home, but oddly attractive.

As they walked down the hill towards the river and the waiting barges Kit found to his surprise that he was talking to her without his usual instinctive withdrawal. He asked her if she was going to be at the ball to be given next week in honour of the French ambassador and when she assented he added with a faint warmth in his cheeks, 'I hope you will dance with me, mistress.'

Her smile widened as she inclined her head, and there was a hint of amusement in her veiled eyes, but she only said: 'Thank you, sir. You will find me with her Majesty.'

A week later, dressing for the ball, Kit regarded himself in the mirror with some despair. It was no use—he would never make a gallant and this new coat was too elaborate with its silver lacing and wide, turn-back cuffs. He was too tall and thin for magpie stripes of black and white, albeit Monmouth had assured him the King had set the fashion for these colours, and impatiently changed the coat and waistcoat for a plainer suit of heavy dark-green satin. It felt more comfortable and looking into the mirror he knew it became him better. He hoped Ann would think he looked well.

It was plain she did for her eyes swept over him from his long fair hair, over the dark-green silk, to his white stockings and plain black shoes.

'You dance well,' she told him as they moved through a bransle together. 'What court lady taught you these steps?'

'None,' he said, smiling, 'but Mr. Gohory, the Duke's dancing-master, and I am not yet very practised.'

'I will remedy that,' she assured him, and looked up into his face. There was something almost boyish in her frank manner and certainly no mistaking her interest in him.

He returned her glance, wishing he could suppress the embarrassing flush that would come, until, unable to look into her face any longer, he lowered his eyes and saw that her dress of bronze satin, rich and full in the skirt, was so tight in the bodice and so low cut that her breasts were pushed up into two soft mounds. It was fashionable to have it so, but he became instantly aware of her as he had been of no other woman.

His hand tightened involuntarily on hers and he wanted to draw her closer, but the music ceased and they stepped apart. He led her off the floor to a small couch where she sank down, fanning herself.

'It is very hot.' She patted the seat. 'Come, sit down beside me. They call you Kit, do they not?'

The furious colour came again at this further step in their intimacy and he wished he could make effortless small talk. Instead he spoke out what was in his mind. 'I shall remember this evening.'

'Shall you? I wonder why?'

He had a feeling she was teasing him and did not know what to say, but he was saved from having to explain what he did not understand himself by the arrival of Colonel Richmond.

'I am sorry to disturb you,' the latter said, 'but I must take Kit away for a few moments—a matter that will not wait. Will you forgive me, Mistress Ann?'

'I will not!' But she was laughing as she added, 'You interrupted a conversation that promised to be very interesting.'

'I did not know you were acquainted with Mistress Ann,' Richmond said, when they were out in the corridor. 'I knew her father well and it was a thousand pities he died, for those boys of his are wild and unprincipled and may well have imparted their ways to Ann. Lady Ratcliffe is too indolent to bestir herself on her daughter's behalf and I believe that half the time, in that ancient barn of theirs in Westmoreland, Ann wears her brother's clothes and rides bareback about the countryside. I hope she has not been allowed to grow too lax.'

'I do not think . . .' Kit began stiffly, and then decided to change the subject by asking why Richmond had come to fetch him so urgently.

The Colonel paused in the dimly lit corridor. 'His Majesty wishes to see you.'

Kit turned in astonishment. His mind searched rapidly over the last weeks to try to find some reason for this summons, but he could think of nothing.

Richmond smiled at his concerned expression. 'You have committed no crime. The King is conferring a great trust upon you.'

He looked gravely at his ward, thinking how the boy had changed since he had brought him, shy and undeveloped, to England and the court. He was only a little under six feet now, but he still had too little flesh on him—no doubt with chasing after the energetic Monmouth, Richmond thought. He had learned to carry himself well, however; how to behave in the most exalted company; how to meet all manner of men without becoming either subservient to those above or patronizing to those beneath. He was of use, well liked, and rapidly making a name for dependability. 'Ask Kit to do that,' Monmouth would say and know it would be done.

Thinking of what the King was going to ask of him, all this gave Richmond more confidence that it would turn out well enough.

Kit, having no idea yet what it was all about, followed his cousin in growing curiosity along the passages until they reached the door of the King's closet. This was his private sanctuary which no one, not even his brother York, might enter without first encountering Chiffinch, the keeper of the closet. And Chiffinch was at liberty to use his discretion as to whom he admitted when his Majesty wished for privacy. Tonight he received Kit as one who was expected. They were to come to know each other well during the years that followed.

'His Majesty awaits you,' he said quietly, and opened the door.

So for the first time Kit entered the closet. It was a small room and it reflected the King's excellent taste for it was filled with all manner of art treasures, pictures, tapestries, fine Italian glass, Dutch china and clocks—a dozen of them ticking in all parts of the room.

Charles himself sat by the fire, his feet on a footstool, one dog curled on his lap and another stretched out by the stool while yet a third lay comfortably asleep on the velvet cushions of the window-seat. He had changed his ball clothes for a silk dressing-gown and he nodded informally to Richmond as they entered. Then he smiled at Kit.

'Good evening, Mr. van Wyngarde. Pray be seated, and you too, Harry. Put that tiresome animal off the window-seat if you wish.'

They sat together, Richmond declining the seat and taking a chair while Kit modestly sat on a stool beside him. For a long silent moment, to Kit's intense embarrassment, the King studied his face.

Then Charles leaned back in his chair. 'They tell me,' he said lazily, 'that you spend a good deal of your time looking after that bad boy of mine.'

A little taken aback, Kit must have shown his embarrassment for the King laughed.

'The more you know of me the more you will realize that I am aware of everything that goes on in my palace. Well, that was one of the reasons why I put you into his service. At the moment, however, I need you to serve me. Are you willing to do that?' The appeal of his personality, as he chose to exert it at that moment, was overwhelming.'

Kit said quietly, yet aware of a rising sense of anticipation: 'Yes, sire. I would serve you in any way I may.'

Charles's black eyes were hard on his. 'In *any* way?'

Certain that this was an important question, that his answer mattered, Kit considered for a moment before he replied. For some reason he remembered Rupert's warning—yet surely one could trust a Stuart king? And Charles's smile would have charmed away stronger doubts than any he entertained. He inclined his head.

'Your Majesty may use my services as they may be most needed.'

Richmond made a sudden movement, but he said nothing.

Charles leaned back in his chair and relaxed, one hand fondling the silky head of the dog on his knee. 'Then, Mr. van Wyngarde, I will tell you what I want you to do. I want you to go home for a short visit—and while you are there pay your respects to the Prince, my nephew.'

'The Prince, sir?' This was the last thing Kit had expected.

'Yes,' Charles went on smoothly, but he was watching Kit from beneath his black lashes. He explained briefly the unhappy change in William's situation and saw the angry flash in the grey eyes opposite. 'I see you feel for my nephew. I understand from the Colonel here that you were in part educated with the Prince and would therefore have no trouble in gaining access to him. Is that so?'

'Yes, indeed, sir. The Pensionary may have sent away the English servants, but I do not believe he would dare to antagonize such families as mine or the Bentincks or the Overkirkes by keeping us from his Highness' company.'

'This is as I thought. Now the war is in some measure a protest against his treatment and to show de Witt that he cannot with impunity so slight a member of my family. But I wish to know the true situation at first hand and ascertain my nephew's mind.'

'Forgive me, sir, but . . .' Kit hesitated. 'I do not understand. The Prince is not yet of age and can do nothing alone.'

'I am aware of that, but I had to be a man at sixteen and with England to support his claim he might well take what should be his own.'

Kit was silent for a moment. The possibilities this opened up were limitless and to one nurtured on intense loyalty to the house of Orange overwhelmingly attractive. Then he looked up at the King.

'What does your Majesty wish me to do?'

'You may give it out that you are going to Holland to visit your home. Jamie goes to sea shortly with my brother, as you know, so you will leave at a convenient time. No one, not even Jamie, is to know that you do more than pay a purely social call on my nephew. You must, however, contrive to see him alone.' Charles picked a letter from a table by his side. 'You will give him this. It says little but that you come directly from me, but I would not wish it to fall into the wrong hands, if only because it would render you useless in the future. You follow me? Good. Now you are to assure my nephew of my goodwill and tell him that, when the time comes, I will aid him.'

There was a slight pause.

'Is that all, your Majesty?'

'What more could there be at this moment?' Charles saw the slight disappointment on the young man's face and added: 'My dear boy, I cannot cross the Channel with an army and set my nephew free, however much I might like to. These things take time and patience, and you must bear with me. I am giving you a great responsibility. You will be required to pay occasional visits to his Highness which must appear wholly innocent; observe all you can, listen to gossip and rumour and carry any messages his Highness may wish to send me. Is that not enough?'

Seeing his smile, Kit felt his disappointment vanish. Of course, sir. Indeed I am more than grateful that you should think me fit for such a task.'

Charles held out the letter. 'Then off with you, boy. You will have to travel to France and ride overland to Holland, so be on your guard and take care of this letter. Destroy it rather than let it fall into the wrong hands.'

Kit tucked it carefully inside his coat. 'Your Majesty may trust me.'

'I believe I may. Make your report to me as soon as you return. Chiffinch will be instructed to admit you privately.'

Kit bent the knee and kissed the outstretched hand. It seemed like the fulfilment of a dream, that he might serve both Holland and England. The desire to serve, that he had hugged within himself, half ashamed of it in the easy-going world he lived in, flared up again, giving purpose to the years of training here at Whitehall. Flushed and inarticulate, he bowed himself out.

4

On such a journey, Richmond said, Kit needed a personal servant to travel with him, and knowing of a suitable young man at Tolbrooke sent for him. At the end of the week Jeremy Hodge arrived in London, his honest rosy face beaming with pleasure. He was a sturdy fellow, a year older than his new master, a good hand with horses and ready and eager to learn his duties. Before they reached The Hague, crossing to France and travelling overland, Kit knew that Jeremy was exactly the servant he needed, friendly yet respectful, cheerful yet unassuming.

On arriving at Breda, Jeremy began his usual practice of searching the bed-linen for the kind of inmates not to be desired and looked up in surprise when told it was unneccessary.

He scratched his head. 'Sir, I ain't never seen an inn yet where there wasn't no fleas nor bugs neither.'

Kit laughed. 'You'll find none here. We think a great deal of cleanliness in Holland.'

Jeremy looked slightly shocked. 'That ain't natural, sir. My old grandfather always said a little dirt protected a man against the ill-humours. If he be too clean they'll lodge in his body, and we all know where that ends,' he finished darkly, and stumped off to the stables to hire horses for the last stage of their journey, leaving Kit smiling over his tray of supper.

On the following evening they rode into The Hague. Kit looked around him with mixed feelings. There were few signs of war in this old city with its tree-lined streets and freshly swept paths, but he noticed one or two houses of business with English signboards were closed.

As he entered the Huis van Wyngarde the first person he encountered was his aunt Sophia.

Her opening remark was not propitious. 'So you have condescended to visit us at last?' Her eyes swept over him. 'You seem to have taken to decking yourself out like a Whitehall popinjay. Have you, may one ask, adopted their frivolity as well?'

It was not exactly a promising start to his visit and he wished his aunt had been on their country estate at Herensdyke. She was a thin bony woman, struggling to preserve the last remnants of her former kittenish beauty, and she treated her nephew, as always, with a playful malice. Even as a child he had sensed that Sophia resented him, though he had no idea why. He had the curious feeling that something more than mere dislike underlay her attitude, and was glad that his grandmother came down the stairs then so that he was able to turn from Sophia to greet her.

Sophia flounced away to her own room and his grandmother's first words drove all thoughts of her from his head.

'I hope Colonel Richmond realizes that your stay in England must shortly come to an end,' Mevrouw said pointedly. 'The Prince will soon be of age and you will be needed here.'

He stared at her in appalled silence. He could not tell her that his very presence in Holland was in the Prince's interests, nor that the mere thought of leaving Whitehall and all his friends, to say nothing of Monmouth, to say nothing, a small voice added, of Ann Ratcliffe, filled him with horror. His consternation must have shown in his face.

'Well, well,' she said gruffly, 'we'll not talk of it today.'

He felt penitent, sorry to have distressed her, but he realized how far he had moved from her world and how slender now was the thread that bound him to Holland.

In the morning he rode out to the Huis ten Bosch, the charming 'house in the woods' where he learned William was residing, and there was surprised to be ushered with unusual formality into a small, sparsely furnished room.

Thinking of the lavish, untidy apartment where he struggled to keep Monmouth's affairs in order, he smile a little and found the smile surprised on his face by a soberly dressed man of about thirty who sat at the desk. He glanced at Kit with pale intense blue eyes that offered no response to that inadvertent smile.

'Your business, mynheer?'

Used to entering or leaving the royal apartments with some freedom, Kit took an instant dislike to the man.

'The servant must have informed you that I wish to see his Highness. You are clearly new to your post or you would know that I need no specific business to call upon him.'

The pale eyes gleamed. 'I know well enough who you are, but we are at war, mynheer, and I am instructed to use the utmost caution concerning whom I admit to the Prince's presence. I will, however, inform him you are here. Pray have the goodness to wait.'

Ten minutes later he returned and requested Kit to follow him.

William was in the garden, looking intently at some dark-red roses. He had grown a little in stature, but he was still small for his age, thin and pale, his pallor accentuated by the dark curls that hung to his shoulders. His deep-set eyes above the strong hooked nose looked even more luminous against so transparent a skin. He appeared far older than his sixteen years.

'Well, van Wyngarde, it is pleasant to see you again.' He held out his hand and stood immobile while Kit brushed it with his lips. 'Do you admire these roses? My uncle sent them from England last year.'

'They are very fine, sir. The English pride themselves on their roses.'

'As on their seamanship,' William commented. 'I do not imagine you find it very pleasant being a Dutchman at the English court just now.'

'As to that, sir, I do not find anyone bears me ill-will because I am Dutch.'

The Prince raised an eyebrow. 'Indeed? Do you tell me the war is unpopular in England?'

'Not exactly that, sir, but his Majesty does not favour it. He wishes for peace.'

The heavy lids fell cautiously. 'Does he? Yet he makes no effort to bring it about.'

Kit came a step nearer. 'Highness, that is not so. Have you—have you not thought the time may soon be ripe for you to take your rightful place? When I came through the streets it seemed to me that there were more orange ribbons decorating hats than ever I recall before.'

Over William's face there came a curious mingling of emotions: rage, grief, stubborn determination. 'The preponderence of orange favours is one of the reasons why the Pensionary has seen fit to make my life even less tolerable.'

'I know, sir, and I am very sorry. It is damnable that he should force such measures on you.'

'He does what he will,' William said broodingly. The lines deepened about the thin mouth that as yet carried no beard. 'But it will not be for ever. By the living God, I will not endure it for ever. I will match my strength with his, my hold over our people with his domination——' he broke off, and pulling a rose from one of the bushes held it to his nose with a hand that shook a little.

Looking at him Kit saw his loneliness and his courage, saw that he held an untenable position with tenacious determination. He, a mere boy not yet out of his teens, was challenging the all-powerful, mature statesman that de Witt undoubtedly was, and it was this solitary fight to hold on to what was his that had defeated his boyhood and brought him to man's estate when others of his age were enjoying their youth.

Kit moved a little closer to him. 'Highness, it may be my privilege to help you to your goal earlier than might otherwise be possible. If we could speak in more privacy I have a letter from your uncle that will explain my visit.'

The Prince looked sharply up at him. 'Come into the house, then. My study is the best place.'

Once there, with the door shut, William sat down at his desk and held out his hand. Slowly Kit withdrew the letter and handed it to him. Still in silence he read, his face betraying nothing. Once he glanced up, but he made no comment.

When he had finished he stared for a few moments out of the window. 'You think my uncle means to aid me?'

Kit leaned forward eagerly. 'I am sure of it, sir. Only have patience and you will see.'

'Patience! It is a virtue I have had to cultivate, is it not?' He picked up a bell on the table and almost as soon as he rang it the secretary appeared. William looked at him, still holding the letter between his fingers.

'Piet, this is not for de Witt's prying eyes, but it informs me that

Mynheer van Wyngarde is my uncle's accredited agent. You are to admit him whenever he comes.'

Kit was aghast. 'Sir! This was to be a confidential matter.'

A faint smile crossed the Prince's face. 'You ought to know by now that though I have many supporters I have few about me that I can trust—two only perhaps with my life, William Bentinck and Piet Daagen here.'

Kit stared across the room at the slight figure of the secretary, his disbelief only too obvious, and Daagen met his look with one equally hostile.

'Highness.' It was the latter's turn to protest. 'Whatever news this man brings out of England, I do urge you to be cautious. He is over-young to act as a go-between. Such ticklish work needs a man of soberer years.'

'If King Charles had thought so he would not have sent me,' Kit retorted, stung, and at once William held up his hand.

'Gentlemen, do not let us waste our time and tempers. I need not urge discretion on you, van Wyngarde; you know the need for it. And you, Piet, take that frown from your face. I tell you that van Wyngarde is to be trusted. Now go and order some refreshment.'

Daagen went, his mouth drawn into a thin line, and William glanced at Kit. 'You must forgive him. He thinks only of my safety.'

'Your Highness is sure of him?'

William sighed. 'If there is one thing my life has taught me it is to judge men. Piet would die for me.' He said it coolly, without any bravado. 'We wait—knowing that when God wills it my time will come and then——' A sudden spasm of coughing seized him and Kit, who had seen these spasms before, poured a glass of the cordial which always stood ready.

When it had passed the Prince leaned wearily back in his chair and went on as if he had not been interrupted, 'and then I shall require your presence here, not in an alien country.'

A little stiffly Kit said: 'Your Highness must know that by acting as an emissary I am endeavouring to serve both you and the King——'

William laughed, a harsh sound without much mirth. 'A difficult task, my friend. Indeed, I think you too honest for this game.'

Kit allowed himself a faint smile. 'Is it impossible for an honest man to serve princes, sir?'

William held out his hand to signify the end of the interview, his face expressionless. 'That, van Wyngarde, is something you will have to find out.'

5

Kit returned to England to find the country aflame with excitement over an English victory at sea. He listened to the news with mixed feelings, rejoicing for the navy and all his friends aboard ship, but feeling at the same time that war with his own people seemed pointless and a waste of men and money. The seas, surely, were large enough for all?

He rode into London, untidy, dirty lecherous London that he had come to love so greatly, to find the sprawling city sweltering in a heat-wave and already on several doors large white crosses drawn in chalk and underneath the words 'Lord have mercy on us.'

The plague had come to London and Kit turned his head away as a cart for the dead rumbled past to await the night and its gruesome cargo, but the sickness came most summers and he took little notice of it. A good rainstorm would clean up the city.

On reaching Hedge Lane he learned that his Grace was out hunting, so he went to his room to change his clothes. Cleaned and refreshed he then repaired to Whitehall, where he slipped unnoticed into the quiet corridor that led to the King's apartments. No one was in sight and he knew this was the time he was most likely to find the King alone.

Chiffinch came immediately in answer to his knock and stood aside for him to enter. The keeper asked no questions, merely asking him to take a seat while he informed the King.

Presently Chiffinch returned and told him he might go in. In the closet Kit fell on his knees and kissed the hand he was beginning to know. The only other occupant of the room was the King's brother to whom he bowed as he rose.

Charles motioned him to a stool, studying his face in the searching way he was beginning to expect—it seemed to be the prerogative of princes.

'Well,' the King said at last. 'You may tell us how you have fared.'

Kit began, wishing that York was not present, for the Duke's chilly manner took away the ease he would have felt in speaking only to Charles. However he did the best he could.

The King listened in silence and then turned to his brother. 'What did I tell you? We have a diligent and careful messenger. Well, boy, so you think my nephew will be a man to be reckoned with?'

'Yes, sir. I believe he dreams of nothing but attaining his father's place.' Encouraged by the King's manner, he leaned forward impulsively. 'Your Majesty, forgive me—but I do beseech you to aid him as soon as it may be possible. If you could but see him'—he searched for words that would impress his listeners—'you would know that he has courage enough for a dozen ordinary men. He is very much alone and he lives in a world where he can trust few. He would turn to you.'

York glanced at his brother, frowning, but the King was looking blandly at Kit.

'Have I not said I will aid him?'

In a rush of gratitude Kit bent over the King's hand again. He believed Charles implicitly—why indeed should he not with the King's hand in his and Charles smiling openly down at him?

.   .   .   .   .

He found his Grace of Monmouth returned from his experiences at sea bronzed and fit and only too eager to recount his adventures on board his uncle's ship.

'He may be sour-faced and stiff,' he told Kit, 'but he's a damned fine sailor. Even Rupert for all his dash is not his equal. Odso, it was exciting, only . . .' He paused, the smile fading from his face. 'Kit, do you recall Lord Falmouth that my father loved so dearly. He was blown to pieces while he was standing between my uncle and myself. It was the first time I realized what war means.' But a moment later his face was alight again and he was talking of their triumphal ride into London. Finally it occurred to him to ask how his friend had fared in Holland.

'Tolerably well,' Kit said, 'but my aunt says I've become a Whitehall popinjay. I'm glad to be back.'

He had not admitted, even to himself, how glad he was, glad that he might see Ann Ratcliffe again. But that evening in the card-room she was engaged at the Queen's table, helping the little

Portuguese lady with her hand, and he had perforce to stand in converse with young Kit Monk and others of Monmouth's set until the game was ended.

As soon as he could he went to her and she smiled up at him.

'You are soon returned, Mr. van Wyngarde.'

'It was Kit before,' he said in a low voice, and his eyes swept over her.

'Kit, then.' She laughed. 'I do believe I have missed you. Mr. Pepys tells me the cherries should be ripe now at Rotherhithe. Will you take me there?'

They rode out the next day. She astounded him by arriving at their meeting place clad in a suit of her brother's clothes, claiming they would have more fun without her petticoats, and throughout the long hot summer day she teased him, talked gaily, laughed with him until the last vestiges of his shyness fled. He had never met any-one so engaging and thought she looked enchanting in her stuff breeches and brown, gold-laced coat.

They ate their fruit in the shade of a large cherry tree near the river-bank and watched the river craft go by until the sun began to sink. At last, reluctantly, he half rose and, kneeling, took her hands to help her up. He felt them warm in his and then, whether she pulled him towards her or whether it was an involuntary move-ment on his own part he did not know, but he was pressing his lips to hers.

When he raised his head she was smiling.

'Kit! Was there never a girl before me?' And when he mutely shook his head, she took his face in her hands and put her mouth to his with slow deliberation.

A moment later, tantalizingly, she sprang to her feet. 'Come, we will be late for supper and the Queen scolds if we are not all in attendance.'

She went, laughing a little and running lightly between the old trees, half boy, half woman. Confused and shaken, he gathered up his cloak and stood for a moment gazing after her.

He had thought kissing no more than a soft pressure of the lips, had not known it could be the hot sweet intimacy she had made it. He put a hand uncertainly to his mouth, and then hurried after her. There was, all at once, a leaping joy within him.

.   .   .   .   .

As the weeks went by no rain came to wash London clean. The heat grew intense and more crosses appeared on the doors, the stench became almost unbearable.

At night Kit lay naked on his bed listening to the tolling of the death-bells in the distance and every morning ate figs stuffed with rue which Jeremy assured him were a certain guard against the disease. One of the first victims at court was young Tom Spinney. Kit had been on his way to sup with him when Tom lurched from the door of his lodgings, vomited, and fell in a huddle at his feet. By the time Kit bent over him he was dead, the death tokens visible on his body. Nauseated and shaken by the sudden and lethal nature of the disease, Kit leaned trembling against the wall, a kerchief held to his mouth.

Prayers were said in the churches for rain but still the dry heat remained and in August, when London had become a charnel-house, when disease struck hourly regardless of rank or position, the court left for Salisbury, joining the stream of carts and horse-men fleeing from the scourge.

Kit accompanied Monmouth with great relief. He was no hero, he decided. Tom's death was not easy to forget and London just now was more than he could stomach.

After a month at Salisbury the court moved on to Oxford, and the city was hard put to it to accommodate its royal guests. Kit, to his disgust, was separated from Monmouth who lodged with his father at Corpus Christi. Old Sir Henry Lightfoot had been too un-well to make this progress and consequently Kit found himself having to conduct Monmouth's affairs from a room at the Mitre Inn, unaided except for some desultory advice from Tom Ross, who was busy enjoying himself.

But it was not all work. The court was in a holiday mood and there were daily picnics and hunting parties, tennis and bowls and horse-racing, as well as dancing and gaming by night. Kit spent every spare moment with Ann. Her beauty, her liveliness, her frank manners that had at first shocked him now seemed wholly desirable. Deep in his first love, he found it hard to concentrate on his work and the miracle of her response to him was such that it drove all saner thoughts from his head. Any doubts he might have had about her feelings were dispelled one morning when he was returning from some business of the Duke's and was taking a short cut through New College.

Ann was coming in the opposite direction, carrying a basket of flowers, and seeing Kit she laughingly handed it to him and told him he might carry it to her lodgings. She led the way up a narrow grey-stone stair and along a gallery to the far end before she paused.

'There, this is where I lodge. Thank you, Kit. The flowers were a gift from Lady Sedley; they are beautiful, are they not?'

'Very,' he said, but his eyes remained on her face. 'Do you—do you have to play cards tonight or'—he blushed in anticipation of what he was going to say—'could we perhaps walk in the gardens? There will be a full moon and it is still warm. Since that day at Rotherhithe I have longed——'

She put one finger against his lips. 'Kit—my very dear Kit, you are learning fast. But I fear I must play cards. Still'—she opened the door—'if you should not wish for sleep, you know now where I lodge when my duties are done.'

The door closed. Alone in the silent corridor Kit stared at it, his pulses racing uncomfortably, his hands pressed against his sides. There was no doubting what she meant, no mistaking the tone of her voice. For the first time in his life he was vividly aware of his body and its demands.

The day passed with intolerable slowness. After dinner Monmouth took him to visit the Master of the Royal Household, that stately old cavalier the Duke of Ormonde, and for what seemed an interminable time he listened to his Grace's stories of the late wars which at any other time would have fascinated him. Today, however, he sat on the edge of his chair and wished the minutes away. At length they went.

'What's the matter with you?' Monmouth asked. ''Pon my soul, I think you've a fever.'

'It's nothing,' Kit answered, and began hastily to talk of something else. He could not confide this even to Monmouth.

At supper he saw Ann in attendance on the Queen and later at the card table. They exchanged a quick smile but there was no chance to speak and at length he slipped away from the noise and chatter and music and went out into the quiet of the college garden.

He sat on a stone bench, his hands clenched on the edge of the seat, half afraid of this new thing within him. Despite the inculcation of his grandmother's stern morals, desire rose in him. He could not suppress it and would not if he could nor think where it might lead. He did not want to think, only to feel and at this moment he was all feeling, throbbing with it, burning with it. He was a man now and he needed to know, to experience. Ann had at last driven away his shyness and although a nervous apprehension turned his stomach to water he knew now that there was a cure for it. He had to seek that cure and find it in his own manhood.

Presently the music ceased and he watched the college lights dim one by one.

At last when it was quite dark he rose and crossed the court, letting himself in by a side door. It was even darker within but he felt his way along the passage to the main staircase, where a solitary lamp still burned, and then up and along corridors until he found her door. His heart beat frantically as he tapped on the panel. He waited for what seemed an unbearable time, wondering if he had mis-understood her, if she had changed her mind, if she was not there at all. But at last he heard the bolt withdrawn and a slit of light fell across the passage.

'Come in,' she said softly, and, as he slipped through the door-way, she closed and bolted the door behind him.

For a moment he stood blinking in the light. A sconce of candles burned on a table and beside it stood wine and glasses and a plate of sugar cakes. Thick curtains were drawn over the window and in the corner stood a bed, its hangings drawn back to reveal the white linen, the red silk covers. He glanced swiftly at it and then away to Ann.

She had changed her dress for a loose wrap of white silk and her hair hung freely down her back. Through the material he could see the firm line of her breasts and dropped his gaze as she put her head on one side and smiled at him.

'So you have come. I thought you would.'

'You knew?' he stammered. 'You meant . . .'

She turned aside that he might not see her smile widen. 'Did you doubt your welcome?'

'No—that is—I was not sure,' he muttered awkwardly as she moved to the table to pour wine into the glasses. She handed one to him but he put it down untouched on the table beside him. Her smile grew more provocative.

'Do you not want your wine? Perhaps you would like a little cake? They are delicious.'

He stood still, clenching his hands by his sides, his cheeks burning.

'No, no.' He was still stammering a little. 'I—I do not want anything to eat.'

She looked across at him. 'My poor Kit!' she said softly, and leaning forward blew out the candles.

In the sudden darkness he heard the soft sound as her wrap fell and the faint creak of the bed. Fumbling a little he flung his coat from him and with trembling fingers began to undo the buttons of his waistcoat. They were stiff and in his clumsy haste one broke and rolled away.

.   .   .   .   .

For three months he was wildly, incredibly happy. Blinded by Ann's yielding, satiated with love, he cast all his dreams with one abandoned gesture into her lap. She had given him fulfilment, she had made him a man, and he would have done anything she asked of him.

A generous mistress, warm and welcoming, she taught him how to employ his passion to give her pleasure; how to be master of his body and yet to yield aptly to its needs. She took his youth, though he did not know it, and shaped it to her own desires.

The inevitable teasing of his friends concerning his preoccupation with a certain lady worried him not at all for, newly confident, he was able to return their banter with an ease he had never had before. But he told no one, not even Monmouth—though the latter guessed—the extent of his relationship with Ann. It was a secrecy he owed her.

Colonel Richmond, who could not fail to notice that he spent a great deal of time at her side, merely raised an eyebrow and said, 'You find the fair sex not so terrifying as you once thought, eh, Kit?'

Richmond was in lodgings near the King and in the pleasant informality at Oxford he and Kit saw more of each other than was possible at Whitehall. They were supping now at the Mitre, and Kit, feeling more on a standing with his guardian, asked a question he would not have risked a little while ago.

'I am surprised, sir, that with an estate like Tolbrooke you have never married.'

Richmond looked up, a little startled, and then, as a slight embarrassment crossed Kit's face, answered equably: 'I have no objection to your asking me that. I was betrothed once, but she died of the smallpox before we were married. It took me a long time to get over it—now I am an old bachelor set in my ways. Tolbrooke will be yours, Kit.'

Kit dropped his knife and his easy colour flooded up. 'Mine? But, sir, I am no more than your cousin. Surely there must be someone else who——'

'No one. My only brother was killed at Naseby. He fought for Parliament.' Richmond paused, an old sadness passing fleetingly over his face. Then he looked up and saw Kit's confusion. 'My dear boy, I know that you have an inheritance in Holland, but I think you have come to love England too—and I doubt you'll leave his Grace of Monmouth as long as he needs you.' And when Kit shook his head, he added, 'I would have you marry and see your heirs at Tolbrooke.'

The very aptness of these words, quite apart from their amazing generosity, produced such an expression of astonishment coupled with an obvious warmth that Richmond was curious. 'Had you thought of marriage?'

Kit smiled a little, holding his secret close. 'I will think of it now,' he said.

.   .   .   .

Throughout that autumn the Dutch war dragged on, but at Oxford the court continued to make merry in its usual uproarious fashion.

In London the citizens were fighting a final and victorious battle against the plague, but even after the first frosts had driven the disease from the streets the court remained where it was. My lady Castlemaine was to bear the King's child, and refused to undertake any journey until after she was delivered.

'So we are all to sit here on our backsides,' Bab May said irritably. 'Damme, there's not a tavern we've not drunk dry of any palatable liquor.'

Shortly before Christmas Kit began to feel that the state of affairs between himself and Ann should be regularized as soon as possible. He had, to his mind, seduced a girl of good family and the sooner the situation was put right the better, but whenever he mentioned it to her she laughed and said that 'there was time enough'. Since the Colonel had told him about Tolbrooke, however, he felt more confident of himself as a suitor and determined to set the wheels in motion.

They had managed, in a court where there were few entanglements free from the gossip-mongers' tongues, to keep their meetings secret. The very privacy of his nocturnal visits to her rooms had at first lent an added aura to the whole affair, but now his inherent honesty had begun to assert itself over the blind desire that had taken such a hold of him.

He no longer wanted secrecy—he wanted to own her before the world. Their meetings too had become more difficult. Several times she had told him she must take another maid of honour into her bed in order to free a room for a court visitor and he knew that when they returned to Whitehall it would be impossible to seek her out in her apartments there. He sensed too a slight change in her. She seemed to tease him more, to spend less time in public with him, though she told him this was to fox the gossips.

He watched her, in a restless mood of jealousy, dancing with the Duke of York, smiling up at him as they turned in the set, and in something like agony saw the Duke's hand stray further than decorum permitted. He hated himself for his jealousy, while Ann only laughed and told him not to be foolish.

In the end he could bear it no longer and a few days before Christmas sat down at his desk and began a letter to his grandmother. She would be difficult, no doubt, as she disapproved of young people choosing their own marriage partners, but he suggested she should write to Colonel Richmond who would be able to set her mind at rest as well as act for him in approaching Lady Ratcliffe.

He had however written no more than half a page when the door burst open to admit, apparently simultaneously, Monmouth, Bab May, Rochester and Mark Rainsford.

'We've sent your man for some ale,' the Earl told him cheerfully. 'There's good news at last.'

He and Bab pushed aside Kit's papers without ceremony and seated themselves on his desk while Mark went over to the hearth and kicked the logs to send the sparks flying.

'Aye!' Monmouth straddled a stool and held out chilled hands to the blaze. 'Come, Kit, put down your pen for a moment and listen.'

He turned to face them all, still half preoccupied and absent-mindedly rescuing his letter from beneath Bab's velvet breeches. 'Why, what has happened that drives you gentlemen of leisure here? I've enough to do keeping his Grace out of a debtors' prison!'

Bab grinned. 'How unsociable. Anyone would think you weren't pleased to see us. Anyway it's good news. Castlemaine has slipped a filly, so now, thank God, we can all go home.'

Kit's heart sank a little. It meant the end of his freedom. He must finish his letter as soon as possible.

'I feel sorry for any children that woman bears,' Mark said curtly. 'She treats them like lion cubs. Now when my son is born...' He had married six months before, Isabel Trelawny, the daughter of a Cornish gentleman of property.

'Your *son*?' Rochester took a mug of the ale that Jeremy, well used to exalted company in his master's rooms, was handing round. 'Don't count your chickens, my boy. Wanting seldom makes a thing so, though'—he glanced round his friends—'have any of you noticed Mistress Elizabeth Malet who came to court last week?' No one appeared to have done so, so he went on: 'A fair wench, with the yellowest hair I've seen. I've a mind to wed her.'

'Good God!' Monmouth sat up in surprise. 'Never tell me, my lord, that you're set on virtue so soon?'

'Who said anything about virtue?' Rochester enquired mildly, thus sending his companions into howls of laughter. 'But a man must wed and she's taken my fancy.'

Bab shrugged his shoulders. 'I've yet to know why a man must wed. I do not intend to.' He looked from one to the other. 'What with his Grace married, your lordship contemplating it, and Mark here about to become a father, you and I, Kit, are the only true Hectors left.'

Kit smiled a little. 'As to that, I think I may not keep you company too long.'

Bab groaned. 'Oh lord, not you too, and not, I pray, that Ratcliffe girl you've been dancing attendance on all summer. Odds-fish, man, have your fun, but if you must tie yourself up in a marriage knot don't look to York's latest mistress. He'd not thank you for it, neither I think would she. She's set on being "the lady" to his Highness.'

A sharp snap broke the silence that had followed this speech, and they all turned to see Kit sitting, white as the paper before him, a broken quill crushed between his fingers.

Monmouth gave Bab a swift angry glance and a muttered injunction to hold his damned tongue, while Rochester, in the act of swilling his ale, put the pot down and looked at Kit in pure astonishment. Mark half rose and then sat down again.

'Oh damme,' Bab said softly. 'Never tell me you did not know? Why, these last three weeks . . .' Before the stricken expression on Kit's face his words trailed away and he stared down at his empty pot.

Kit said nothing. His love, recovering from the shock, cried out that it could not be true, that it was court gossip—and yet at the same time it explained so much, brought an instant and vivid picture of her as she had been last night, dancing with York and smiling up into the Duke's face. God, had he been thus cuckolded?

He wanted to shout to them all to go away, to leave him alone, but he could not speak, only with an effort wrenched his eyes from Bab's face and looked down at his clenched hands.

Bab himself, with sudden resolution, got up and, exchanging a glance with Monmouth, took the Earl and Mark each by the arm and propelled them out of the room, leaving Kit alone with the Duke.

When they had gone Kit got up and with his back towards Monmouth took the letter, tearing it slowly across and across before putting the pieces on the fire.

'I'm sorry,' Monmouth spoke close behind him. 'God knows I would have done anything to prevent that.'

Kit lifted his head, but he did not turn round. 'You knew?'

The Duke went back to the desk and began to fiddle with the quills lying there. 'Yes, but I thought—indeed I did—that it was no more than a passing fondness on your part. After all, you've never bothered your head much about women.'

Unable to see that this was the key to the whole situation, he tried in his kindly but tactless manner to alleviate his friend's distress. 'None of us thought you serious—not with a girl like Ann Ratcliffe. She's a scheming ambitious bitch and when you wed you deserve better than a——' He broke off, aware that this was not likely to administer much comfort. 'Kit, don't take it so hard. The world is full of wenches.' Then, as there was still no answer, he blundered on: 'Anyway, you will not need to see her for some while if you don't want to. We are going away for Christmas.'

His last words roused Kit. 'What did you say? We are going away?'

'Yes, to my lord Crofts at Saxmundham. Buckingham will be there, and Bab and Rochester, and a number of others. We shall leave the day after tomorrow, I think.'

For a moment Kit's face quivered. 'Thank God at least I can go away from here.' He made an effort to master himself and succeeded. But the hurt inside, he thought, how would he ever master that?

He went back to his place behind the desk and spoke in as natural a voice as he could command. 'If we are to go so soon I must pay the tradesmen in the town and there are these letters to be despatched. If your Grace would sign them. . . .'

Yet as he laid out the letters he could not keep his hands from shaking a little. He could think of nothing, see nothing, but Ann lying with York as she had lain with him, using the same words perhaps, the same gestures of love. He thought of York's long lugubrious face, his heavy earnest manner, his straying hands. . . .

God in heaven, how could she? Revulsion rose in him. He began to feel sick, in mind as well as in body.

BOOK TWO

The Trade of Kings 1668-1672

'LOOK!' Monmouth said. 'There is the coastline.'

Kit followed his pointing finger and in the distant mist of a summer evening saw the faint thread of it outlined against the horizon.

They were aboard the Duke's yacht with a retinue of some fifteen persons, twenty horses, numerous chests of clothes and plate and gifts for the French royal family, as well as a small chest of coin on which at this moment Kit had one foot firmly planted. It was his responsibility to see it reached Paris safely, to be available there for the Duke's pocket, and he was taking no chances.

'Paris,' Monmouth said speculatively, and leaned on the rail. The wind was with them and it blew the curls of his periwig about his face. He had recently adopted the wig, though his father, and Kit too for that matter, thought he looked better wearing his own thickly curling brown hair. He sent his companion a mischievous look. 'French coats, French wine and French women. What more could we want?'

Kit sighed. He could see he was going to be hard put to it to keep the Duke's hand from dipping too freely into the chest beneath his foot. Since Sir Henry Lightfoot had died last year he had become comptroller to the ducal household and now had two clerks under him, both of whom he had left in London in charge of Monmouth's new lodgings at the Cockpit in Whitehall. The Duchess, recovering from a hip dislocated by a fall, was remaining at home and Kit could see the Duke was not sorry.

'I wonder if my aunt will have changed much,' Monmouth was saying. 'I imagine marriage to Monsieur of France can be no sinecure. My father must know Phillipe is as objectionable as everyone says or he would not have ordered me to treat him with great respect.'

Kit smiled. 'Your father knows your talent for saying the wrong thing. I'm afraid he thinks Paris may go to our heads.'

Monmouth threw back his own and laughed. 'He doesn't know me if he thinks it won't or you if he thinks it will!'

They found the French capital *en fête* for them and in a mood for celebration. There was peace everywhere now, for Charles, eyeing Louis' new acquisitions in Flanders, had made his own treaty with de Witt.

'My nephew's day will come,' he assured Kit, and sent him to William with conciliatory messages. He had by this time sized up his courier and, with unerring judgement, dispelled Kit's disappointment by pointing out that his policy was keeping the French King's armies from pouring over Dutch soil. Kit believed him. Now the King had entrusted him with a letter to be delivered privately to his beloved sister 'Minette' and he could not help but be gratified at being so trusted.

They rode into Paris through cheering crowds who flocked to see '*le beau Duc*'. Kit found the French King somewhat formidable. Tall, flamboyant, magnificently dressed, Louis ruled his palace, his household and his people with a power and a dignity that Kit imagined his own King would have found oppressive. But he could see that for all the charm Louis exerted to make his guests feel at home he was shrewd, ruthless and as cunning as a fox.

His brother Monsieur, Phillipe, Duc d'Orleans, was a very different person. Small and pot-bellied and teetering round the palace on the high heels he wore to give himself another inch or two, Kit wondered how so pretty and delightful a person as 'Minette' could bear to be tied to so repellent a creature. One of the more confidential courtiers when in his cups confided to Kit the extent of Monsieur's various perversions, and though he turned from such gossip he heard enough to know that if a quarter of it was true then the truth was appalling.

He looked at Madame with new pity, but at the moment she was too caught up with delight in seeing her nephew again to reveal any other feelings. She and Monmouth dined, hunted and danced together; walked in the gardens hand in hand and talked in English which Monsieur did not understand. Within a week he was in a jealous rage, convinced that 'Monsieur de Montmout' was making love to his wife. All the Duke's carefully rehearsed speeches fell therefore on deaf ears and it took all Louis's tact and authority to prevent his brother either calling Monmouth out or setting cut-throats to murder him by night.

Kit had a feeling that in private Monsieur retaliated by making his wife's life a hell, but despite these difficult undercurrents he and Monmouth enjoyed themselves through some weeks of glorious summer weather.

The French King with his vivid mistress, Madame de Montespan, on his arm, treated his visitors to every kind of entertainment. A magnificent hunting-party was held at Versailles and Kit wandered enchanted through the wonderful gardens, gazing at the rare trees, the marble statues, the fountains and shaded walks. He saw an orange tree planted just after the battle of Agincourt and glided in a boat along the grand canal; he saw fantastic birds in the aviary, the famous Grotto of Thesis and in the city itself visited the theatre to hear M. Molière's new piece *Georges Dandin*.

At last at the beginning of September Monmouth said regret-fully that they must go home, and it was then that Kit received a message by one of her ladies that Madame wished to see him in her apartment. He found her, in an undress robe, sitting at her desk and sealing a letter.

She smiled up at him and gave him her hand to kiss. 'Mr. van Wyngarde. My brother tells me I may trust you implicitly, that you are prepared to serve one Stuart as well as another.'

He bowed. 'That is true, madame. You have only to command me.'

'It is a very simple matter. I wish you to take this letter to my brother as you are returning so soon—only privately, you under-stand?'

'Of course, madame.' He took the letter, tucking it into his pocket, and she looked at him curiously.

'My brother tells me he never had so reliable a courier, yet you are a Dutchman, are you not?'

'Yes, madame, but a Dutchman who has learned to love England.'

She looked up at him, not smiling now but a little sad. 'Once one has learned to do that, Mr. van Wyngarde, one cannot be truly happy anywhere else.'

·   ·   ·   ·   ·

When he returned to the Duke's luxurious quarters, Monmouth glanced at him and then dismissed his valet.

'Well?' He sat down on the bed while Kit knelt to remove his shoes and stockings. 'You look mighty solemn. Are the revels here too much for you? I saw you looking down your nose this evening at two silly gallants who were squabbling over the right to hand Madame her fan.'

Kit shrugged. 'King Louis seems surrounded by even more fools than we have at home.'

Monmouth leaned forward and shook him gently. 'Kit, you are becoming caustic and it does not suit you. I think some fine French lady must have turned you down.'

'No, sir. You know I do not amuse myself in that way.'

Monmouth sat still, bare feet dangling. 'Why will you not forget what is past? It is three, nearly four years ago.'

Kit shrugged again. 'As to that I lose no sleep over it any more, but I don't meddle with court ladies.' He took the Duke's coat, laid it on a chest and fetched his nightshirt.

Monmouth stood up, stripping off the rest of his clothes. 'We are in a parlous state, you and I. Here am I tied to a woman I do not love and you tied to the memory of one you did love. We are not very fortunate.'

Smiling a little, Kit flung the nightshirt over his head with one deft movement. 'I've not noticed that your Grace lacked diversion, and you know very well I am not unconsoled in London.'

'Of course not, but neither of us is as fortunate as your friend Mark and his enchanting Isabel. A happy marriage like that seems a rare thing.' The Duke climbed into his large ornate bed where he sat hugging his knees like a boy. 'My poor aunt has not found it. She is very pretty, is she not? I think I am a little in love with her.'

'You are a little in love with every pretty woman you meet! And I think you flirted with her these last two months as much to annoy Monsieur as for any other reason.'

'Well, who would not? Phillipe is a pompous, effeminate mincing pimp. And'—he shook a finger at Kit—'only my father's injunctions keep me tolerably polite to him. That's the worst of being born into a family such as mine. One cannot do what one chooses.'

'As far as I can see you do exactly as you choose.'

The Duke pulled a face at him. 'You are in a mood tonight. But you must admit my wife was chosen for me. Heyday, poor Anna. I fear she is too clever for me, and, oh, Kit, so dull! She tries hard and so do I, but it is no good. I must have gay company and Anna can never be that.' He lay back against the pillows, his arms behind his head. 'I think my father giving me a place in Rupert's guards was the best thing that ever happened to me. It is good to have something useful to do. Which reminds me, why are you so serious tonight?'

Kit folded away the last of Monmouth's clothes. 'No reason—but I feel sorry for Madame. She seems to me to be a very lonely person.'

'My father will persuade Monsieur to allow her to visit us and then she will be happy again,' the Duke said confidently. 'You will see.'

Kit thought he was probably right and a week later, when he presented Madame's letter to the King, saw that the latter was also hopeful.

Charles sat by the window in the closet reading the letter and nodding over it while Kit stood by, looking out on to the river where, as the fine summer lingered, there were still pleasure boats out.

Finally Charles looked up. 'You thought my sister well?'

'Well, sir, yes.' Kit hesitated and then, sure that the King wanted the truth, added: 'But not happy, except in the prospect of a visit to you.'

Charles's face shadowed for a moment. 'You are very perceptive. No, she is not happy and I sometimes think it is not the prerogative of the Stuarts to be happy.' He braced himself as if putting aside something he did not want to think about, and standing, put one hand on Kit's shoulder. 'My boy, you serve me well and with admirable discretion. I am grateful and would reward you. Is there anything you want?'

Taken by surprise, Kit answered a little confusedly that he was more than well paid as his Grace's steward.

'Are you so? Bless me if I should think myself well paid on the pittance you earn—and earn a dozen times over if I know my son!'

'My needs are simple, sir. I have few expenses.'

A wicked look came into the King's eyes. 'Certainly if one limits one's pleasures life is less expensive.' He saw a faint colour come into Kit's cheeks and laughed again. 'Oh, I know all about you, Christian,' he added, thereby increasing the young man's embarrassment and his own amusement—but despite his confusion Kit noticed with pleasure the King's use of his given name. It struck him, years after, as odd that Charles, the informal, never used the shortened version.

'Is there no way I can recompense you?' Charles was asking. 'No trifle you would like?'

He shook his head again. 'No, sir, thank you. I am well enough as I am.'

'Then you are a rare specimen, my boy.' The King seemed about to dismiss him and then, changing his mind, dived into a glass cabinet and brought out a watch, a lovely delicate thing in pale-blue enamel with sprigs of yellow flowers and a tracery of green leaves round the edge. 'What do you think of this, eh?' He moved the hands a little and then passed it to Kit to hold as it gave forth a tiny bell-like chime.

Kit looked at it lying in his palm. 'I've never seen one like it.'

'Good,' Charles touched his shoulder lightly. 'It is yours.'

For a moment Kit stared at him. 'But, sir, so valuable a gift—indeed I cannot——'

Charles took him by the arm and led him to the door. 'Of course you can. You will not let me reward you any other way, but you cannot refuse a gift from your king.'

He tried to express his gratitude, to stammer out his thanks, but before he could say more than a few words the door opened and James of York came in. Kit stood aside at once, bowing stiffly, the four-year-old revulsion crystallized into an icy disdain that made him step back so that York might not brush against him.

The Duke, however, barely glanced at him, and as he bowed himself out he heard York say eagerly, 'Are there letters from France?'

   .   .   .   .   .

He left the palace and went out into King Street, busy as always with traffic, coaches, carts and drays blocking the narrow thorough-fare, so that the unfortunate pedestrians had to take refuge behind the rows of hitching-posts. He walked along by the houses that crowded together and, aware of a rich smell issuing from the King's Head, realized it was near supper time and he was hungry.

He took out the watch and looked at it. It was the most astonishing gift he had ever had, and he saw it as a mark of confidence, a sign of a king's trust, to be treasured as such. His position was now one that any man might envy. Close to Monmouth, serving him day by day, treated with open friendliness by the King and with respect everywhere, he had become a familiar figure at Whitehall. He had his own suite of rooms at the Cockpit, two offices, quarters for Jeremy and stabling for his horses, and it was difficult now to imagine living anywhere else.

Far away in Holland old Mevrouw van Wyngarde wrote peevishly, telling him his time in England was run out and he had best come home to his duties, but always he had begged for a few months more. Now there was no need to ask. His grandmother was dead, had been found dead one evening, her hands clasped on her ebony stick and sitting in her high-back chair, as stiff and straight as ever. It was typical of her, he thought, that she should not die in her bed. He mourned her, but the loss was softened by the years he had spent away from Holland.

Attending the funeral, he informed his aunt that he proposed to leave the estate in the efficient hands of their steward, adding that he hoped she would consider herself free as always to live in whichever of the family homes she preferred.

'I should hope so,' she retorted, and tossed her head. 'A fine thing it would be if you dared to suggest anything else.' There was an oddly significant note in her voice.

'My dear aunt,' he answered mildly, 'I can't think why you should suspect me of such uncharitableness.'

'No, you can't think why,' she returned, 'I am well aware of that——'

'But while we are on the subject may I suggest that you use a little more discretion when inviting guests to this house. I understand from Hans that the Pensionary's brother is a frequent visitor here, and as you well know our loyalty has always been to the house of Orange.'

'Loyalty! You, of all people, have the least right to talk of loyalty. And'—she walked to the door—'if I choose to entertain Cornelius de Witt, I shall do so. It is not your affair.'

He shrugged his shoulders. Living so far away he had no means of enforcing his will on her and had to let the matter rest. After two more days of her vagaries and innuendoes he returned to Whitehall with relief.

Much had happened during these years. A great fire had destroyed acre upon acre of the London he had learned to love and he had laboured for a day and a night, blowing up houses, organizing the carrying of water from the river and supervising the rescue of the trapped from burning buildings.

Slowly London recovered, but Kit walked sadly through the rubble and over the miles of blackened ash that covered the city.

He called on Mr. Pepys at Seething Lane and took a pot of ale with him, listening to the little secretary's tale of how he had ferried his wife and goods down the river to safety and buried his gold in the cellar. But Mr. Pepys's house was not burned and Kit, who liked the cheerful, uninhibited fellow, was glad. They called each other, very correctly, Mr. Secretary and Mr. Comptroller, but the liking was mutual.

Rochester had married his Elizabeth Malet and Rupert, now living in somewhat lonely splendour as Constable of Windsor, had rather surprisingly taken a mistress, Mrs. Hughes the actress. When she gave him a daughter he asked Kit, to the latter's intense pleasure, to stand god-father to the child, who was baptised Ruperta.

Castlemaine's day was seemingly over, though the King was too kind to turn his back on her, but his attention was now taken with Eleanor Gwynne and Moll Davies, both from Drury Lane Play-house. Kit went with Monmouth to see Sir Charles Sedley's play *The Mulberry Tree* and thought it witty but silly. He was far more interested in Mr. Milton's new work *Paradise Lost* and now, pausing at a bookstall, bought a copy for Monmouth's duchess. Jamie, he thought amusedly, would hardly appreciate such a gift.

Presently he turned into Axe Yard and thinking of the welcome awaiting him in the comfortable rooms high up in the old house at the far end, his step quickened.

The time that had passed since the end of his unhappy affair with Ann Ratcliffe had gone some way towards healing the wound but it had hurt, damnably, for he had been at an impressionable age. After hours of miserable, tormenting indecision he had eventually confronted her with the gossip. She had laughed at him. They had had three months of happiness, she told him, and he surely could not blame her if she was flattered that a royal duke should take a fancy to her. She had a mind to fine jewels and gowns and a house of her own. Stunned, he had left her and never spoken to her since.

Now, as he said to Monmouth, he lost no sleep over the affair. He could see her, dancing with York, wearing his jewels, or driving in his carriage, and turn away with no more than a brief contempt for her and for himself that he had given his heart so easily to such a woman. But Ann had destroyed more than she knew and a certain cynicism crept into his nature that had not been there before. He could not love lightly and pass on as Monmouth did.

And now he had Cathy who was no maid of honour to ogle him with sidelong looks or betray him with a laugh.

He had met her a year ago. He had been walking by the river when something floating by caught his eye, and he leaned over to see what it was. A moment later he heard running steps and a pair of hands seized him while a voice implored him 'not to do it'.

He turned to see a girl, garishly dressed, painted and perfumed but with a natural prettiness that was still unspoiled. Mildly he enquired what he was not to do and she explained she had thought him about to throw himself in, and hated to see such a fine young gentleman come to so miserable an end.

He assured her he had no such intention and then, the humour of the situation striking them both, they began to laugh. He took her to supper at Hercules Pillars and over the meal she talked with irresistible frankness and coarse humour of London and her life there since she was fourteen years old. Later when he took her back to her rooms it seemed natural that he should stay with her. They talked on by her fire and in a desire to ease his own mind he confided to her his unhappy love for Ann and its wretched ending. She listened with a surprising sympathy, and when at last they did lie together it was with more mutual pleasure than if they had not had that long intimate conversation.

'You're not like most of the men I entertain,' Cathy told him candidly. 'They've no wish to talk to me—nor I to them. But you are different.'

It was soon apparent that their relationship was going to be of some duration so he took her from her sordid lodgings, setting her up in a convenient apartment in Axe Yard, close by Whitehall. With consummate ease she threw off her past and devoted herself to him, gentling him out of his lonely bitter distrust of all women; he on his part taught her how to eat more delicately, how to use one of the new forks instead of a knife and her fingers, and he showed her how to clothe herself with taste, nor would he let her spoil her face with paint or use cheap perfume. He took her shopping and bought her gowns and gloves, shoes and stockings until she clapped her hands with a delight that he found oddly touching.

On one of these expeditions, seeing Monmouth's carriage, he left her to look over some silk while he went across the road to speak with the Duke.

'Cathy needs some new gowns,' he explained rather absently. 'I'll not have her parade in those trashy things she has.'

Monmouth sat on the seat in his coach and laughed until the tears ran down his cheeks. 'Rat me!' he said when he could speak. 'Only you, sobersides, could take a mistress and reform her at the same time.'

For a moment Kit was indignant. 'You make me seem a prude, Jamie.'

Monmouth shook his head. 'Of course not, but we've not named you sobersides for nothing.'

'Rochester and Bab call me "the Puritan" too—oh yes, I've heard that, but God knows I don't merit it.'

'Indeed you don't,' the Duke said cheerfully. 'Now go back to your desirable Cathy or I shall come a-wooing her myself.'

She was desirable but Kit was not in love with her. As time went on his affection for her grew, mingled with a desire to make up to her for her wretched past, but it remained no more than that.

Tonight, mounting the stairs to her rooms, he was disappointed to find them empty. There was a fire burning and the beginnings of a meal set out on the table, however, so he sat down in his large chair before the hearth and put his feet up on a stool. This, for the time being, was more entirely his home than the Huis van Wyngarde, or Tolbrooke or even his lodgings at Whitehall. Warmed by the fire, he fell comfortably asleep.

Presently the door opened and Cathy came hurrying in. 'Kit! Mrs. Jenkins told me you had returned.' She ran across the room and perched herself on his knee to kiss him. 'I have missed you so much. Tell me about Paris. Was it full of pretty women in fine clothes? What did you do? Were there balls and banquets?'

'Give me a moment to wake up,' he said, smiling, 'and I cannot answer all your questions at once.'

He gave her a roll of French velvet he had bought for her, watching her eyes sparkle with pleasure, and over supper entertained her with a vivid description of the fireworks at Versailles. After the meal they sat together by the fire, Kit in his chair and Cathy on a stool, her head against his knees.

'What have you been doing while I've been gone?' he asked. He wondered sometimes if in his absence she was with other men.

'Oh.' She turned to face him. 'I have become so respectable! I have taken to helping Mrs. Gunn down the street. Imagine, Kit, she has fifteen children, all living. She needs help, believe me.'

He was at once ashamed. Cathy had accepted his protection, had accepted him, and, by her code, rough though it might be, would not betray him while she ate his bread under a roof he paid for.

He caught her to him, his hands caressing her small breasts, his mouth on hers, seeking the oblivion from himself and his own thoughts which was perhaps the thing above all that he looked for in her company.

Yet much later, lying in the darkness of their bedroom with her sleeping body beside his, he was aware of how often he did not like his own thoughts. He wondered if Bab and the others had not nicknamed him rightly, yet he had no cause to be censorious hence his shame, his determination to root out that trait in himself, and his desire for Cathy, for her gaiety and her matter-of-fact philosophy that made mock of his own introspection.

She stirred beside him now and, half asleep, turned towards him, fitting herself into the curve of his body. He drew up his knees so that she lay more comfortably and a welcome drowsiness stole over him. But there was still, despite the intimate comfort of this curtained bed, the old dull ache in his heart that a gentlewoman had cruelly betrayed him and it was a prostitute who had been kind.

2

On the sixteenth of September, a bright blustery day, the Life Guards and Foot Guards, smart in their red-and-yellow uniform, were mustered in Hyde Park to receive their new commander.

Kit was standing with Mark Rainsford and young Tom Bruce—Lord Ailesbury's son and newly come to court—and together they watched Monmouth's arrival. He was strikingly clad in a yellow velvet coat, rich with heavy gold lacing, brown thigh boots and a large brown hat decorated with a mass of yellow ostrich plumes. He had set this at a new angle on his handsome head, cocked at the back, and he was riding a magnificent black horse, a gift from Prince Rupert especially for the occasion.

As he moved along the lines with a quick word for one man and a smile or a nod for another, one by one they tipped their hats on to the backs of their heads.

'The Monmouth cock,' Mark said. 'I'll lay any odds that'll be the rage all over town by tomorrow morning.'

Presently the King arrived with a number of gentlemen, including his brother York, Rupert and Buckingham. In the breeze Kit heard only part of the King's speech, formally handing over the command of his guards to his son before he delivered the written commission, but Mark's sharp ears caught one surprising omission.

'Kit, did you note that? His Majesty said "my beloved son". That won't please his Grace of York.'

'He'll have the "natural" put in before the day is out,' Kit said grimly. 'I'll wager that!'

Bruce glanced curiously at him. 'You hate York, don't you?'

'He has cause,' Mark intervened before Kit could answer, and added, rather irritably, 'and I can tell you I'm getting a little weary of being in his Grace's household. He's a fine Admiral but when you've said that, you've said it all.' He narrowed his eyes in the bright sunshine, watching Monmouth riding now at the head of his troops. 'I think I would like a commission in the Guards. Your duke is infinitely preferable to mine, Kit.'

A cheer had broken from the front ranks of the Foot Guards as Monmouth rode by and a moment later every man was flinging his hat in the air and shouting, 'A Monmouth—a Monmouth!'

Kit threw his own hat with the rest and saw Monmouth's face, flushed and triumphant and lit by a smile of genuine pleasure at this tribute. Then, sharply defined, he caught a glimpse of the Duke of York's long features. They were grim and unsmiling. Seeing reflected there the cold heart of the man Kit became aware of the birth of a small, intangible but very feal fear.

Monmouth could not have been more honoured, more loved, more popular with the people had he been Prince of Wales. But he was not.

Over the months that followed the fear remained, thrust deep inside. Honours were heaped on the younger Duke. He was his father's constant companion, fêted by visiting dignitaries, given further commands, and in the following spring, on the eve of his twenty-first birthday, admitted to the Privy Council. Small wonder, Kit thought, that he believed nothing to be beyond his reach.

A week after his birthday he was away to Harwich with his father to inspect a new yacht, and Kit, taking advantage of this, went down to Tolbrooke with his cousin.

Richmond had resigned his commission in the Guards when Monmouth took command. 'Your Grace needs younger men about you,' he said, smiling but firm. The King promptly gave him a baronetcy and he rode home to Tolbrooke as Sir Harry Richmond.

On Easter Sunday he and Kit walked across the park to the

village church and sat in their pew, firmly boxed in, to listen to the familiar words of the gospel for Easter day. Kit stared at the east window, changing colour in the fitful April sunshine, and realized how he had come to love the Anglican liturgy; it was, he thought, dignified, peaceful yet exhilarating, and containing more to comfort a man than the strict Calvinism of his youth. He had adopted it as easily as he had adopted England.

The village in return had adopted him; Jeremy's family treated him to home-brewed sack and dough cake when he visited them, the country folk doffed their caps to him, calling him 'young master', and up at the big house Richmond treated him as his heir. It was, somehow, satisfying in a way that his visits to his Dutch estates were not.

When the service was over and the congregation streaming out through the old low porch, Elizabeth Rainsford danced over to him and asked if Mark was come with him.

'Not this time, Imp,' he said smiling. 'Your brother is too busy with his new duties as a soldier.'

'Well, I'm glad,' she said plainly. She was an unusual child with a long bony face and straight fair hair that refused all her nurse's efforts to curl it. 'He was cross last time he came. He smacked me and I bit his hand. I wish you were my brother.'

'If that is how you would treat me I am glad I am not!'

'Oh, I would not do that to you,' she answered confidently, and held his hand the rest of the way home to Westfield where he and Richmond were to dine.

Lady Rainsford was expecting her eleventh child but her lord was unperturbed. 'The midwife tells me we need not look for the birth for a few days yet,' he told his guests; and added, with rough humour, 'We can be certain of eating our dinner in peace.'

After the meal the talk turned on Monmouth's recent admission to the Privy Council.

'God knows what things are coming to,' his lordship grumbled. 'When I was young the council chamber was only for grown men and to my mind for men of honourable estate. Monmouth is a likeable fellow and I'll not say a word against him, but he's a bastard and some say more like Colonel Sidney than the King.'

Kit sat stiffly in his chair. 'Those who say so, say it for their own reasons. Why, you have only to look at him to see his likeness to the King's father.'

'That is true,' Richmond admitted slowly, and then went on, it seemed unwillingly, 'but however the King chooses to honour him he will remain—what he is.'

Shaken by the turn of the conversation, Kit spoke hesitantly. 'Mr. Pepys says there are rumours the King will make him Prince of Wales.'

His lordship laughed shortly. 'Nonsense. Put such ideas out of your head, boy. The King would have spoken had there been anything to tell—surely you know that?'

'Perhaps,' Kit said uneasily. He had the feeling that he was being forced on to say more than he had admitted so far even in his own mind. 'Yet perhaps not. Maybe it has not been politic to do so. But if the Duke of York turns papist——'

Richmond dropped his knife with a clatter. 'What makes you think he might?'

'Rumour has it, and Mark who has after all only recently left his household believes it is true.'

Lord Rainsford frowned heavily. 'Then Mark should not spread idle gossip and I shall tell him so.' He glanced up and saw Kit staring across at Richmond who was sitting pale and silent and twisting his glass in restless fingers. 'Come, we must not spoil our dinner by talking of state affairs—they're enough to give a man a bad digestion. Harry, tell me what you think of Christopher Wren's designs for rebuilding our poor city. You have seen them, have you not?'

Obediently his guests followed his lead, but neither could give his mind to the topic and, as soon as they had taken their leave and were out of earshot of the house, Kit turned to his former guardian.

'It is true, isn't it? About York, I mean?'

Richmond turned up his collar and pulled his hat down, and Kit wondered whether it was to keep out the unusually cold April wind or to hide the truth on a face that ever found it hard to dissemble.

'I don't know—no one knows. It is his Highness's private affair.'

'It cannot be any such thing if he is to be King. The people won't like it.'

'Whether they like it or not, he is his brother's heir.'

For a few moments they rode in silence beneath an avenue of chestnut trees where already the fresh young leaves had burst into green fronds. Quite involuntarily Kit shivered.

'I begin to see something,' he said at last. 'Something I have not seen before. There is the King whom we both serve and there is the

protestant duke who has my love. There is also the papist duke—
don't deny it, sir, we both know that if it is not already the truth it
is likely to be—and he, I think, has your loyalty. Why? Would you
see a papist on the throne?'

Richmond moved uneasily in the saddle and his mare shook her
head, jangling her harness. 'I would see the King's rightful heir on the
throne,' he said steadily, 'and you, Kit, are near to talking treason.'

Kit glanced sharply at him and then away at the long line of
trees. A silence fell, a silence that seemed ominous. Neither broke it.

Only as they mounted the steps did Richmond speak, sliding his
arm through his cousin's.

'Come, my dear lad, you must not see trouble where there is
none. Let us warm ourselves with a glass of wine and put such
thoughts out of our heads.'

But years after, when it was all settled for ever, he remembered
this day and knew that Kit had been right, that he himself had
deliberately refused to face the truth.

.   .   .   .   .

The long-planned visit of Madame was at last arranged for May
and Kit accompanied the court party that went to meet her.

For three weeks she was royally entertained at Dover, her
brother's delight in her presence communicating itself to everyone
there. Yet Kit thought it was a feverish gaiety, a snatching at something so brief and precious that it might not be stayed.

And there was something else, too, an underlying current of
feeling between the King and his sister that was hard to define, long
private meetings behind closed doors—natural enough, Kit told
himself, but nevertheless he felt curiously uneasy.

All too soon her time was up and he saw her embrace the King
again and again, unable to check her weeping. She reached up to
kiss tall Monmouth and he too had tears in his eyes as she lingered
for a last clasp of the hand.

Only a few weeks later Kit was awakened one morning from a
heavy sleep in Cathy's lodgings to find, most unexpectedly, that
Jeremy was shaking him by the shoulder.

'Sir, his Grace . . .'

Instantly awake, Kit flung back the bedclothes. 'What has
happened? Out with it, man.'

'Nothing to his Grace, sir, but it must be bad news. He is very upset and will admit no one but you.'

Kit hurried into his clothes and ten minutes later was at the Cockpit. He went straight to Monmouth's rooms and entered without knocking.

The Duke was standing by the window of his bedroom, one hand holding the velvet curtains and in the other a crumpled letter. Tears were streaming unheeded down his face.

Kit went swiftly to him and laid a hand on his arm. 'Jamie, for God's sake, what is it? Not your father?'

'No.' Monmouth turned and pressed the note into Kit's hand. 'It is Madame, my aunt. She is dead. Some say poisoned—I do not know. I only know she is dead and three weeks ago we were dancing together at Dover.' He pointed to the bed. 'My father sent me that.'

Kit looked across the room and saw, laid out on the yellow damask bed cover, a royal purple cloak of mourning.

3

Long afterwards he came to think that Henrietta Stuart's untimely death was a turning point in Monmouth's life. Not only did the Duke mourn her sincerely but at her memorial service he stood behind the King with his uncle and Prince Rupert, clad in royalty.

Day by day his popularity increased and though remaining outwardly friendly his uncle of York watched him with increasing wariness. In October it crossed York's slow mind that he had another nephew to watch, for William of Orange, visiting the English court for the first time, was formally acknowledged next in succession after York and his family.

For Kit the visit turned out to be one of distinctly mixed feelings. Hitherto Holland and William had been identified in his mind; England with Charles and the lively court. To see the two together was something of a shock.

William was only twenty but he carried himself with maturity and his cool self-possession was unshakeable. Every effort was made to entertain him, but he sat silent and unmoved through the private theatricals put on for his benefit, refused to dance or play cards and seemed bent on pinning his uncle down to serious discussions on his position at home.

On the second morning Kit came to the Prince's rooms to pay his respects. William received him in his bedroom where the sour-faced Piet Daagen was writing letters for him and William Bentinck supervising the laying-out of his clothes.

'Well, van Wyngarde, I am pleased to see you.' He held out his hand.

'Welcome to Whitehall, sir. I hope your stay will be a pleasant one.'

'I think that unlikely. I can only hope it may at least be a profitable one,' William told him, coolly. 'The English seem to eat too much and wash too little. I find this place shabby and none too clean.' He caught hold of a piece of tapestry and shook it a little. A cloud of dust emanated from it and he coughed, putting a kerchief to his lips. 'Ugh! I could not live in such squalor.'

Kit felt instantly on the defensive. 'Highness, do not judge Whitehall from its outward appearance. I know it falls short of your palaces in cleanliness, but the people here are eager to welcome you and the King wishes to help you—he told me so himself.'

'Did he, indeed?' William queried drily and Daagen looked up from his writing to give Kit a look of patent disbelief. 'But I am not here to enjoy myself,' the Prince went on. 'I want my mother's dowry, which was never paid, and English aid for my cause.'

He said it as if he had doubts of either materializing. Kit was disappointed and not a little irritated that William, after all this time, should approach the visit in so pessimistic a mood—yet William's past life was likely to have soured a far less proud nature, and he looked at the Prince in some perplexity.

And then William, with his extra-perceptive knowledge of men, smiled and held out his hand. 'Forgive me, van Wyngarde, if I seem ungrateful. I know you at least wish me well.'

The smile, curiously, made Kit think of Rupert in one of his mellower moods and that evening, when he and Monmouth accompanied the royal guest to supper at Rupert's house in Beech Street, he saw an astonishing likeness between the cousins.

Monmouth and William shared a passion for hunting, and Rupert invited them to hunt in the park at Windsor and dine with him afterwards, entertaining them with his fund of military anecdotes. Both of them keen soldiers, they listened with an eagerness which the rest of the court, who had heard all the Palatine's stories before, did not exhibit.

'Discipline is the greatest need of a soldier,' he told them. 'I had none in my youth but I learned it—and judgement too. Without these qualities you will never defeat your enemies.' He looked across at his guest. 'But I think, Cousin William, I do not need to tell you that.'

A little warmth stole into William's pale face, and Kit felt instantly grateful to Rupert for paying so subtle a compliment. They came often after this and Monmouth told Kit frankly that he liked 'Dutch Billy' whatever the rest of the court might think.

Not so happy was the time at Whitehall. It was soon plain that the Orange and his uncle were not getting on well together, and the former emerged from more than one private interview with a stormy expression on his face. Kit began to fear that William might indeed be the ruin of his own hopes.

Matters came to an unfortunate head. Buckingham issued, at the King's request, invitations to a select supper party a few nights before William's departure. Charles himself was to be there with Rochester, Sir Charles Sedley, Lord Buckhurst, Monmouth, Harry Killigrew and Bab May.

'The finest set of rakes in town,' Kit heard Bab informing a crony. 'His Majesty wants to see if there is more to the Orange than the leathery skin on the outside.'

It was hardly fair, Kit thought, and tactfully suggested to Bentinck that an egg beaten in milk might be a good precaution for his Highness to take before the party.

Whether or not William took his advice he did not know and as he was asleep when Monmouth came to bed that night heard nothing of the affair until the next morning. He called on William at ten o'clock as he had been in the habit of doing, and he felt the atmosphere as soon as he entered. William was pacing up and down, his face even more colourless than usual, his large eyes burning with scarcely suppressed rage and an attack of asthma causing him considerable difficulty in his breathing.

'I was a fool to come,' he burst out, before Kit could open his mouth. 'I can see that I waste my time if I expect anything here but levity. This is a court for tosspots and lechers, not fit for decent men.'

'Highness,' Kit began, thunderstruck by this biting attack. 'I do assure you——'

William turned on him. 'As for you, van Wyngarde, I wonder that you, a Dutchman, can endure to live here. I am surprised you have not returned home in disgust.'

'Highness . . .' Kit began again, but nothing could stop the breathless diatribe.

'It has taken me all this time to squeeze even a portion of my mother's dowry, owed these twenty-one years, out of the Treasury. It is a mean nation that can hold back such a payment. And no one will listen when I speak of my needs at home—indeed I wonder why I was invited at all. As for my uncle, all he wants is for me to——' He stopped abruptly. Family loyalty held, and closing his lips he turned his back on his silent listeners and stalked away to the window.

Kit exchanged a glance with Bentinck who shook his head and indicated the door. Kit bowed himself out.

Presently in the gallery he came upon Rochester and drew him aside. 'My lord, you were at the Duke of Buckingham's supper party last night. If anything occurred to distress the Prince of Orange I do beg you to tell me.'

Rochester flung himself down on the window-seat. 'Distress him? Well, I don't know about that—the boot was more like to be on the other leg.' He went off into a peal of laughter. 'Lord, Kit, but it was funny. I'll be hanged if I've laughed so much for years.'

'I do wish you would tell me what happened.'

Rochester took out his kerchief and wiped his eyes. 'Well, his Majesty told us to ply the Prince with wine to try and shake him free of his Dutch sobriety—saving your presence, Kit, he's a dashed dull dog when sober and we thought he might be pleasanter drunk.'

'Go on.'

'We had a good supper—one of Buckingham's most lavish affairs—and on my soul I've seldom seen so much good French wine drunk at one meal.'

That, Kit thought, was saying something even for Rochester, and he glanced at him now as he leaned back against the window-frame. The Earl was still no more than three and twenty years old but he bore already in his face the marks of his restless search for excitement, for sensation, perhaps for some inward fulfilment. Even his wife, whom he loved, had not been able to satisfy his questing spirit, and he had the reputation of being more or less permanently drunk. It was, like all gossip, only partly true, but true enough to make Kit see what William, used to abstinence at home, had had to face. No more seasoned topers than the guests of last night could have been assembled to set about drinking him under the table.

'Poor Dutch Billy,' Rochester was continuing. 'He tried so hard to refuse us, but then all of a sudden he seemed to take to the wine and began to sing a Dutch song none of us could understand. We tried to join in and he jumped up on to the table the better to teach us. Of course he fell off, but he thought I'd pulled him down and set about me. Monmouth had to hold him off. By heaven, Kit, when he's roused he can put the fear of God into you!'

He paused, and Kit stared at him in astonishment. This was an unknown William.

'What happened next?'

'Next? It's hard to recall for we were all pretty merry but about midnight, or it might have been later, the Prince shouted out that we needed some feminine company and he was off like a streak of lightning down the corridor towards the maids of honour's apartments. His Majesty, who was laughing his head off, sent us after him and we caught young William in the courtyard. We told him he must at least keep away from respectable young ladies, though no doubt we could find him other company, but he pushed us off and smashed a window into the bargain!' The Earl collapsed into helpless mirth again. 'Bab and I got hold of him at last and brought him back, and after that he collapsed on the floor so that we had to carry him to bed. Odso, it was an evening I'll never forget.'

Neither, Kit thought, would the Prince of Orange. With sudden intuition, he realized that William could better accept defeat on a battlefield than the petty victory Charles had gained over him last night.

'It was unfair,' he said hotly. 'His Highness has lived so sheltered a life that he's no match for all of you.'

'Lord, Kit, don't be so stiff-necked,' Rochester answered easily. 'We all think the better of him now we know he's as human as the rest of us. It was mild enough fun.'

'You got him so drunk that he made a fool of himself when he is on a State visit. I don't think that very amusing.'

The Earl roused himself and looked closely at his companion. 'No, by God, I can see you don't. Well, I suppose one could not expect the Puritan to approve, but I thought that by now you'd know us well enough to realize we meant no harm.'

Kit met Rochester's stare, too concerned for William to take any personal offence at the last remark—and indeed he did know

Rochester too well to believe that any was intended. Rather wearily, he got to his feet.

'No one ever means any harm,' he said, 'but harm is done all the same.'

.   .   .   .   .   .

Befor Christmas came he knew what William had meant by his half-finished censure of his uncle, and guessed the rest. A treaty had been signed, but this time a treaty between France and England for the specific purpose of waging war against the Dutch republic, and a treaty arranged, it was understood, by Charles and his sister at their last meeting at Dover.

'The only way to help the Prince is to defeat the Republican party in Holland,' Richmond said when the news came out and he saw his ward's reaction. 'Don't you see that if de Witt's position is weakened it will strengthen William's?'

'I suppose so,' Kit said reluctantly, but it seemed a specious argument—especially as the King was to receive a vast sum from Louis for his share in the war. It did not, however, begin immediately and during that winter and the following spring Kit had other things on his mind. Even Ann Ratcliffe's break with York, and her marriage to the Earl of Carrisford, failed to distract him from his preoccupation with Monmouth's affairs.

If the Duke was working hard at his soldiering he was also playing harder. He was scarcely ever at home and whereas a few years ago he had been a boy struggling to keep up with the men of his world, now he was one of them and took his pleasures with a man's virility. Sometimes Kit thought that only constant exercise and hard riding kept him fit enough to take the less creditable of his excesses in his stride. He did not blame Monmouth, for it was no more than the way of their world, but at times the playing got out of hand.

On one occasion a member of Parliament, Sir John Coventry, chose to be somewhat impertinent in the House concerning the King's preoccupation with the ladies of the theatre. Two nights later two of Monmouth's officers and some of his guards laid in wait for him, and catching him in a dark alley slit his nose to the bone. It was a common enough form of revenge but Kit was disgusted and told Monmouth so.

'My fellows went further than I intended,' the Duke said, with just enough defiance in his voice to show that he was aware of some guilt, 'but the scurvy knave had to be punished for his impertinence.'

'Not like that,' Kit retorted. 'There'll be trouble over this.'

There was, for the House rose as one man and called the outrage an attack upon their freedom of speech. Monmouth's two officers were banished and he himself the subject of stern criticism together with a telling ballad from the hand of the Member for Hull, Andrew Marvell, and addressed to 'The Haymarket Hectors'.

'But was't not ungrateful in Monmouth ap Sidney ap Carlo,
To contrive an act so hateful, O Prince of Wales by Barlow?
For since the kind world has dispensed with his mother,
Might he not have spared the nose of John brother?'

The Duke read these lines with a face dyed crimson and without his usual light 'let them say what they will'. This hurt, but he let no one see it except Kit.

'They will think differently one day,' he said, between tight lips. 'I tell you, Kit, the truth must come out and then——'

'What truth? And what then?'

Monmouth turned away, tearing the ballad-sheet into small pieces. 'You understand me well enough.' He braced himself then, flinging off his anger. 'But we'll not talk of it now. Let the devil take the scandal-mongers and Mr. Marvell in particular. Find Rochester and Bab and we'll go to Hercules Pillars—we'll show the town the young Hectors are not banished yet.'

There was nothing to do but go with him. But Sir John was nephew to the Duke of York's secretary and Kit knew York would take the whole affair as a personal insult. Consequently when, some time after, there was another incident to be chalked up in the Duke's accounting, Kit felt impelled to take Monmouth to task. It was the only occasion on which they had ever quarrelled and it nearly ended their friendship.

Lord Mulgrave had a mistress by the name of Moll Kirke, a promiscuous girl without heart or feeling, and York had a mind to her. He pursued her in his usual blundering manner and she treated him cruelly. Monmouth, for some inexplicable reason, decided to rival his uncle, and, as Moll was one of the Duchess of York's ladies, the whole court watched the rivalry with interest and some speculation.

'Though anyone giving odds on York is likely to lose his money,' Bab said, and invested ten guineas on Monmouth's chances with Lord Buckhurst, who was of the opinion that Mistress Kirke wanted to keep her place with the Duchess. Lord Buckhurst lost his bet, for one night Monmouth ordered a few of his guards to keep Lord Mulgrave entertained until dawn, by which time he had succeeded where his uncle had failed. Mulgrave's revenge was to tell York what his nephew had done. The Duke was furious but there was nothing he could do except to add it to the list of Monmouth's sins until the day came for a full reckoning.

Kit heard the tale next evening at Whitehall, and when he returned to the Cockpit, even though it was late, went straight to Monmouth's bedroom and stood by the hearth awaiting him, too angry, not so much with Monmouth as for him, to allow sleep to bring him to a more amiable frame of mind.

When the Duke came in he took one glance at Kit's face and dismissed his attendant. He looked tired, an unusual thing for him, and as soon as they were alone spoke without his usual pleasant tone.

'Well, Kit? What in hell ails you that you stand there looking at me like a Jeremiah about to rebuke the heathen?'

It was obviously not a propitious moment to speak, but for once Kit had lost his tact. Without preamble he remarked that Whitehall was seething with unseemly talk. 'One is used to ordinary tittle-tattle, but I must confess I found tonight's subject ill-befitting the high names it concerned.'

The Duke had gone to his bedside where he stood with his back to Kit, winding his watch. 'May I ask what you mean by that?'

'I mean that though your affairs of the heart are none of my business at least in the past they have been conducted with discretion and without the lechery that is now occupying the court babblers.'

Monmouth swung round, his face dark with a rare anger. 'You are quite right,' he said icily, 'in that my affairs are none of your business. I think you forget yourself.' He turned on his heel and the door slammed behind him.

The next morning, after a miserable and sleepless night, Kit was at his desk, uneasily sorting through some bills, when Kit Monk, now Albemarle in his father's place, entered with Captain Churchill. Kit cursed silently, for it meant there would be no chance of speaking to Monmouth alone when he came in, however he bade them good morning and Churchill, neat in his scarlet uniform, sat down astride a chair.

The more impatient Albemarle paced up and down. 'Where is his Grace?' he demanded. 'He made an appointment to ride with us an hour since.'

'I've not seen him this morning,' Kit said, and went on with his work.

Churchill leaned his arms on the back of the chair. 'What? Has our good Kit mislaid his duke? Well, I'll be damned if I'll wait any longer, I'm on duty in an hour.' He got up and started towards the door just as it opened to admit Monmouth, already dressed in riding clothes.

'Good day, Jack. Ah, Albemarle, you are here too.' Ignoring Kit, he apologized for keeping them waiting, but after a moment or two sent them down to the stables, promising to follow immediately. Then he came across the room and stood looking at his silent steward.

At length, dropping his gaze, he began to twist the diamond ring King Louis had given him. 'You were extremely outspoken last night. I take such censure from no man—unless it be my father. Perhaps if you feel like that about me you would prefer to seek other employment?'

Too stunned to answer, Kit stood rigid, scarcely able to believe it was Monmouth who had spoken such words. Yet perhaps he had merited them—it was the old nagging thought—they called him the Puritan and he hated himself for having earned that name. Only on this occasion he knew he had been right, that the censure had been justified.

'You know me better than that,' he said at last, and met Monmouth's stare without betraying his own miserable anxiety.

'Do I know you so well? You surprised me last night.'

Kit shrugged. 'I have always spoken my mind to you and I suppose I always shall. But by all means send me to the Tower if you will. Rochester spends half his time there for being rude to your father.'

Monmouth hesitated, but only for a moment longer, and then he burst out laughing. 'Damme, I believe you would enjoy it. You've the stuff of the martyr in you, old sobersides.' He put his hands on his shoulders. 'But I cannot, nay I will not, quarrel with you.'

'Nor I with you.'

'Then find your hat and gloves and come riding with us. Oh, by the way, I'm leaving Mistress Kirke to those who wish to fight over her. I've done. As for my—what did you call them—lecherous ways, why, I'll stop when I find someone to stop me.'

After that there were no more such incidents. Kit took no credit to himself for this, knowing the Duke had no liking in reality for such sordidness, but he could not help wondering if Monmouth would ever find any woman strong enough to 'stop him'.

Presently, when the Duke told him that Anna was carrying their first child, he hoped it might herald a more settled life for them, but he knew it was not Anna who would ever hold James of Monmouth.

4

Inevitably the war came. Louis invaded Holland by land and the English fleet put to sea, while day by day the regiments drilled in Hyde Park and recruits were summoned by drumbeat. The old war horse, Rupert, emerged from Windsor to join York in conducting the sea fight.

'But I don't like it,' he told Kit privately, 'I've a great respect for your countrymen—particularly now they have thumbed their noses at de Witt and elected young William Captain-General. God knows I don't wish to fight him but war, it seems, is the trade of kings and we must go where they lead.'

He departed to Chatham and presently Monmouth, eager to try himself in the field, went to Paris to join the French King and his army. Kit, at his own request, remained behind. The fact that William was now leading the Dutch entirely changed his view of the war, and as the French began to over-run the Low Countries he dreaded each day's news.

Time passed slowly and wretchedly. He haunted Whitehall, eager for any scrap of news, or visited Mr. Pepys who might be relied on to have the latest piece of intelligence. Once or twice he went to Tolbrooke, but knew himself to be poor company—except perhaps to young Elizabeth Rainsford in whose eyes, apparently, he could do no wrong. He walked with her in the autumnal woods and talked of Mark who had gone with Monmouth, while she searched for sweet chestnuts to roast by the fire, but he was restless and seldom stayed more than a few days away from London.

A letter came from his aunt Sophia, the usual acid missive complaining that his steward kept her short of funds—a manifestly false assertion as he well knew. She also wrote bitterly that her good friend Cornelius de Witt was in prison and for no more than refusing to see William proclaimed Stadtholder as well as Captain-General. Thinking of William's own long and bitter captivity, Kit threw the letter aside with impatience, but while such things were happening in Holland he could not help fretting at his own inactivity.

Then, suddenly and surprisingly, action came.

On an August morning Charles sent for him and with a bland smile gave him a letter to take to the Prince of Orange. Seeing his look of utter astonishment the King laughed.

'You don't understand, do you, Christian?'

'No, sir,' Kit answered honestly, 'I do not.'

'You thought I had deserted my nephew, eh? Come, admit it.' Charles looked searchingly at him until he gave a helpless gesture. 'I thought so. I see I must explain. King Louis wants the Low Countries for part of his empire. I do not want him to have them, but I need money. If my Treasury is empty I cannot do anything for anybody, can I? Now Louis will pay well for my help. On the other hand my nephew needs English aid and if de Witt is defeated I can then persuade Louis to treat with William, even if it is at a price. Between the two we may achieve much.'

Kit sat uneasily on the edge of his stool. 'With all respect, sir, that seems to me to be dishonest.'

'It is diplomacy, my boy, and the only way to keep too much power from falling into one pair of hands. If you do not understand it, leave it to wiser heads than your own.'

The reproof was mild enough. Kit accepted it—and that the intricacies of politics were beyond him.

Three days later he reached The Hague. As soon as he and Jeremy approached the gates, however, he knew that something was happening for they were greeted by a curious noise, an indefinable wave of sound that clarified, as they entered the gates, into the ominous yelling of a mob gone wild. He exchanged a glance with Jeremy and set spurs to his horse.

Once inside he saw crowds of excited people stretching away towards the square. In every hat there were Orange favours and a pedlar with a tray of orange ribbons was doing so fast a trade that he could scarcely keep up with the demand.

Kit dismounted and threw his reins to Jeremy. 'Go to that tavern over there,' he ordered, 'and wait until I return.'

Then, without pausing to listen to Jeremy's protest, he turned and made his way through the crowd. Everyone was talking excitedly and there were periodic outbursts of cheering and cries of 'the Orange! the Orange!'. There were yells too of 'Death to all traitors! Down with the de Witts!'

Kit caught hold of a man in the apron of a butcher and asked him why the people were out.

'The de Witts are dead,' the butcher told him, and spat cheerfully. 'Hell rot their stinking hides.'

'Dead? How, in heaven's name?'

The man jerked his head towards the Binnenhof, dark and forbidding across the square. 'Did you not know Cornelius was shut up there for refusing to recognize the Stadtholder? Well, brother John got an order for his release and came this morning to take him out of the city, but we weren't going to let the traitors get away. They've done harm enough.'

A fat woman smelling of garlic pushed herself up against Kit and stuck an elbow in his ribs. 'The good days of William the Silent will come again, eh?' She raised a raucous voice and yelled: 'God bless Prince William. He'll drive the bloody French into the sea. See this button, mynheer?' She waved the object in Kit's face. 'This was on the Grand Pensionary's coat not an hour since.'

The butcher grinned, exhibiting rotting teeth. 'Well done, old woman.' He leered at Kit with a blood-lust in his face that was revolting. 'I'm not a butcher for nothing and it was I who set John's head on a pole.'

Kit felt his gorge rise. To be torn to pieces by a mob wild with an animal desire for blood was a fate he'd not have wished on his worst enemy.

He turned from the man and elbowed his way through the straining, sweating press of people. There was something in the whole atmosphere, in the animal licking of the lips after the fiendish job was done, that nauseated him.

Making his way in the direction of the Huis van Wyngarde, he came out at last into an alley, turned into the street at the end of it, and then he was going up the familiar steps. To his surprise the door was half open and he entered quickly—but there in the hall he came to a sudden and awful halt.

The place had been wrecked. A hat and discarded cudgel lay by the entrance, one of the shutters had been torn loose from the long windows, curtains ripped down and several pictures flung from their places above the stairs. A mirror lay broken on the floor, while scattered wildly were the remnants of a statue of a Greek goddess, a favourite possession of his grandmother's.

In the middle of all this chaos, in a corner, old Hans the steward was crouching, rocking back and forth and moaning, his hands over his face.

Kit leapt over the mess of broken glass and china and caught the old man by the shoulder. 'Hans! What in God's name has happened?'

Hans had cowered in terror as he approached but hearing the familiar voice dared to look up. Seeing his master he burst into tears.

Kit pulled his travelling-flask from his pocket and held it out to him. The old man drank a little and then, trembling, brushed his hand across his mouth.

Kit helped him to his feet. 'What has happened?' he asked again. 'Come, there is nothing to be afraid of now.'

'They did it,' Hans stammered, 'that wild mob out there.'

'But why? Why?'

The old man was still trembling, but he sent Kit a swift shrewd glance. 'You did not know what was going on, young master. You've been so long away.' He was an old enough servant for there to be a hint of reproach in his voice. 'But since Mevrouw van Wyngarde died, Mevrouw Sophia——'

'Yes—what about my aunt?'

'She—it was the Ruart de Pulten, sir. He and his friends were here nearly every night, and Mevrouw Sophia at the head of the table, welcoming the Prince's enemies in a way that would have made your grandmother turn in her grave, God rest her.'

'And today?' Kit stared slowly round the ravaged hall. 'Was this the crowd's revenge?'

'Yes, sir. After they'd killed Cornelius and his brother they came here, but thank God we had word they were storming the Binnenhof. Mevrouw packed her jewels and told the coachman to take her to Herensdyke. Some ruffians tried to stop the coach but the driver beat them off. Then they came to the house. I tried to keep them out, Master Christian, but'—he was weeping again, his gnarled hands clasped together—'they broke down the door and I could do nothing. I am an old man, and the other servants ran away.'

'You did all you could, and at least my aunt got safely away.' Kit put his hand on the steward's shoulder. 'My poor Hans. You must think the family you've served so long has fallen low indeed when our own people turn on us.'

The old man straightened. 'A mob is a wild thing, Master Christian, and not to be regarded.' And then he added a little uncertainly, 'But these mad fellows did set our Prince in his proper place at last.'

Kit said nothing, moved by the truth of this remark. William indeed had his freedom now, but he wished it had not been bought with blood and terror and violence.

5

The murder of the de Witts caused a stir that travelled the length of Europe. King Louis, convinced that he had all but defeated the Dutch, prepared a final onslaught, but Charles, remembering his last meeting with his nephew, sent the Duke of Buckingham to The Hague to persuade the Prince to treat with England and France.

Meanwhile the Dutch, wild with excitement, watched with wholehearted joy the way in which their young Stadtholder assumed immediate control of the country. The fact that he stood alone against the armed might of England and France was not likely to deter William now.

On the day after the rising Kit applied for an audience and was told that the Prince had gone to the front, but would be holding a levée at the Honselaarsdjik on the following evening.

In the meantime, leaving old Hans to restore order at the Huis van Wyngarde, Kit rode out to Herensdyke to see his aunt.

He found her sitting in her room, crouched over the fire. Her hair was uncurled and hanging untidily about her shoulders, and to her nephew she seemed to have aged beyond all recognition.

As soon as she saw him she burst into a sobbing tirade against the mob, the wild beasts who had murdered her friends, against William who, she said, had incited them, and against himself for no more than not having been at home when he was needed.

'They would have killed me too and burned the house above my head,' she flung the words at him, 'but you care nothing for that!'

'My dear Aunt,' he protested, mildly, 'I am very sorry indeed that you should have been exposed to such danger, but you must admit that I did warn you. . . .'

She hardly seemed to hear him. 'They said I was his mistress, but it wasn't true. I only entertained him——'

'In a house that is mine and where the Orange has always been acknowledged,' he broke in sternly.

'In a house that should never have been yours!' An angry flush rose to Sophia's cheeks. 'I suppose you'll turn me out of Herensdyke too—though you've no right to that either.'

He stiffened. 'May I ask exactly what you mean?'

For a moment she seemed startled, as if she had inadvertently said more than she meant to. Then her eyes gleamed maliciously. 'You do not know?'

'I know that you never liked me, but that's not sufficient reason for what you have just said. What is behind all this?'

She drew herself up in her chair, her body rigid with emotion. 'You are no true van Wyngarde,' she said, and her voice shook. 'You took everything, everything that should have been mine.'

Astounded, he came forward to face her. 'What are you saying, Aunt? You cannot mean——'

'I do mean just that,' she interrupted spitefully. 'I don't know who begat you, but I do know Hendrik van Wyngarde was impotent.'

There was a deadly stillness in the room. Kit felt all the colour drain from his face. The room, his aunt, the familiar view outside, all took on an unreality, a quality of nightmare. A little of his horror must have shown on his face for when he took two steps towards her she gave a little scream.

'I shall not hurt you.' He put his hands behind his back. 'But you will tell me at once all you know of this.'

'Nothing more,' she stammered, 'nothing, I swear. When Hendrik brought your mother here from England they were already married. You were accepted as Hendrik's child. Old Mevrouw never said anything, and I had no proof.' Her eyes lit with hatred again and her face was flushed in ugly dark patches. 'I had no proof, but I knew a bastard child had taken the van Wyngarde heritage.'

Hoarsely, searching for some logical explanation, he said: 'You are saying this because you are, you always have been, jealous. I cannot, I will not, believe you.'

'You must,' she said in angry triumph. 'When I was young it was Hendrik I wanted, not Dirk, but he was always too busy with his books and experiments to——' She broke off and then went on in a rush: 'When my father and I were staying here once I went to Hendrik's room. I—I thought that if he compromised me he would have to marry me.' She giggled in a manner that horrified her nephew. 'That was how I found out about his—disability.'

He recoiled from her, his brain reeling, but Sophia had lost control of herself and nothing could stop the flood of words. 'What I lost in Hendrik I might have had when Dirk died: this house, all the land, everything. If your mother had not behaved like a whore——'

She stopped because he had caught her shoulders in so hard a grip that she was momentarily terrified. She moaned, her eyes rolling, and he released her so suddenly that she fell back in her chair.

He felt the sweat standing on his forehead. 'I'm sorry. But if ever you speak my mother's name again like that I'll not be answerable for the consequences.'

He straightened his back and walked away to the window where he stood looking out into the garden with unseeing eyes. He recalled little of his mother, but his father had taught him to venerate her memory. His father! He remembered the long happy hours they had spent together, the shared affection—and then he remembered too Hendrik's scholarly approach to life, his remoteness, his lack of social contacts. Sophia's accusation could be true—it was possible!

At last he said harshly: 'You cannot be certain, madame. These things are not always irrevocable. But I do know this. My father wished me to remain ignorant of—what you have said, or, if I am his son, then there is nothing for me to know.' He came back across the room and stood looking down at her. 'I think it would have been much better if you had not said what you have this afternoon. We shall never know the truth and now we cannot forget.'

She was sobbing, the tears running ruthlessly down her ageing face. 'I've told you the truth—it's time you knew. Now go, leave me——'

He went—out of the stuffy room, down the stairs and out of the house, as if the shock of her revelation was stifling him so that he must have air.

It was still raining a little, but he was glad of the drizzle for it cooled his hot forehead as he crossed the path and went out into the lime avenue beyond, pacing restlessly the length of the gravel drive.

He was too stunned to think clearly and Sophia's words pounded meaninglessly at his brain. He wanted to believe she had only spoken out of grief and envy but her voice had the ring of truth. Was he or was he not his father's son? And if not, how had it come about that Hendrik van Wyngarde had always treated him as if he was? Who could have been his father? Had his mother betrayed Hendrik whom she had married and whom he had loved so dearly? Oh God, that was too horrible an idea to entertain! And yet, if Sophia had spoken the truth, that was what must have happened.

He swung round, unable to bear that thought. There was no one left to whom he could appeal for the truth, no one who could tell him if he had any right to the name he bore. Only Sophia's words would remain to fill him with doubts for the rest of his life. Anger rose in him, an impotent rage that she had spoken after years of silence, that she had so completely and devastatingly destroyed his peace of mind.

He began to walk back down the drive and then, hearing a distant church clock chiming the hour, recalled that he was to present himself at the palace in two hours' time. He hurried back to the house, shouted for Jeremy, and then rode off at such a pace that Jeremy was hard put to catch up with him.

He arrived back at The Hague utterly spent in mind and body.

There were still bands of unruly apprentices and excited citizens roaming the streets, bonfires blazed in the square and already a ballad-monger was selling his verses on 'the dying of two traitors' or 'the Stadtholder's triumph'. Riding down the street towards his own house Kit found himself wishing William had achieved his aims any way but this.

At the gate of the Huis van Wyngarde there were some half-dozen apprentices hanging round the railings and looking up at the shuttered windows.

'Let me through, lads,' he said, quietly. 'There's naught to be gained here.'

One stalwart boy leapt forward with a yell.

'Pull him down! Seize him! He's nephew to that bitch who held court here.'

He flung sinewy arms round Kit's waist and taking him by

surprise succeeded in pulling him off his horse while two other lads went for Jeremy. Kit struck out, dimly aware of Jeremy shouting furiously, but the big youth lunged at him, catching him a blow on the chin that sent him reeling against the railings. He managed to steady himself and as the boy came on again punched him twice, first and very hard in the stomach and secondly on the jaw. His assailant staggered away, half conscious, and it was as he was gathering his scattered wits that another youth came at him. He was half the size of the first but in his hand he held a knife.

In the semi-darkness the horses were trampling wildly, Jeremy was dealing out blows with flailing fists, and in the stress of the moment Kit did not see the weapon. He went for the boy, meaning to send him after his friend, had one glimpse of a pale vicious face and then, too late, saw the rise of the steel. The next moment he reeled back from the impact of the blow and felt the youth wrench the blade free.

As he fell, clutching at his side, the boy yelled, 'Come away, come away—it's done.'

As swiftly as the fight had started it was over. Jeremy tried to hold one youth by the collar but he wriggled free and disappeared into the darkness. Then he saw his master fallen to his knees by the railings. 'Sir! Are you hurt?'

Kit shook the rain and sweat out of his eyes, and taking the outstretched hand got to his feet. 'No—at least, only a little. And you?'

'The young cut-throats winded me, that's all. Let me help you in, sir.'

Together they went up the steps and into the house where old Hans, hearing the noise of the scuffle and terrified that the mob had returned to burn the house, was holding high a lantern in a hand that trembled so much that the light flickered wildly. Jeremy turned anxiously to his master, and, eeing in its light blood oozing through the fingers pressed to his side, gave a faint cry of alarm.

'It's nothing,' Kit said, and indeed did not feel much pain, only breathlessness and exhaustion. 'Fetch some linen and strap me up and then lay out my clothes. I must be at the palace in half an hour.'

'But, sir,' Jeremy cried, aghast, 'you can't go now, not with that wound. You must get to your bed and I'll send for the surgeon.'

'You will do as you are told,' Kit snapped, in no mood to argue. Hans, get linen and warm water. Jerry, my clothes if you please.'

Half an hour later, suitably dressed in a coat of black satin with silver ribbons and a collar of Brussels lace, he was on his way to the palace.

All The Hague society was there, great families who had always been devoted to the House of Orange, and a good many people spoke to him with a slightly doubtful courtesy. Sophia, it seemed, had not been popular lately. Presently he took his turn in the line approaching the young Prince.

William sat in his chair as unchanged and inscrutable as ever. His hazel eyes watched the crowds in between the long scrutiny he gave each person who came before him, and when he spoke it was quietly and unemotionally as usual.

When it was his turn Kit came forward and bent the knee. He was becoming aware that he was feeling a little odd, and he had some difficulty in rising. William's eyes flickered over his finery.

'Ah, van Wyngarde.' He lowered his voice. 'I understand you wish to see me. Be in my private study at eleven o'clock.'

Kit bowed. 'As your Highness commands.'

He passed a somewhat unhappy evening, increasingly conscious of a burning sensation in his side, and a sharp altercation with Piet Daagen did not help matters.

He encountered the secretary in the reception hall.

'Well, mynheer,' the latter said. 'You see us in somewhat different circumstances tonight.'

'I rejoice for his Highness,' Kit bowed formally.

'And he has succeeded through his own merits, without the machinations of those that would use him for their own ends.' There was a distinctly malicious note in Daagen's voice.

Kit turned angrily to face him. 'If you are referring to King Charles then I tell you that you lie—and I would hardly call the blood-lust of a mob the merits of the Stadholder.' But there was no strength in him to reinforce his anger and seeing Daagen's face whiten he walked away into the crowd lest it should come to blood-spilling between them. Presently at the appointed hour he made his way to the study. There was a fire burning in the hearth, for it was a cool damp evening, and the Prince was holding his thin hands to the blaze and coughing a little as he sat in his winged chair. He indicated a seat opposite and Kit all but collapsed into it.

After a moment, however, aware that he was required to say

something, he sought for the right phrase. 'I rejoice at the change in your Highness's fortunes. It has come at last, as we dreamed it would when we were boys at our Latin.'

'I have long since ceased to feed on dreams,' William answered, as one who had put his boyhood far from him and did not wish to recall it. 'I have heard of the attack upon your house, van Wyngarde, and regret that your aunt, however mistaken her political leanings, should have been thus manhandled. When the people rise in a just cause their zeal sometimes exceeds reasonable bounds.'

A neat way to dismiss the blood-lust of an uncontrolled mob, Kit thought wearily, but William had already pushed the subject aside.

'Now, tell me why are you in Holland?'

Kit produced the letter from his pocket. 'This, Highness, was of course written before the sudden change here. I am sure his Majesty will be delighted to know that you are at last in the place of your fathers.'

'When he makes war on me?' William took the letter and read it slowly. Then he tore it into small pieces and threw them in the fire. 'You have my answer. Go back and tell King Charles that my people have restored my rights and that I shall surrender them to no man.'

'But, sir,' Kit tried to protest tactfully. He was finding it increasingly difficult to keep his hold on this conversation.

William held up his hand. 'And I have something to say to you personally. It seems to me that as head of your house you would be better employed serving mine than the king of a hostile state.'

It took a few seconds for the full meaning of this to penetrate Kit's brain. When it did a flush rose to his cheeks. 'Your Highness would have me leave England?'

William's piercing eyes held his. 'I would.'

Kit put a hand to his head. This was something he had always known he must answer but which he did not think he could come to terms with tonight. 'Highness,' he said at last, and haltingly, 'you know that I have lived now for eleven years in England and served the King in a particular capacity, quite apart from my place in the Duke of Monmouth's household. You will not deny I owe his Majesty, and the Duke too, some consideration.'

'No, I do not deny it, but neither did I think to have to remind you of your promise to me, given long before any you have made my uncle. You are the head of an illustrious house, long bound to my own, and your duty is here.' The Prince's rare smile came, illumining the pallid face and giving light to the large watchful eyes. 'If I offer you a place about myself, will you accept it?'

The heat of the room, the buzzing in his head and the curious sensation that consciousness was slipping from him made Kit clutch at the arms of his chair for stability. William's voice seemed to come from a long way off, but the impact of what he said, the offer itself, reached through the muffling fog that seemed to be enveloping him. His promise had indeed been given to William but that was so long ago, before he had gone to Whitehall, before he had known Charles and Monmouth, before Sophia had flung her revenge at him. And if what she said was true, if he was a bastard, then he could not be the head of his house. At Whitehall he was wanted and trusted, no one there cared whether or not he was a van Wyngarde, the King had only to send for him and he would come, Monmouth had only to call 'Kit' in his ringing voice and he would be there.

He put the other hand to his head and half rose.

'I cannot.'

'Cannot? I do not understand you, my friend. What is there to prevent you from returning to the position which even my time-serving uncle must admit is your heritage?'

'I cannot,' Kit said again. He felt unbearably hot, burning now with a heat that came from the throbbing fire in his side more than from the fire in the hearth. Sweat began to trickle down the sides of his face. 'There are reasons——'

'What reasons could there be? Van Wyngarde, you had better explain yourself.'

But now Kit could only shake his head. Even if he could think clearly, he could not explain, could not tell William the whole truth. He got to his feet and the movement jerked his side so that he gasped with pain. He felt a warm stickiness against the bandage and knew his legs would not bear him from this room. He clutched at the back of his chair.

'Your Highness—if you would pardon me—I fear I am un-well——'

Above the roaring in his ears he heard William saying: 'Yes, I see that you are. Sit down, van Wyngarde. Let me help you.'

He heard the familiar little bell ring, and was dimly conscious of the Prince himself holding a glass of brandy to his lips. . . .

The sun was already dipping into the west for it had shifted while he slept and the tree no longer shaded him from its rays, but Kit lay for a little while with his eyes closed still, absorbing the warmth, reluctant to emerge from his doze. He was lying on a day-bed in the garden of a house on the Sicilian coast and from the shore below he could hear the faint sound of waves breaking on the rocks. It was a soothing sound and had lulled him to sleep so that his book lay unopened by his side.

But at last he yawned and sat up, feeling pleasantly relaxed. At home in England it would be winter, with ice on the ponds and frost encrusting the evergreens in the park, and, looking across the green lawn and the profusion of flowers in the beds to the distant blue of the sea, he found it hard to realize that it was already three days after Christmas.

Footsteps sounded on the terrace, and turning he saw Sir Harry Richmond coming down the steps and across the lawn.

'Ah, Kit, you are awake. How do you feel?'

Kit swung his legs to the ground. 'A fraud, sir. I am really quite well and just being disgracefully lazy.'

Richmond studied him critically. 'Yes, I do think you are recovered. You are ready to journey to Rome tomorrow?' And when Kit assented he went on: 'It is a wonderful city—I shall never forget the years I spent there during my exile from England. And talking of England'—he put his hand in his pocket—'there are letters for you.'

Kit took them eagerly: one from Monmouth, one from Mark Rainsford and a third from Cathy. He opened the latter first and smiled at the badly written, ill-spelt scrap of paper. He himself had taught her to read and write but she was not yet very proficient.

Honoured sir, she began, in a stilted manner so unlike her that his smile spread. *I trust you be much recovᵈrᵈ. I am well. Mistress Jenkins has give me a littel dog. It dos do puddels on the floor. I beg that you will com home soon to*

Yʳ devotᵈ
Catherine Shaw

He laughed out loud and, when Richmond looked up enquiringly, said: 'Cathy has a puppy which is not house-trained. I fear she will find it a handful.'

He had made no secret of his liaison with her. Knowing Richmond's wish that he should marry, he had to make it clear that such was not his intention at the moment. He turned to the second letter.

'Mark says that Monmouth is very much the man of the moment, praised by no less a person than Marshal Turenne for his leadership. They went home as his Grace wanted to see how his son fared—he found the child thriving. Now they are in Paris and the Duke received royally. King Louis has given him a sword set with diamonds. Well, Louis always was ostentatious.' He paused, thinking of the last time they were in Paris, he and Monmouth. Madame had been alive and they had had two golden summer months with her.

He sighed a little sadly and went back to the letter. 'Mark also says York is busy refitting the fleet after the trouncing it got at Sole Bay. The navy is furious because a French admiral failed to come to Rupert's support in the fight—God's death, what allies have we taken to ourselves? There is talk that York will take a foreign princess for his second bride. Why, he's not been widowed a year yet.'

'No, but of all the children Ann Hyde gave him only the two girls are living. Perhaps he wants a male heir,' Richmond suggested. 'The King has none.'

Kit said nothing. It was not a subject he wanted to discuss. Instead he opened Monmouth's letter. 'His Grace hopes I am better. He is obviously in his customary health from all the activities he has been pursuing. He says Jack Churchill is the best officer he has.'

'That young man has promise,' Richmond nodded. 'What else does his Grace say?'

Kit laughed. 'You know Monmouth. To sit still for long enough to pen even half a page in his own hand is quite an achievement.' He folded the letters. 'I think I will go and write an answer to him before supper.'

They strolled back to the house together, but once in his own room Kit sat for a while by the table in the window, staring out towards the sea, blue and calm on this December evening. He felt, as he had told Richmond, fully recovered at last after months of weakness and lassitude. The wound he had received that night at The Hague had done more harm than he had supposed at the time, and his insistence on going to the palace had set up an internal bleeding which nearly cost him his life—as Jeremy was never tired of telling him. He had lain for a week in a raging fever so that the doctor despaired of his recovery. Jeremy, panic-stricken, had sent for Richmond who travelled post-haste to Holland, and when Kit at last returned to full consciousness it was to find his former guardian sitting by his bed. Monmouth sent urgent messages and required news of his progress to be sent every day, William also asked to be informed of his condition, while Rupert wrote a long letter suggesting various remedies and a cure for green wounds.

His recovery was slow and tedious, but Kit was considerably moved by all this concern for his health. Gradually it improved and as winter was approaching and the war still dragging on, Richmond suggested they should travel south where the sun would do the invalid more good than the fogs and damp of an English winter.

As he had lain day by day in his bed he had been tormented by the doubts his aunt had planted in his mind. There could be no answer to them, nor was there, as yet, an answer to the choice William had put before him, but both gnawed at his peace like a wretched canker and he was only too glad to go away for a while, to have a chance to think it all over.

Yet after all here, in this lovely place, he found he had not wanted to think of it. He read, lazed in the sun, swam in the sea while nature, intent on the cure of his body, dulled the normal alertness of his mind.

Wrenching his gaze at last from the view of the cyprus trees and the sea, he began his letter to Monmouth, telling him of their forthcoming journey.

Rome astonished him. Richmond proved an excellent guide and showed him the wonderful churches, the incredible magnificence of St. Peter's, the fountains and gardens, and the ruins of ancient Rome that he thought surpassed the present city for sheer beauty. But presently he began to see other things. There was poverty in London, but it was as nothing to the poverty and filth here in the meaner part of the town. They called this the Holy City, but at times its degradation sickened him, and as things turned out he was to have no very pleasant memories of it.

Richmond seemed a little on edge during these days, as if he sensed Kit's reaction to Rome, and several times, on the pretext of visiting an old acquaintance, went out alone. Kit was surprised, for this kind of uneasiness was not like Richmond.

One evening as they were at supper a servant came in to say that there was a gentleman below asking for the Signor van Wyngarde. Surprised, for he had no acquaintance in Rome, Kit went down the stairs to the crowded taproom of the inn and there, to his even greater astonishment, standing aloof by the door and wrapped in a black cloak, was Piet Daagen.

They had not met since the night of the Prince's levée and Kit bowed stiffly, his greeting cool. Daagen's manner was equally chilly, for he merely asked if there was somewhere where they might talk privately. Kit led the way up to his own room, and once there did not ask his guest to sit down, nor do so himself.

'Well, mynheer?' he asked abruptly. 'I need hardly say it surprises me to see you here.'

'I am in Rome to consult with his Highness's ambassador,' Daagen answered frigidly. 'I happened to see you in the street this afternoon and noted that you came into this inn. When I return to Holland I shall report to his Highness all that I have learned here.' He laid particular emphasis on the last part of the sentence.

'You choose to be ambiguous. I presume you have some more obvious reason for seeking me out.'

'I have, indeed. I have made it my business to ascertain why you are here and in whose company.'

Kit felt his temper rising. 'I have been travelling for my health, as you surely know, and in the company of my cousin. I cannot conceive why this should interest you.'

'Very plausible,' Daagen sneered, 'but it so happens that I know the true purpose of your visit is to act as emissaries from the King of England to the Pope.'

Kit stared at him as if he had taken leave of his senses. 'What in God's name are you talking about?'

'You are a king's courier. You have carried letters to us, and, as we now know, to France. Do not expect us to be too gullible, mynheer.'

'What nonsense is this?' Kit demanded impatiently. 'If you think I am here for any other purpose than to see the city then I must conclude you paused too long in the taproom below.'

Daagen drummed his fingers on the mantelshelf. 'Don't try to defend yourself by attacking me. Surely you don't think we believe you entirely ignorant of what was in the letters you carried, not only to us but to our enemies in France.'

Startled by this particular accusation, Kit was more bewildered now than angry. 'But of course I did not know what was in them. The King never discusses his private business with me, and anyway I never carried letters of any State importance to France.'

Daagen smiled a little, but it was not a pleasant smile. 'Don't try to dissemble, van Wyngarde. We found information among de Witt's papers, provided by his intelligence service, that you helped arrange the meeting between the King and his sister which resulted in that infamous Treaty of Dover.' He laughed scornfully. 'We understand well enough now why you told his Highness that there were reasons which prevented you entering his service.'

Kit stiffened angrily at this piece of misconception. 'My reasons were purely personal and known to none but myself.' And no concern of yours, he hoped his tone conveyed.

Daagen shrugged. 'You can look at it any way you like, but I suppose that having taken part in bringing about a treaty for the purpose of making war on us was reason enough for even your conscience to jib at accepting a place about his Highness.'

'That was not my reason,' Kit exploded furiously. 'Damn you, I knew nothing of that. It was something quite other . . .' He stopped. There was no way to clear himself of this indictment, nor to clarify why he had said what he had. And what could Daagen mean about the treaty? He groped for some answer, some explanation. 'The treaty has been made public now,' he said slowly, 'and even if I did carry letters concerning it—though how you can know about that I can't imagine—I cannot see that I can be held responsible for anything in it.'

'Responsible, no. But you must have known that there was more to it than was made public—else why the secrecy? France is no doubt paying England well, not only for the war but also for the King's conversion to the Romish church.'

Kit stared at him in undisguised disbelief. 'What are you talking about? There was nothing in the treaty about the King becoming a Catholic.'

'You are very naïve. Of course there was not. I imagine your English Parliament might have treated him very much as they did his father if they knew, but does it not occur to you there may be some secret clauses? We do not know for certain, but our spies are convinced of it. Why don't you ask Sir Harry Richmond? I believe he will know.'

Kit strode across the space dividing them and stood trembling with rage before the Dutchman. 'I tell you, as I did once before, you are a damned liar,' he swore. 'The King upholds the Protestant faith and if you say otherwise you will answer to me.'

Daagen shrugged his shoulders. 'As you wish, but you are being very obtuse. Sir Harry had an audience with Cardinal Vezziano yesterday morning and it was known that he represented King Charles.'

Kit put a hand to his head. 'Yes, yes, he was out then—but you cannot know for certain——'

'It is my business to know. Men can be bribed and I must give his Highness all the information I can as to how his enemies plan to act against him.'

'You are no more than a miserable spy,' Kit said in utter disgust, and the Dutchman turned on him.

'What, then, have you been all these years?'

In silence they stared at each other, Kit in a growing horror. What indeed had he been?

At last, rather desperately, he said: 'King Charles doesn't wish to act against the Prince. He wants to aid him.'

Daagen gave a scornful laugh. 'Yet he sends the Duke of Buckingham to his Highness with proposals no true Dutchman could accept—and when Buckingham told him that in that case he would see his country lost, his Highness replied that there was one way never to see it lost and that was to die in the last dyke.'

'It was a brave thing to say.' Kit could almost hear William saying it. It was so like him, and he would mean it. 'Perhaps it will take time to reach agreement, but the King told me that when de Witt was gone he would make peace.'

Daagen laughed again. 'How truly simple you are. King Charles wants money. He wanted it from the Prince as the price for his help and when his Highness refused he turned to France. I believe he would sell his soul for money—which is probably what he is doing,' he added.

White now with anger, Kit said: 'You will please go. I've no wish to hear any more lies or insults.'

Daagen gathered up his cloak. 'As you will. But I may as well tell you that, before I left, his Highness had given orders that you were no longer to be admitted to his presence. He thinks your loyalty doubtful, and when I tell him what I have learned here——'

Kit caught his arm. 'He cannot—he cannot believe that *I* have ever been disloyal to him.'

Daagen shook his arm free. 'No? Yet you carry correspondence that forces war on us, you consort with papists . . .'

Surprise overcame Kit's anger. 'I? I have never consorted with papists in any particular.'

Daagen looked at him with genuine contempt. 'Surely you cannot expect me to believe that you did not know your cousin to be a Catholic?'

Kit had recoiled. '*What?* It—it cannot be true.' And immediately a number of incidents came into his mind—Richmond's refusal to come to church last Easter at Tolbrooke on the flimsiest excuse, his preoccupation with certain friends, his frequent departures on mysterious business, even his behaviour the last few days. . . .

Daagen's voice broke into his thoughts. 'I have an acquaintance in employment at the Vatican and I know that this at least is true. Everyone there believes the King writes of his desire to be admitted to the Romish church, but that I cannot vouch for, though I do think it likely.'

Kit's anger flared again. 'God's death, if I believed all the idle rumours I heard at Whitehall——'

'You believe too little.'

He stood silent, fighting conviction. All his natural feelings revolted at the truth, rejected it, flung it from him even while a deeper, cooler reasoning prepared to accept it.

He looked up at the man standing silent now by the hearth. 'Why should I trust you? Why in God's name should I believe you, who would, I think, like to see me discredited?'

It was Daagen's turn to flush. 'You must believe me because I speak the truth and you know it. I think only of the Prince and I tell you, you will not be welcome at his palace. You had best return to that bawdy court and bawdy monarch where no doubt they are not too particular what kind of man you are.'

He stopped, for Kit had crossed the room in two swift strides. 'As God sees me I'll not bear that,' he said, and struck the Dutchman hard across the mouth. 'Now go, go, damn you, before I do worse!'

For a moment Daagen's eyes blazed and his hand went to his

sword-hilt, but then, surprisingly, he pulled out a kerchief, wiped his chin and without another word left the room.

Kit waited until he heard the latch fall and then, sinking into a chair, covered his face with his hands. How long he sat there, his mind mazed with shock, he did not know; but at last he got up, and, knowing he must face it out, went along the passage to Sir Harry's private parlour.

When he entered Richmond glanced up and then, seeing the expression on his face, sprang to his feet.

'My dear boy, what in heaven's name is the matter?'

He poured some wine, pushed Kit into a chair and stood over him while he drank it. 'What is it? Do you feel unwell again?'

'No, no, I am not ill,' Kit said, a little wildly, and then, in a rush of words, went on to repeat every accusation the Dutchman had made. When he had finished he did not look at his companion but leaned both arms on the table, overturning the glasses so that the dregs ran unheeded on to the white cloth.

Richmond's shoulders had sagged and he looked suddenly much older, but he seemed to make an effort not to show the shock Kit had in turn inflicted on him.

'Come,' he said gently, 'it is not as bad as he made out.'

Without looking up, Kit asked, 'That part about you—is that true?'

Richmond lifted his head. 'Yes,' he answered steadily. 'I became a Catholic a year ago.'

'Why did you never tell me?'

'I have tried—several times.' He saw Kit's jaw tighten and went on swiftly: 'You think I was afraid to speak. Well, perhaps I was, but I wanted you to understand.'

'I think my understanding is going to be sorely tried.'

'Tried, yes,' Richmond retorted astringently, 'but you are man enough to bear that.'

At these words Kit sat up and faced him, but he wondered if Richmond knew just how much he was asking. 'Can you deny that I have been used to betray everything that mattered to me?'

'No, I cannot deny it. I can only say you were warned. If one wishes to serve princes it asks a very single-minded devotion.'

Kit grasped his hands together, aware that nothing could coat the bitter pill of betrayal. 'I am a Protestant, yet you and the King have used me to attempt to restore the Catholic faith in England.

It would be an odd kind of devotion that would bear such usage. And can you deny that there are secret conditions in that treaty, that France wants the King to become a papist?'

'It is not my business to pry into such matters,' Richmond answered, and scarcely recognized his own harsh voice. 'If the King wishes it, then it is his right.'

'It is not his right to try and force an alien faith down England's throat!'

'Nor will he do so. You should know Charles better than that.'

For a moment Kit did not reply. Then he said slowly: 'I thought I knew him well, but I see I was wrong. He sent me, a Dutchman, to the Prince of Orange with preposterous suggestions that were, in fact, no more than bribes. It was dishonest, despicable. No wonder William would not accept.'

'You don't understand. The King wants peace—yes, he does— but he must keep the heel of France from England's neck. You know Louis would give much to have us in his power, don't you?'

'Yes, I suppose so, but——'

'This treaty will stop him, though people at home would never believe it; that is why any understanding he and Charles have must be kept secret.' Richmond sank down rather wearily in his chair. 'The King will get peace in his own way and in his own time.'

'Then I doubt his ways are mine,' Kit said, with a finality that made Richmond glance sharply at him. 'I can carry no more letters for him. I should always wonder what intrigue they might contain.'

'You don't mean that?'

'Yes, sir. If I may serve him in other ways, I will; and I will never willingly leave Monmouth, but that other must end—even if it means he dismisses me from court.' He got up and walked away to the window, looking out at the stars above the skyline of Rome.

Richmond came to stand beside him.

'I would have given anything to have prevented this happening,' he said, in a low voice. 'Believe me, I had planned to tell you of my own conversion, at least before we left Rome. As for the rest, well— Charles's wishes have always come first with me. I knew what we were risking and I am to blame, but he wanted you, and I agreed to it. You have every right to be angry.'

'That at least is honest,' Kit said, his eyes on the distant sky. 'I remember Prince Rupert warned me, years ago. He told me not to

put my whole faith in princes, let alone a Stuart prince, and I see that
he was right. The King lied to me——'

'Of course he lied to you,' Richmond interrupted sharply. 'Did
you think he would tell you what you carried? No one, not Rupert,
not even his closest ministers, knew what he was doing. Why then
should he tell you?'

The harsh truth of this was somehow harder to stomach than all
the rest. 'I don't know,' Kit said wretchedly. 'I see now there was
no reason why he should. But—I have defended his integrity.' He
thought of his furious vindication of Charles, flung so confidently
at his Dutch enemy, and a slow flush spread over his face. He
turned and crossed the room.

'Where are you going?'

'I don't know. Away—somewhere quiet. I must think.'

He left Richmond still standing by the window and went out,
closing the door behind him.

Dawn came up quickly as he rode out of the city. He set his
horse's head towards the blue rocky hills, allowing the animal to
pick its own way unhindered along the stony road. His head ached
and his eyes were heavy with lack of sleep but these discomforts
were as nothing compared to the burden on his mind.

It seemed almost impossible to grasp the fact that Charles, to
whom he had given faithful and honest service, should have so
abused it. He had trusted Charles, believed him to have William's
welfare at heart, believed that he wanted peace while all the time
Charles wanted nothing but money and his own security. It was
incredible. All his desire for plain dealing revolted at such duplicity
—yet surely, surely, there must be mitigating circumstances?

He would have to try and understand. He had not lived all these
years at Whitehall without knowing that a certain amount of deception was inevitable. He thought of the King's inveterate friendliness,
his pleasing smile and easy manners, his numerous kindnesses, and
could not believe that Charles had wanted to betray his trust, or
force England back to Catholicism.

He thought of Richmond, converted to that faith, working for
it no doubt with York whom everyone knew to be a papist. How
could it be? He did not know, only felt a weary disgust. His world

which he had been so sure he knew, accepting its faults and follies, was even less commendable than he had thought. Perhaps William had been right, perhaps Whitehall was the cesspool of iniquity he had called it. Perhaps that curious instinctive streak of puritanism that he had tried to root out of himself had been right too?

He rode on, turning the whole thing over and over in his mind without taking account of where he was going. At noon he became aware of an overwhelming thirst and stopped at a farm for a mug of milk, but he refused the good wife's offer of a meal. His stomach turned queasy at the mere suggestion of food.

He finished his milk and rode on. It was very hot now and he shifted stiffly in the saddle as he reached the top of a hill. Before and below him lay a panorama of Italian scenery, but as his horse came to a standstill he found himself looking, not at the magnificent view of purple hills, lush valleys and low white dwellings, but at a way-side Calvary. It was old and had fallen to one side, and the sun had long since burned away the paint that had once adorned it. Carved perhaps by some country craftsman, it had a simple primitive beauty coupled with a hidden agony that stirred Kit profoundly.

He dropped the reins and slid to the ground, leading his horse under the trees. There he flung himself down in the shade and closed his eyes, while his horse cropped gently at the grass.

A terrible despair took hold of him. He was a bastard, he was certain of it now; his father whom he had loved was not his father; his guardian whom he had trusted was not worthy of that trust; the King whom he had served so joyfully had not valued that service at any worth, and—one part of his mind whispered—the only woman he had loved had thrown his love back in his face. Even William, on whom he had unconsciously relied, had thought him a traitor, had condemned him without even a hearing. He remembered once asking William, with happy confidence, if it was impossible for an honest man to serve princes—and he saw now, with awful clarity, that his very confidence had made him appear the traitor he most assuredly was not.

Oh God, was there no faith left in the world, no one in whom he could place his trust and not fear to be betrayed?

Moving restlessly, as though his body sought for ease as his spirit sought for peace, his eye fell again on the Calvary. The sun had gone now and no longer lay across the face. It seemed shadowed, peaceful, less agonized.

And slowly his tormented mind emptied, was left naked, thirstily waiting.

It was thus that the answer came to him, into that empty stillness. He must go back to England. He must go back, face the King, abide by his decision, accept the consequences of that decision. It was as simple as that. He had only to find the courage for that one step and he would know—it would be given him to know—what to do.

He got to his feet, utterly exhausted, but the valley of decision was behind him and, though he did not yet realize it, he had defeated his Appolyon.

.   .   .   .   .

By the time the first snowdrops were out he was back in England. He rode into Whitehall late one evening and went straight to his own rooms at the Cockpit. There, to his surprise, one of the servants told him that the Duke had arrived home from France for a few days; he was out at the moment but expected back in the morning. Eleanor Needham, Kit thought, recalling the latest mistress —there were times when Monmouth's virility astonished him.

Then, because he did not like postponing the unpleasant, he went out to Will Chiffinch's rooms, asking when he might speak with the King. As luck would have it Charles was alone in his laboratory, and a few minutes later the keeper conducted him into the King's presence.

Charles was measuring liquid into a little bottle and without looking up enquired what had brought him home, hazarding that it was a letter from Richmond.

'No, sir.' Kit was conscious of a rising apprehension that turned his palms damp. He gripped his hands together wishing himself anywhere but here, having to say what might bring down a king's wrath upon his head. 'No, sir, though it is because of the mission he carries out in Rome that I am here.'

Charles swung round. 'What do you know of that? Harry had no right——'

'Your Majesty, I beg you to let me explain.' He hesitated, aware of the black eyes fixed on him, of the black brows drawn heavily together, but he had to bring out the words and he began, telling the story so baldly that he knew it made him sound more condemning, more rebellious than he was. Only of the change in his personal standing, of Sophia's charge, did he make no mention.

When he had done Charles swore roundly, told him he was a damned idealistic fool, threatened him with the Tower and then asked what the devil he did want?

Kit stood immobile, facing the blast. 'Only to stay with the Duke, sir. I know I have failed you, but, though I can't carry your letters as before, anything I have learned, particularly in Rome, I will never divulge to any man.'

'No, by God, or you would soon find yourself out of harm's way!' Charles's eyes flashed for a moment. He continued to stare disconcertingly at Kit. 'I believe that once I too hated deceit, but I have long since learned that one must play the game according to the prevailing rules. I suppose you have forgotten that I warned you in these very rooms that I would use you without scruple.'

'No, sir, I have not forgotten. I—I did not understand what it might mean.'

Charles laughed harshly. 'I see you did not. Well, it meant that you are dispensable—the Crown is not.' He swung away from Kit, replacing the stopper in a bottle on the table. 'Go back to Monmouth, then.' He glanced round in time to see relief flood into the face opposite him. 'I must say your request surprises me a little since you censure my ways so forthrightly. I should not have thought Jamie's principles in keeping with such high-mindedness.'

'Sir, I do not confuse principles with prudery,' Kit protested, and was aware how stiff it sounded. 'If I hold to the first I need not be accused of the latter.'

'Maybe not, but why you should attach yourself to the greatest young rake-hell in town I can't conceive.'

Kit forced a smile. 'Perhaps it is because he is all the things I am not.'

'I would not be sorry if he were some of the things you are,' the King said honestly. He sighed a little and added: 'I wish you had trusted me, Christian. I am not the black-dyed villain you seem to think. I want the welfare of England and I am not going to force popery on her whatever you may suspect. As for my conscience— that, I believe, is my own affair.'

Kit's face burned. 'Your Majesty, forgive me. You have always been generous to me and if I may serve you in any other way——'

Charles left his bottles and jars and came to stand facing him. 'But only as it suits your conception of what is right, eh? Odso, that's how they talked to my father! It seems I got me a puritan to carry my letters.'

'Yes, sir.'

Charles's eyebrows shot up, and then he laid a hand on Kit's shoulder. 'Well, at least I know I can trust you with what secrets you have learned. I don't think we can serve any useful purpose by going over the matter any further. Go back to your office, Mr. Comptroller; keep Jamie out of debt and out of mischief, and it is I who will be in your debt. Fortunately you are able to take to an honest profession—I am not!'

The grim lines around his mouth relaxed, Charles Stuart laughed, and Kit was able, this time, to laugh with him.

So the interview ended. It had been so much easier than he had expected that he felt now only a warm gratitude towards the King. He would be able to tell this to Richmond when he came home; for the latter, his business in Rome unfinished, had remained behind and they had parted unhappily. The King's understanding, Kit thought, would help to heal the breach that neither wanted.

He woke the next morning to find the ever-energetic Duke dressed and standing by his bedside.

'Well, sobersides, so you've come home at last, and looking as brown as a nut too! 'Pon my soul, we have all missed you prodigiously.'

Kit sat up, shaking the hair out of his eyes. 'Your household seems to have survived without my care,' he said amusedly and then, because he was so relieved to be back with one who had no part in his disillusion, he held out both hands: 'Jamie, you'll never know how glad I am to see you.'

'And I you. Nothing is the same without you to frown upon my nonsensical ways. Up with you, now. I'm away to St. Martin-in-the-Fields to show myself a good Protestant. Will you come?'

'Of course.' Kit pushed back the bedclothes and began to dress. 'I heard some talk in an inn at Canterbury that the Duke of York has laid down his commission and all his public offices. Is it true?'

Monmouth pulled a face. 'Aye, it's true. When Parliament passed their Test Act we all had to take the Sacrament according to our Anglican rite or withdraw from office. My uncle refused and declared himself a papist, though everyone knew it long before that. Now he has nothing to do and walks in the park every day looking a picture of misery.'

Kit said nothing. York's unhappiness aroused no sympathy in him.

Monmouth sat himself astride a chair and went on: 'I tell you, Kit, our good English folk like this war less and less. They prefer an enemy they know to a friend they can't trust. Shaftesbury says he doubts we'll have the French for allies much longer.'

'Thank God for that.' Kit rang for his shaving water and then wrinkled his brow. 'Shaftesbury?'

'Yes—Ashley Cooper, you remember him? He's Lord Chancellor now and since Clifford resigned because he's a papist and Buckingham's in disgrace—I forget quite why—little Shaftesbury is my father's most influential minister.' The Duke leaned his arms on the back of the chair and watched Jeremy wrap a towel about his master's neck. 'He's a great man for all he's less than five feet tall. He leads the new country party that will have peace with Holland. They want England for the Protestants and no papist alliance and so I am with them.'

Kit swung round, narrowly escaping having his throat cut and drawing a disapproving grunt from Jeremy. 'Sir! For God's sake, don't you turn politician. That would be more than I could bear.'

The Duke looked surprised. 'I? Why, our Whitehall gossips will tell you, and truthfully, that I've not the head for it. But I do think Shaftesbury right in what he believes to be for the good of the country.'

He talked on cheerfully, absorbed in his subject, and asked no questions of Kit, for which the latter was grateful. Only as they left the Cockpit he felt he must explain, in as discreet a manner as possible, that he could no longer act as emissary for the King, partly because he too hated the French alliance.

'There are other reasons as well,' he finished, rather lamely. 'I will tell you it all some time, Jamie, but not now.'

'As to that,' Monmouth answered lightly, 'I've never questioned what you did for my father and if your conscience—God bless it—won't let you do it any longer, why, I'll have more of your company myself.' He laughed and took his arm as they went downstairs.

To Kit, after his weeks of unhappy bewilderment, it was balm to be wanted for himself alone.

When they reached the church it was to find that the service had already begun, had in fact reached the consecration prayer. Dr. Tenison, the vicar, saw them enter and paused as Monmouth walked slowly forward.

A whisper ran round the church, quiet at first, and then with gathering strength.

'God bless the Duke of Monmouth.'

'God bless the Protestant Duke!'

Kit glanced sharply at Monmouth. This was a new warmth, a new intensity of feeling; he had always been popular but this was more than popularity.

When they reached the chancel steps they knelt together while Dr. Tenison finished the prayer. Then before the silent congregation Monmouth, and Kit after him, received the Sacrament.

It was what every avowed Protestant was required to do, but stealing a glance at Monmouth's face and seeing the absorbed devotion there Kit knew that it was far more than that to him. Exactly what it did mean he learned when they reached the privacy of the Cockpit.

Monmouth had been unusually silent on the way home and now with a gravity he rarely exhibited he turned to Kit.

'I had a purpose in going to St. Martin's this morning. Did you know my old tutor, Tom Ross, was dead? No? Well, when he was dying he told me he had seen my mother's marriage lines. I believed him, Kit. I believe my mother was truly married to my father and that the proof is somewhere to be found—but even if I do not find it I believe it exists. Tom saw it and that is enough for me.' He paused and then added quietly: 'You see what it means? I am the legitimate heir to England, the Protestant heir——'

The Protestant heir! And that, England's greatest need! With his mind racing to assimilate this, Kit stood silent, his eyes on Monmouth's face. He knew that mobile countenance so well that he could have recognized any deception, but he saw none. Monmouth's faults were legion enough, but he did not lie and he was incapable of duplicity.

And then, startlingly, Kit saw also that here was the answer to his own problem. Here was a prince to serve, a prince to be trusted; here was his cause, his purpose, where it would not matter whether he was a van Wyngarde or a nameless bastard, where the faith he held was held with equal tenacity, where friendship and loyalty would never be in question. Stronger than any call of duty, stronger than any other loyalty, was his love for Monmouth.

Slowly he went down on one knee.

'It is enough for me also,' he said in a low voice, and for the first time put Monmouth's hand to his lips.

BOOK THREE

A Prince Persuaded 1678-1685

'The enemy are well entrenched,' Mark Rainsford said, screwing up his eyes in the sunlight. 'See, Kit, the abbey lies along that ridge and those slopes are covered with thorn bushes.'

Kit followed his pointing finger. 'They won't be easy for the cavalry to scale.'

'No, but Monmouth has ordered the gunners to clear the woods of snipers on each side of the escarpment. We'll go up there.' He glanced at his friend. 'Are you ready?'

Kit knew he referred to more than the immediate moment and he nodded. 'Yes, but I wish my captain hadn't taken a fever. I'd rather not be leading the troop myself.'

Mark took his arm. 'You've no cause to fear on that score. I've seen how you drilled your men in the park at home.'

'Maybe.' Kit added quietly: 'By the way, should anything befall me in this fight Jerry has all my personal papers and instructions to deliver them to Sir Harry at Tolbrooke. Perhaps in that event you would see he gets safe away.'

Mark gave his arm an added pressure. 'Of course, but nothing will happen to you. It's your first fight but not likely to be your last, nor mine, please God.' There was just enough gaiety in his voice to give confidence to the sentiment.

'Amen to that,' Kit agreed, 'but I wanted you to know.'

Mark's smile faded a little. 'You are right, Kit. A man is a fool if he deludes himself that he is less likely to fall than any other. If I should die, I have left my affairs in order—only perhaps you would be good enough to see that Isabel gets my personal effects.' On his thin dark face the struggle to suppress the fear, not of death but of the parting with his wife, was painfully obvious. He was a dedicated man, his whole life devoted to only two objects, his wife and his soldiering.

Presently he went off and Kit inspected his own troops. To him this campaign was like the realization of an old dream, for England and Holland were united at last against France and their armies led by Monmouth and the Prince of Orange.

Not many months ago Parliament had refused to continue financing the war against Holland, and the King, finding there was no more money to be screwed out of Louis either, did a neat *volte-face* and allied himself with his nephew. He forced the Duke of York to give Princess Mary to William as his bride, despite the entreaties of the father and the tears of the daughter, and Protestant Europe welcomed the alliance.

Kit promptly begged a place in one of the regiments to go to Holland and Monmouth, considerably amused, made him a lieutenant in his own troop of guards. Kit applied himself with his usual thoroughness to his new job. He was out in Hyde Park every day, training and drilling his men, but they had little enough time for all that needed to be done and after only a few weeks, with all the arms and equipment that could be collected, they were shipped to Ostend.

Now, with their Dutch and Spanish allies, they faced the French some fifteen miles south-west of Brussels. Monmouth was Lord General of all the English forces, a title that had made his uncle of York rage with impotent jealousy—even his insistence on the word 'natural' in his nephew's commission had not made up for the loss of an office York himself might have held but for his religion.

The years since Kit had pledged himself to Monmouth's cause had indeed seen an advancement of that cause. York grew daily more unpopular as Monmouth's star ascended. The younger duke was now Master of the Horse, Chancellor of Cambridge University, a Privy Councillor and Commissioner for the Admiralty, as well as holding numerous smaller offices. He was also the figurehead for the growing Country party which opposed the King's policy and which was governed by the powerful Earl of Shaftesbury.

At the back of Kit's mind, barely acknowledged, was the old certainty that one day it might come to a clash of arms between the two dukes, papist and Protestant, and he was glad now of the chance to learn to be a soldier.

It was two o'clock when the bugles finally sounded the advance, the guns opened up and Kit sat his horse, Chimera, at the head of his squadron. It was a hot sultry afternoon and his hand felt sticky inside its leather gauntlet, while his buff coat was already causing him to sweat profusely. Behind him, equally sweating and earnest, his lads waited, and he found himself praying that he might lead them well, with vigour and enterprise, yet without undue hazard of their young lives.

Only as they began to move forward did it occur to him that he had never killed a man, and even now, facing a hated enemy, had no desire to do so.

Half an hour later, there was no time for such thoughts. It was kill or be killed and strongest of all was the desire not to die.

They found less difficulty than anticipated in surmounting the hillside for the gunners had done their work, but at the top the enemy were firmly entrenched in the abbey and the château. Monmouth, riding furiously along the whole approach, called out to his captains to attack the north side of the abbey where the outbuildings lay; as he passed he gave Kit a quick reassuring smile which Kit answered by a salute with his sword.

His own troop faced a low wall that flanked the monks' kitchen garden and forming the line he saw enemy musketeers crouched behind it. 'Come on, boys,' he called, cheerfully. 'It's a lower wall than many I've cleared in the hunting-field and we'll take the enemy by surprise if we go straight over it.'

Along the lines trumpeters sounded the advance and they emerged from the shadow of the trees into the sunlight at a full gallop, crossing the short space with a thundering of hooves and a flying of dust that brought every man to battle-pitch. Kit held hard to the reins, dug his heels in and took Chimera over the wall with ease.

The musketeers had opened fire as they charged and a few shots had found their mark but Kit sensed that most of his men were over and in; he bawled the order to wheel and it was then that he saw the result of the weeks of training, for his troop turned as easily as if they were still in the park at home.

Excitement seized him, a rising exaltation that swept him on. He rose in his stirrups and saw the enemy had formed a line, the officers with drawn swords and the men, with no time to reload, preparing to use the butt end of their muskets.

At the head of his troopers he rode at the line, churning the neat rows of cabbages as he went. An officer came at him with a long curved sabre, but he deflected the blow and Chimera, rearing wildly, knocked the man off his feet, trampling him beneath plunging hooves. Kit heard his scream, but there was no time for pity, for two musketeers were converging on him, swinging their weapons. He struck out and drove his sword deep into the first man's chest, wrenching it free just as the second man lifted his musket and caught him a blow on the shoulder. He swayed a little, grabbed the reins to steady himself, thrust forward with his sword. French blood spurted over his breeches and Kit plunged on.

They fought it out among the cabbages and beans, and after less than fifteen minutes the few remaining Frenchmen threw down their arms and cried for quarter. Kit called his men off and at last, panting and trembling a little, had time to look round. He could see that Mark's troop had done their work further along and Mark himself was riding along the line, while beyond the stables a crowd of surrendered French dragoons was being rounded up by soldiers in Dutch uniform—and striding across the courtyard, on foot, hatless, and with a bare sword in his hand, was William himself.

'The abbey is ours, lads,' Kit said in triumph. A quick glance told him he had lost only three men, though several were nursing wounds. 'Re-form—close order.'

As they moved to obey, he became aware that his shoulder was painful, his right arm ached, his clothes were dyed with alien blood and his sword still red—but the revulsion had gone. It had been a clean fight, against an enemy he could see, the odds equal, the issue plain, and he could look at the bloodied corpses among the cabbages and thank God that no more than three of his men lay there.

That night they bivouacked where they were. Kit went the rounds seeing that his injured men went to the surgeon and checking the number of dead, until at last, deadly weary, he was free to stretch himself on the ground, his head on his folded cloak. Jeremy had come up from the baggage waggons, bringing miraculously a jug of hot soup, and now all he needed was sleep.

He closed his eyes, but he had scarcely begun to doze off when an orderly came up calling his name. The Lord General, it seemed, needed him at once.

He got to his feet, groaning inwardly. Surely even Monmouth must be tired! But he found the Duke writing rapidly, using a drum for a table.

'Kit!' He looked up at once. 'How did you fare today?'

'Well enough, but I confess I would have liked to sleep tonight!'

Monmouth laughed. 'I'm sorry—you can sleep later. There's news just come in—a peace has been signed at Nimwegen. So your war is over. We can go home and Cousin William has his boundaries safe for a while.'

'Thank God.' Kit sat down astride an empty powder keg.

'Why? Did you hate the fight so much?'

'No,' he answered honestly. 'To tell you the truth, I like soldiering better than I would have thought possible. If we cannot live in peace on this earth—and it seems we cannot despite the treaties that are made—then I would rather fight this way than through politics.'

'Of course you would,' Monmouth said at once, and with vigour. 'So would any sane man. Now I'll tell you why I sent for you. I'm going back to Brussels to find the rest of our English regiments as Cousin William wishes to review them, and then I'm for home to report to my father. I'll take you and Mark with your troops as my guard. Can you be ready by dawn?'

Kit turned his eyes heavenwards. 'Must you always be off at a moment's notice? Yes, we can be ready, though my men are desperately weary.'

'I know, but I'll rest them later. We'll snatch a few hours' sleep and then be on our way. The quartermaster will see our wounded get proper attention. Incidentally, you might like to know that your Stadtholder fought like ten men today—on foot, like any private soldier!'

It was typical of Monmouth, Kit thought with a warm glow of pride, to be so generous to William.

At that moment the Prince himself came up, looking tired and drawn and coughing a little, but none the less in command of himself. He nodded to Monmouth and looking beyond him saw Kit.

They had not met nor spoken for six years, not since that night when Kit, with a knife wound in his side, had visited the Prince in his palace at the Honselaarsdjik. After that William had believed him a traitor and pride kept him away.

Now William surveyed him dispassionately. 'So,' he said coolly, 'we have fought together, van Wyngarde.'

Kit inclined his head. William grew in mental stature every time he saw him, he thought. 'Yes, Highness. It was always my wish.'

William subjected him to a disconcerting stare and it was Monmouth who covered the awkward moment, for once saying the right thing.

'Aye,' he put a hand on Kit's shoulder. 'Lieutenant van Wyngarde has for many years wished us allies, cousin, and today has proved we do very well together.'

William nodded again, his eyes still on Kit's face, lit by the lantern on the drum. 'If I misjudge a man, van Wyngarde knows well enough that my past life did little to incline me to trust my fellows.'

'Highness . . . ' Kit began and then stopped. William would give no more, he knew that and sensed that the matter was best left alone. His relationship with the Stadtholder would never again be what it once was.

He bowed, took his leave of Monmouth, and went away into the darkness to inform Mark of the Lord General's orders.

.   .   .   .   .

Three days later they were back in London. There they found Whitehall deserted, except for officials, for the court was gone to Windsor, but Kit, crossing the Matted Gallery, came rather surprisingly upon Rochester sitting alone by a window, looking curiously forlorn. His face was ashen pale and his hands, lying limp in his lap, seemed skeletal. He turned when he heard steps and immediately sprang to his feet, both hands outstretched, his welcome almost pathetic in its gladness.

They sat exchanging news for a while but when Kit queried why his Lordship was alone at Whitehall, the Earl evaded the question and muttered something about having affairs to see to in London.

Kit laid a hand on his arm. 'My lord, the Duke and Mistress Needham are to sup with me tonight in Axe Yard, and Mark too. Will you join us?'

A pale smile crossed Rochester's face. 'Thank you, Kit. To be honest I was sitting here wishing for an evening in the company of old friends, none of whom seemed to be in town. I have sworn off women for a while so if you will tolerate me unaccompanied . . . '

'Of course,' Kit answered at once. This was a rather strange

Rochester and he wondered what was wrong. 'Mark is coming alone too—he is thinking only of riding home to his wife tomorrow.'

'He is a fortunate fellow,' Rochester said, and sighed. 'To know what one wants is a greater blessing than we realize—but how to know, that's the rub, eh? Will six o'clock suit you?'

He wandered away down the passage and Kit, watching him go, was bewildered. But he had no time to ponder over it now and hurried round to Axe Yard to tell Cathy they would have four guests for supper.

She greeted him with a cry of delight and flung herself into his arms. Then, to his astonishment, she burst into tears. She was not given to sentiment or over-emotion, and he put a hand under her chin so that he could look into her tear-stained face.

'Why, what's this, sweetheart? Are you so distressed to see me, or has Mrs. Jenkins turned respectable and given us notice to leave?'

She laughed shakily and, taking his kerchief, wiped her eyes. 'Neither—I am sorry to be so silly.' She seemed at once herself again and when she heard of the invited guests, bustled out to the butcher's crying that he was a wretch to give her so little time to prepare.

It was for Kit a pleasing evening to begin with. Eleanor Needham, still Monmouth's mistress, was tall and fair with a full figure that seemed to Kit depressingly voluptuous; her eyes seldom left his face and her delight in his return was patent. Monmouth, however, was no longer in love with her, and though he could never be anything but kind to a pretty woman, turned from her whenever the conversation held a more masculine interest. Rochester wanted to hear of the campaign and Monmouth began to relate the taking of the abbey, using the table implements to describe his strategy.

Smiling a little, Mark turned to Kit. 'We'll leave his Grace to the story—it makes good supper-time entertainment. I wanted to tell you that I found a letter from my father awaiting me at my lodgings. Kit, you'll never guess who is with the court at Windsor!'

'I shan't spoil your pleasure by trying. You obviously want to surprise me.'

'Elizabeth!' Mark answered, and had the satisfaction of seeing his surprise take effect. 'She is to attend our general's lady.'

'Elizabeth?' Kit exclaimed. 'To attend the Duchess? But she is only a child.'

Mark laughed. 'She is sixteen and it was time she moved into the world. Now that we are home Isabel will join me here in London and it would be lonely for Elizabeth at Westfield. Her friend, Baroness Wentworth, is already at court so she has not come wholly among strangers.'

Kit was silent for a moment. He had not seen a great deal of Elizabeth these last years, but on his visits to Westfield had thought her growing up reserved and shy. How then would she fare at court?

'I cannot think she will be happy,' he said at last, in a low voice. 'She is very young and Whitehall is so——'

'Ah, Kit is bewailing our morals again!' Rochester, his conversation with the Duke at an end, was leaning over Kit's chair.

He sat up at once. 'Why no, my lord, I gave that up long since. I'll go the road to hell with the rest of you.'

Rochester wrinkled his long straight nose. 'How impolite! Well, if you are determined to be damned then at least you'll be in damned good company.'

After the laughter at this Rochester still continued to lean confidentially over Kit's shoulder. 'I've been delivered of a new poem in your absence, my friend. I grow weary of courts and kings, of sycophants and pimps, and I've vented my spleen in some verses. Will you bear with them?'

Together he and Kit moved away from the others to a window-seat where Cathy's little dog, exhausted with chewing at the bones thrown him during the meal, lay curled up asleep. Taking a paper from his pocket, Rochester began to read:

'In the isle of Great Britain, long since famous known

.   .   .   .

There reigns and long may he reign and thrive,
The easiest Prince and best-bred man alive.
Him no ambition moves to seek renown,
Starving his subjects and hazarding his crown;

.   .   .   .

Restless he rolls about from whore to whore,
A merry monarch, scandalous and poor.'

Kit laid a hand on his arm. 'Stop, I beg you. If you let that come to the King's ear, I fear he will find the poem more treasonable than amusing.'

'Do you think so? Is my wit not stronger than my sting?'

'Not this time. Even you cannot make such mock of the Crown.'

Rochester leaned back. 'No? Well, perhaps not; but to tell you the truth, Kit, I think I am past caring.' He looked deadly weary, the shadows under his eyes black in the candlelight.

Kit said sharply, 'My lord, you are ill—forgive me that I did not see it before.'

A strange melancholy crept over the attenuated features. 'Yes, I am ill—sick of the pox and sicker still of the diet-drink the quacks in Leather Lane cram into me. Asses' milk and mercury, or turpentine which is even worse—ugh!' He gave an involuntary shudder. 'I stayed in London these past weeks to sit in their stinking sweat-tubs, but I am no better.'

'I am very sorry. I do wish you well.'

Rochester smiled faintly. 'I know you do. You're a good fellow, Kit. You have never been to my home at Adderbury, nor to High Lodge above Woodstock, have you? I promise you I am a different man in the country—there I can sit at my window and look out upon the summer greenness or the winter's leafless beauty and believe there is peace to be found. Yet I cannot stay. Even though I love Adderbury, and Woodstock too—still I cannot stay.' He looked at his companion with an almost feverish light in his large eyes. 'Do you believe the soul is immortal, Kit?'

Startled by the unusual gravity in the Earl's low voice, Kit answered quietly, 'Yes, my lord, I do.'

'I thought you would. I never did—or I never bothered to think about it. I had my body and it was enough. It ruled me and gave me pleasure and I lived for it; but now—now my body is failing me. It is nothing but a burden and a torture, so I am thinking of my soul. That is odd, isn't it?' He laughed, but in so unhappy a manner that Kit reached out and took his hand in a firm grasp.

'No, it is not odd. You have allowed me to read some of your poems——'

'You mean the few that are not bawdy, or worse!'

'—and no man could write as you do and not possess a soul. But now, I do beg you to let me get a hackney to take you home. You are not fit to be anywhere but in your bed.'

Rochester shrugged. 'As you will. Come and see me soon, Kit. I've a mind to talk with you some more.'

'I will,' Kit promised, and saw him into a coach, aware of an aching compassion. Rochester had been wild, drunken, licentious—all three separately and together—but his mind glowed with a strange brilliance. Now he was dying—for Kit had seen the slow inexorable claim of death marked upon his features—and it seemed a weary waste of talent, riches and opportunities.

Soon afterwards Mark took his leave saying he wished to be on the way to Westfield by dawn, and presently Monmouth, the adoring Eleanor on his arm, departed in the direction of Russell Street where she lived in the house he had bought for her.

Cathy began to tidy the room but Kit, coming back from closing the outer door, took the glasses from her hands and put his arms about her. 'Those can wait until the morning,' he said. 'I've not held you like this for too long.'

He bent to kiss her and felt her mouth cling to his, her arms tighten about his neck. Presently, raising his head to look down at her, he saw that she was near to tears.

'Cathy, what is it? What is troubling you?' He searched her face. 'Why, you are pale and you look very weary. Has something been amiss while I've been away?'

She twisted her head away, laying her cheek against his shoulder that he might not see her face. 'I miscarried of your child before Christmas.'

'Cathy!' Aghast, he put a hand under her chin and forced her to look at him. 'Why didn't you tell me?'

She gave a little shrug. 'You were away and anyway I have always known you did not want me to bear you a child.'

He let her go and walked away to the window. 'You are quite right—I did not.'

She watched him in silence for a moment and then came to him, touching his arm tentatively. But he seemed scarcely aware of her, his eyes fixed on the dark street below. When he withdrew into these strange remote moods, as he did sometimes nowadays, she was a little afraid—not of what he might do or say to her, but of what his conscience might make him do to himself. She had long been aware of the power of that conscience.

'Why, Kit?' she asked at last, a little uncertainly. 'Why do you not wish it? Mrs. Needham has given the Duke four children, Mrs. Barry has borne the Earl of Rochester a daughter and——'

'Then I'll not father another if I can avoid it,' he interrupted, sharply. 'I tell you, Cathy, this world is no place for a nameless man, or woman either for that matter.'

'Kit! Why do you mind so much?'

He shrugged. 'I'm afraid you will have to accept that I do.'

She leaned against him. 'But I want your child.'

'No.'

There was another silence between them. Then she said, her laugh a little forced, 'That is for wives, is it not?'

He swung round at last to face her. 'Cathy! You know I have no wife, nor am I likely to take one.'

'Well, if you're going to emulate your friend Bab May in staying single, you'll be glad of me, won't you? A man, I suppose, must have his solace, and these lodgings are better than Mother Cresswold's bawdy-house.'

He reached out and caught her shoulders. 'Cathy, you're not a bitch so don't behave like one.'

For a moment she stared at him defiantly and then her face crumpled and with a long shuddering sigh she leaned against him. 'Kit, forgive me. I did not mean to be horrid, but—I have had other men before you, you know that, only you see I never cared for any of them and—I love you. That is why I want your child.'

He held her close, her hurried whispered words cutting deeply into his mind. Gently he stroked the dark hair. 'You make me ashamed,' he said, very low. 'Are you truly well again?'

'Oh yes, indeed. I am only a little tired, and don't think I reproached you, Kit. It is not your fault that I have learned to love you so much.'

Unable to bear the sight of her tear-stained face, he turned and blew out the candles. 'Cathy! Come——'

Their loving, that night, seemed to reach a new intensity; as if each took refuge in their physical union to escape the other conflict. Yet, lying with his head against her shoulder, he was still conscious of that now familiar shame.

His friends, he thought, would have laughed at him for such self-probing doubts, and he wondered why life had to be, for him, so fraught with questioning.

He desired Cathy indeed, but she had given him more than mere desire and did not deserve that he should speak so cruelly to her. It was not her fault that she did not understand.

'I'm sorry,' he whispered against her hair. 'If there are some things I cannot give you, at least I swear you will never want for anything.'

He knew at once he had said the wrong thing, that he had added to the hurt, but he did not know how to mend it.

For a long while she was silent and when at last she did speak it was only to ask him to buy a jewelled collar for her little dog.

Slowly he withdrew his arm from her body. He had an over-powering sense of the inherent loneliness of man.

.   .   .   .   .

On the following morning he was up early and away with Monmouth to Windsor. In the courtyard he met Richmond returned from a ride in the park and they entered the castle, arm in arm. They had long since put aside differences neither wanted and which could not be mended, and their relationship, if not quite as easy as it had once been, was nevertheless one of affection, the stronger for the trial it had suffered.

Presently, in one of the castle withdrawing-rooms, he came upon Elizabeth Rainsford.

A lively group was gathered in the room, including the Duchess of Monmouth—looking no doubt for her duke who had gone im-mediately to his father—Sir Charles Sedley with his plain but lively daughter, Lord Bruce, Baptist May, York's duchess and his daughter, the Princess Anne, and Henrietta, Baroness Wentworth.

They were all talking and laughing together and Kit paused for a moment in the doorway, watching Elizabeth. She seemed taller, or was it perhaps the elegant blue-satin dress with its stiff bodice and full skirt that gave her added height? Her hair, still fair as a buttercup field, had been drawn softly from her face, a long curl coaxed to lie on her shoulder, and though she would never be pretty she had a profile that Diana of the Ephesians might envy and she carried her-self with a corresponding dignity.

It was Bab who saw him first and gave a shout of welcome—despite the years, Bab remained raffish—and at once he was be-sieged by them all and answering their questions as best he could. He could only smile at Elizabeth until half an hour later when he had imparted all his news and was able to draw her aside. They sat down together on a window-seat, looking out over the slopes to the Thames winding through the valley below.

'Well?' he asked, his eyes on her face. 'How do you like White-hall?'

She smiled. 'I like it very well—and you thought I was going to say I did not!'

He laughed. '*Touché.*'

She began to talk of a masque in which she and Henrietta Went-worth were to dance before the court next month and glancing across at the Baroness, as fair as Elizabeth but too slim and pale for his taste, he saw Monmouth come in and turn to greet her, apparently with a question. Lady Wentworth gave him a quick formal curtsey, shook her head and moved away at once. He was surprised, for whatever Monmouth asked, he was seldom rebuffed.

'Does your friend, Lady Wentworth, not care for the court?' he asked Elizabeth.

'Henrietta? Oh yes, indeed. She loves the dancing as I do, and the music we have in the evenings.'

He said nothing further, but he saw that for all Monmouth was now the centre of the group, his eyes were still on Lady Wentworth, standing with Tom Bruce by the door.

'Lord Bruce wanted to marry her,' Elizabeth told him confiden-tially, 'but his father thought her not well enough dowered and forbade the match.'

'Did her ladyship mind?'

'I don't think so.'

'And is she betrothed now? She must be a year or two older than you.'

'Yes, but she is not promised.' Elizabeth glanced across at her friend, and there was a curious expression in her face. 'Some girls think of nothing but getting rich husbands, but we are not all like that.'

'Perhaps not,' he said, smiling, 'though no doubt Mark will soon be looking for one for you.'

'Then he can save himself the trouble,' she returned, calmly, and at once went on to ask him if he was back in his place in the Duke's household.

'No, I'm afraid most of my tasks there are delegated to my two unfortunate clerks. I wish to stay in the army—at least for a while.'

Her eyes widened. 'To stay in the army? But why?'

He stared over her head at the group by the door. The Duke of York had come in and no one could fail to notice the coolness of his greeting to the younger duke, nor that he omitted to address him by the usual 'Nephew' and merely called him 'Monmouth'. The latter, his arm about Bab's shoulders, appeared not to notice it and went on talking cheerfully.

Kit turned back to Elizabeth. 'I am staying because I believe that is where I shall be most needed.'

'Needed? But surely now that peace has come . . .'

'Peace with France, yes. Would to God we could as easily sign a peace among ourselves.' He saw the bewilderment on her face, and braced himself at once. 'Come, my dear. I've monopolized you for too long. You must be presented to Monmouth.'

She put her hand on his arm readily enough, but he could see that she was troubled and wished he had not allowed himself the moment of confidence. Yet it was Elizabeth, strangely, who had prompted it. He wondered why.

2

'Then we are agreed, gentlemen? What more evidence or urging could we need?' The speaker, a tiny figure, pale and thin-faced below a huge fair periwig, nevertheless dominated the silent table. His light piercing eyes swept from face to face, his shrewd intelligence, stripped of illusions, summing up each man's reactions.

Kit, lacking the Earl of Shaftesbury's brilliance, saw the gathered members differently, but quite as plainly—only while Shaftesbury tested them for their usefulness to his burning cause, Kit tried to sum up their loyalty to Monmouth whom they had accepted as their leader.

Buckingham he had never cared for. The florid earl, heavy-jowled now, disillusioned and bored, was well aware that his political star had dimmed and was seeking redress, perhaps even vengeance. Halifax was equally uncertain—he talked freely and changed his mind as freely, but his affection for the young duke was genuine enough. As for the Earl of Sunderland and Lord Howard of Escrick, Kit suspected them both of being at least in York's confidence.

Lord Grey of Werke, tall, handsome and ingratiating, probably thought of little but his own advancement, but seated next to him and as different as chalk from cheese, John Hampden, grandson of the famous Hampden who had fought against the tyranny of Charles I, was a straightforward republican, devoted to his country. Also on the credit side, Kit thought, was the Earl of Essex, a sensible man, while Lord Russell, wise and kindly and a devout Protestant, was most to be trusted among this gathering.

At the end of the table sat the 'Plotter', the lantern-jawed, high-coloured Scot, Robert Ferguson, who wrote all their manifestos and pamphlets. Kit disliked him intensely, knowing that such men, by their over-enthusiasm, can be the ruin of the cause they espouse.

They were all gathered in a locked upper room of the Green Ribbon Club which held its meetings in the dining-room of the King's Head tavern on the corner of Chancery Lane. It was a Whig club which Monmouth had long favoured and Kit was content enough to take a pipe and a glass of wine there occasionally and listen to the talk of the eminent men who were among its members. This more intimate meeting was another matter altogether.

Shaftesbury was leaning forward, his pain-lined face burning with an intensity that had long since learned to ignore the body's weakness.

'As you all know I have laid before the House proof of the King's trafficking with France and his willingness to take French money, and we have all had our fill of popish plots. How much more, think you, will the papist duke lean towards France and Rome too when he is King?'

'It does not bear thinking of,' Hampden said gravely. 'My lord, exclusion is the only way out.'

Halifax, a born politician, shifted uneasily. 'Perhaps. But it is not an easy matter to set aside the succession. What is more important is to keep the Established Church inviolate.'

The Scot, Ferguson, snorted with disgust. 'Does my lord Halifax truly think James of York would do that?'

Halifax shrugged and said nothing and it was Lord Howard who spoke next. 'I do not believe his Majesty wishes any harm to come to the Protestant cause. He has always maintained that.'

'His Majesty is indeed the father of his people——' Sunderland was beginning sententiously, when Buckingham interrupted.

'Of a good many of them anyway!'

Grey collapsed into helpless laughter and Shaftesbury banged on the table.

'Gentlemen, this is no time for levity.'

Unexpectedly Monmouth said: 'You are quite right, my lord. If we believe in our cause, to see it threatened should draw from us both the will and the courage to preserve it.'

'Which may well be needed,' Hampden put in. 'The triumph of the court party would put an end to all civil liberty, the liberty my grandfather died for. May God, and our swords if necessary, prevent that.'

There was a little silence. Then Shaftesbury said: 'It may be the only way. I've ten thousand brisk boys ready to do as I bid them.'

Monmouth glanced along the table. 'It's not come to that yet. I'll not shed English blood if it can be helped.'

Kit listened in silence as they talked. It was only talk, but he agreed for the most part. All his old affection for the King remained, but he no longer trusted Charles, and the thought of what James of York would do when he succeeded was enough to throw him wholeheartedly into the Whig party. He seldom spoke at these meetings, feeling himself somewhat among his superiors, but in the next pause, he said quietly: 'I am for the absolute exclusion of the Duke of York. He would persecute all Protestants—it would be the time of Bloody Mary over again.'

Essex sat up and laid down his pipe. He wore his hat at the Monmouth cock and it was decorated with the large green ribbon of the club. 'Captain van Wyngarde is right. There is no making terms with a papist. But there is, thank God, a simple alternative to James of York.'

He glanced at Monmouth, and Lord Russell nodded in agreement, but it was Shaftesbury who rose, glass in hand.

'Gentlemen, I give you the other James—His Royal Highness, the Prince of Wales.'

Ever afterwards Kit knew that this was a moment of decision. For a brief instant there was absolute silence. His hand clenched on his glass. The truth he knew—did they know it, too? Did they believe it? Surely this was what they had all waited for?

Slowly, one by one, they rose—Russell first and then Essex; Grey, with an elegant bow, Buckingham with a more casual air that held little deference, Ferguson with triumph, Hampden with caution.

Monmouth sat still, a grave smile on his face, a warmer colour than usual in his cheeks.

Oh God, Kit thought, are they worth it, any of them? They're using him—will they in the end destroy him? No acknowledgement could have made him happier had he been sure of these men—but he was not.

His anxiety was so great that it must have shown in his face, for a little later when he sat beside Monmouth in the hackney coach that bore them home, the latter turned to him.

'What is it, Kit? Were you not pleased when they gave me my rightful title?'

Kit faced him in the semi-darkness. 'Sir, you know I would give my right arm to see all England call you so. It is just that I do not trust all of them. Shaftesbury is a dangerous man. He knows what he wants and will not care whom he tramples on to get it.'

'He needs me——'

'Yes, he needs you, but God knows to what lengths he will go, or how he will use you. Howard and Sunderland I don't trust, Grey is a fool.'

'Russell and Essex are my friends.'

'They are, sir, and I would beg you to heed Lord Russell above all, but Ferguson is too wild and Buckingham, for all he speaks out for religious liberty, loves his pleasure more and even that he finds a bore.'

'You are hard on them, Master Sobersides. You and Hampden are a pair.'

Kit leaned back wearily. 'I don't mean to be intolerant, but I see, as I think Mr. Hampden does, that it is not always the great lords who have the best interests of the country at heart.'

Monmouth laughed. 'You old puritan! I do believe you would have drawn your sword for Noll Cromwell had you lived twenty-five years earlier.'

'I might have had a hard choice to make and indeed—Jamie, you are laughing at me! But seriously, I do urge you to walk warily with our Green Ribbon friends. They would set a crown on your head, some of them, not for love of you but for their own purpose.'

Monmouth frowned. 'I don't want the crown. I'd rather be a stadtholder, as William is. Anyway, I can promise you to be myself. I cannot dissemble, you know that. They must take me as I am, and they all know I will do nothing against my father while he lives.'

Kit relaxed against the leather seat.

'Thank God they do. And I am with you all in any scheme that will rid us of York.'

Monmouth regarded him in the faint light of the link-boy's torch. 'I think my uncle is the only man you have ever hated. Yet surely you cannot still regret that bitch he took from you?'

'I do not,' Kit said with suppressed violence. 'It only began with that. Now I hate him for what he is, for what he would do to you, to all of us, and I cannot understand why your father does not see it.'

'He sees it,' Monmouth told him with rare shrewdness, 'only it suits his book to keep the French King happy and Papist James helps him do it.'

Kit shot him a quick look, surprised at his perception, but Monmouth, he reflected, had changed a great deal. Gone was the boisterous rowdyism of his youth and now, though he still loved to play, his energies were directed more often to his favourite sport of racing.

Gone too were the succession of mistresses, for Eleanor Needham no longer held him and no one had taken her place. He had turned to more serious things and now seemed prepared to plunge into the political fray. His remarks showed his understanding of his father's opinions, but a month later it seemed that the King had his hand on the pulse of the nation and was aware of the necessity to bend in the wind stirred up by the Whigs. He sent his brother abroad for a while and the members of the Green Ribbon Club shouted their triumph to the crowds in the street below the balconies of the King's Head.

Charles sent for Monmouth and told him to behave himself and not to ally himself so openly with the opponents of the court party. Monmouth said he must do as his convictions directed him.

'Convictions be damned,' Charles retorted, irritably. 'I tell you, Jamie, you're a fool.' At that he stalked out of the room, and for some days afterwards it was noted that Monmouth did not attend Whitehall.

.   .   .   .   .

Throughout that spring Kit felt uneasy, aware that he and Monmouth were slipping into intrigue, the one thing he had vowed to avoid, but where Monmouth went he went too.

Already the story of the black box was going the rounds of the coffee-houses—the box which Dr. Cosin, Bishop of Durham, was said to have left on his death to his son-in-law, Sir Gilbert Gerard, and which supposedly contained Lucy Walter's marriage lines. Kit wished he could understand why the King prevaricated over the business. Surely he would wish to see his loved son as his heir? But the King was too deep to fathom, and he was glad when in the early summer action of another kind broke up the meetings at the Green Ribbon Club.

In May the Covenanters rose in Scotland, rebelling against the proscribing of their religion, and Monmouth, as Lord General, mustered his regiments and rode north to put an end to the trouble. Kit, now captaining a troop of Horse Guards and finding the military life very much to his taste, rode north with him. The army was in good trim and Kit felt proud of his trained, disciplined men, neat in their scarlet and yellow. At Bothwell Bridge they met the rebels, wild fighting men under fanatical leaders, who refused Monmouth's offer of treaty in unnecessarily impertinent terms.

Monmouth ordered an immediate attack and in a short while had taken the bridge and put the enemy to flight—they were no match for his well-equipped troops, and Kit came through the fight with no more than a scratch on his arm.

It was all over surprisingly quickly, but it remained for ever strongly in his memory, for it was here that Mark Rainsford died.

He was about to call the roll of his troop when Jeremy came hurrying up from the baggage-waggons.

'Sir—sir, will you come? Major Rainsford is wounded, dying the surgeon says.'

'God!' Kit flung himself off his horse, called his lieutenant to take over and ran after Jeremy to the rear to where the wounded were gathered. There were no more than a dozen of them. By a waggon, under his scarlet cloak, Mark lay alone. His eyes were closed and his face grey beneath the dust spattered over him, but there was no sign of his wound.

Kneeling down, Kit saw that he was very near death and lifted the scarlet cloak. Nausea rose in him—there was no healing a wound like this.

As he replaced the cloak he saw Mark's eyes, dark now with pain, looking up at him.

'Kit . . . I took a ball . . . in the guts.'

There was little he could do, but Kit took off his coat and rolling it laid it under Mark's head. 'Now you will be more comfortable,' he said as steadily as he could. 'Lie still and rest.'

Mark reached out and took his hand. 'No . . . there will soon be . . . rest enough for me. Kit . . . you must see . . . Isabel. Tell her . . .'

'I know what you want me to do. We spoke of it once before.'

'Yes . . . I remember. But I never believed . . . that I should die . . . like this. It was always . . . some other poor fellow.'

He tried to smile but gasped instead, his thin face contracting with pain and his fingers tightening convulsively on the hand he held. Shocked by the sight of such naked agony, Kit lifted him in his arms and saw, almost with relief, that already his eyes were glazing.

He seemed to be making one last painful effort to speak and Kit had to bend his head to hear the words.

'Elizabeth . . . at Whitehall . . . have a care . . . for her.'

'I will,' he said, 'I will,' and held the dying man close. Mark seemed to relax. His head lay against Kit's breast and he did not move again.

A few moments later Monmouth himself came up. With infinite gentleness Kit laid Mark down and got dazedly to his feet.

'He's dead.'

Monmouth stood beside him, looking down at the still face. 'There are so few dead—that one had to be Mark is damnable.' He glanced at Kit and saw the grief, the nausea, the strained pity. There was only one panacea for this. 'Come—we have work to do.'

.   .   .   .   .

In Edinburgh the bells rang for them as they rode through the streets. The Scottish lords of the council addressed the Lord General as 'your Highness', a title which remained with Monmouth—to his uncle's fury—throughout his equally triumphant journey home.

On their first evening back in London Kit went to Isabel Rainsford to break the news of Mark's death. His heart ached for her, but she bore her grief with proud courage and thanked God for her children.

It was Elizabeth at Whitehall who wept with a passionate violence that startled him and he realized for the first time the depth of her devotion to the brother so many years her senior.

Later in the evening he wandered into the ballroom, looking around for his particular friends.

Bab May, still at forty-odd a sought-after bachelor, was talking animatedly to Rochester. The 'mad earl' had some time ago mistakenly allowed the King to see the poem he had read to Kit and in consequence had found himself packed off for another stay in the Tower. Now, forgiven and restored to royal favour, he was back at court, but he seemed paler and thinner even than before, as if no more than a transparency of skin and bone held him to this world.

Nell Gwynne was dancing with talkative Harry Killigrew, and Richmond was there, standing by the King's chair. Colonel Churchill was partnering pretty and vivacious Sarah Jennings with whom he had fallen in love and Tom Bruce, passing Kit in the dance, invited him to dinner on the morrow.

Presently he saw Prince Rupert standing by the door, aloof and dignified, and went over to talk to him, describing the campaign and particularly Monmouth's generosity to his defeated foes.

'The sign of a great captain,' Rupert said. 'Only the small-minded revenge themselves after victory.'

This commendation and the familiarity of his surroundings all helped to lessen a little the sad gap left by Mark's loss.

It was midnight before the court dispersed, but at last, under a sky bright with stars, Kit walked out into the street and under the Holbein Gateway towards Axe Yard.

Cathy would probably have heard they were back and be waiting for him with her warm welcome, and her body for his loving, and he hurried into the house and up the stairs two at a time.

But the rooms at the top were in darkness. He opened the door of their little sitting-room and went in. It was silent, cold and empty.

Fumbling on the table, he found a half-burnt candle and lit it. The room was tidy, a sure sign that Cathy was not there. The hearth was cleared, the bed neatly made and the cupboards bare. He lifted the candle high, looking all round, and then, hearing a sound, turned with swift expectancy towards the door.

'Cathy! I thought . . .'

But it was only the landlady, Mrs. Jenkins.

'I guessed it must be you returned, sir. Mrs. Shaw has gone, been gone these two weeks, but she left a letter for you.' She held it out, her small bright eyes snapping with curiosity. She saw the astonishment on his face and added: 'The rooms, sir? Perhaps you'd be good enough to tell me if you still want them?'

'Yes, yes, later . . .' He took the letter, waving her away, and when she had gone somewhat reluctantly, he sat by the table to read it.

It was a long letter for Cathy's inexperienced pen, with much scratched out and re-written, many ill-spelt words and blotches, and for a moment he could not make out the first few muddled sentences, but as he read on it became all too clear. She was with child again, the child she had tried so hard to make him give her, that she wanted and he did not. She knew, she said, that he had believed a child was better brought up in a lowly but honourable home than as a rich man's bastard, so rather than encumber him with it she had decided to wed a young farmer who came once a week into London and had long wanted to take her back to the country with him. He would accept the child, when it came, as his own and this way, Cathy went on, she would do what her dear Kit wanted. The letter was smudged with what might have been tears and ended pathetically:

I never lov'd no one els and never will but Tom be a kinde man and will look to me and the babe. 'Tis best this waye. You have been soe good to me, deare Kit, that I would not vex you. Soe goodbye, I will never forgit you, but always be, y^r loving,

Catherine Shaw

He crushed the letter in his hand and clenched both fists before his eyes. What had he done? What had he said to drive her from him? But he knew, knew only too well. He had been cruel, heartless; he had vented his own hurt on her who had not deserved it, and now he had lost her. She was gone, carrying within her the child of his body, the child he would never see and whose coming she thought would vex him. Vex him! He felt his cheeks burn with shame. He could find her, perhaps, trace her to her new home, even provide for the child, but it would do no good. In his heart he knew she was right, that his child would be better off brought up in a lowly home without the shame of bastardy. Yet it hurt, and hurt more than he had believed possible, both that she had not trusted him to stand by her, and that he would never see this child of theirs.

Oh God, he thought, to be caught in my own trap!

He got up, knocking over the candle, so that, rolling away, it extinguished itself. The ensuing darkness was no more complete than the darkness of his own anger and grief and self-castigation, and turning to the bed he flung himself down upon its emptiness and pressed his face into the pillow.

3

Throughout that summer the gossips were busy with the news that the Duke of Monmouth was courting the Lady Henrietta Wentworth, and there was considerable amusement when the lady appeared cool, even indifferent. The less she appeared to care, the more the Duke pursued her to the great interest of the entire court.

Kit was not amused, he was extremely puzzled, for this was most unusual. Monmouth's way had always been light—an easy conquest or he turned elsewhere. Now he seemed anxious and irritable and this was rare enough in one normally sweet-tempered to make Kit ponder the matter. Enlightenment came one bright August morning.

Crossing the cloister near the garden entrance at Hampton Court, he saw Monmouth come in, his face stiff with bewilderment and a rare black frown on his forehead.

Seeing Kit he paused, and without preamble burst out:

'I don't understand it. What ails her that she should not be able to bear me near her?'

'What is the matter?' Kit asked quietly. 'Who has incurred your Highness's displeasure?'

Monmouth swung away from him and leaned against a pillar, looking out into the centre of the courtyard where a little fountain rose and fell in the sunshine.

'You know very well that I mean Lady Wentworth. Kit, you have seen how she uses me—she will not speak more than a few words with me. I asked her just now to take a turn by the river but she would not. Why? What have I done that she should treat me as if I were the worst rogue in Christendom?'

'Perhaps she thinks you are.'

'Kit, don't tease me. I am in deadly earnest.'

'You always are,' Kit said drily, but then something in Monmouth's face stopped him. This was not the spoiled darling of the court, unused to being denied anything he wanted—this was a man indeed in earnest and quietly desperate.

'I want you to go to her, Kit. Speak for me. She will listen to you. Tell her that for the first time in his life James of Monmouth loves—more than himself, more than life. Beg her to hear me. . . .'

Moved despite himself Kit said irritably: 'The devil take it, Jamie, what do you think I am? A ponce?'

Monmouth put his hands on Kit's shoulders, turning him so that they must face each other.

'That was unjust—and if you will look at me you will know that it was.'

'I see,' Kit said, at last. 'But you say she will have none of you. Perhaps she thinks you would use her as you did Moll Kirke or Betty Felton.'

The Duke looked so outraged that it was hard not to smile.

'Good God, she cannot think that! She must understand. If she did . . .'

'If she did, what then?'

'Why then—then I would be no more and no less than she wanted me to be for the rest of my life.'

Monmouth's grasp tightened and all his charm, all that warm compelling personality that bound people to him so effortlessly, now reinforced his present urgency.

'If you love me, Kit! I shall never again ask of you a service so —vital to me.'

Kit gave a helpless gesture. God grant the lady finds it so too, he told himself, and set off on his delicate mission.

But it was not easy to find an opportunity and it was several days before—still not sure he was doing the right thing—he came upon Henrietta alone in the garden. It was a sunny afternoon and she was sitting with a book beneath a lime tree. She had a restful quality about her, and it occurred to him that this must appeal to the restless Duke.

For a while they talked of the beauty of the gardens, of John Donne's poems that she was reading and Mr. Milton's masque *Comus* that had been performed last night.

The last subject gave him his opening. 'You delighted us all with your performance as Sabrina, Lady Wentworth. The Duke of Monmouth remarked upon it.'

'Did he?' She turned away, seemingly without interest, but not before he had seen her pale eyes light up. It emboldened him to go on, but embarrassment and a certain distaste for his task made his voice harsher than usual.

'My lady, I sought you out to day for a purpose,' he began, and went on to repeat exactly what Monmouth had said.

She listened without interruption, an unusual colour rising in her cheeks so that she bent her head to hide it, but he saw that her hands were gripped together so tightly that the skin was white.

'Lady Wentworth,' he said, bluntly, 'I have been the Duke's friend all my life and it is natural that his wishes should be paramount with me, but I would pursue nothing I did not believe to be for his good.'

Her smile was a little twisted. 'Do you think it is for his good that every woman should be ready to fall into his arms?'

'That, no. But I saw it would not be so with you.'

She rose, drawing up her slight figure. 'Then there is no more to be said, is there?'

'A great deal, I think. Will you have no kind word for him?'

She was angry. 'No and no!'

'A little kindness would rob you of nothing and give him so much.'

Henrietta Wentworth turned to look full at him then, her large eyes fixed on his face, too proud to dissemble. 'Captain van Wyngarde, you do not comprehend at all. I *cannot* do what you ask because—because there can be no half-measures between the Duke and myself.'

For a moment he did indeed fail to understand the full meaning of her words, and then, as realization dawned on him, he looked at her in astonishment. 'Lady Wentworth, if that is true . . .'

'It is true,' she answered gravely. 'I have loved him ever since I came to court. At first he did not notice me, but when at last he did I knew that I could not, that I would not, be just another of his women, to be cast aside when he was weary.'

He drew her down again on to the seat. 'You do not know me very well if you think I am come to ask that of you.' But what had he come to ask her? A light flirtation was one thing, but a permanent attachment between herself and the Duke would bring down scandal on them both and on their families. He wished Monmouth had given him any task but this.

Aloud, he said: 'I can only pledge you my word that the Duke does not think thus of you. Years ago he told me he would change his way of living if he found someone to change him. A few days ago he told me he had found that person—you.' He paused, seeing joy struggle with habitual repression on her face, and as she bowed her head he guessed she was combating tears.

'How can I believe you?' she was murmuring. 'How can I? Could Eleanor Needham have believed it?'

'No, but you are not she—no, nor any of the others.'

She lifted her head, holding herself proudly. 'Captain van Wyngarde, what is it you wish me to do?'

He was beginning to see what kind of woman she was, that she had a rare quality of character, that, if anyone could, she would hold the transient Monmouth.

'I would have you save him from a life that will destroy him,' he said at last, and with suppressed intensity. 'You know he was married at fourteen—he had no chance to choose a wife. As it was he amused himself in the manner of the court, and God knows he had temptation enough, but I think I am the only person who knows how often he prays to be free of it.' He heard her draw a sobbing breath and went on, 'My lady, I know him so well and I would stake my life that he is a changed man.'

Very slowly she turned to look at him and he waited in silence. Rochester had once told him that one of his virtues was his ability to wait and listen in silence.

At last she said in a low voice, 'I want to believe you, but—I dare not.'

He laughed softly. 'A Wentworth—saying she dare not?'

Henrietta smiled too, for the first time. 'You are very acute, Captain.'

For a long while then she did not speak but stared down at her clasped hands and he waited, wondering what sort of advocate he had been.

Then she turned to him again. 'If what you tell me is true'—her mouth was trembling, her eyes full of an incredulous happiness— 'then I can only say that you, who seem to understand so much, must know my answer.'

He did not reply but, bending his head, lifted her fingers to his lips. He had succeeded, and all he could do now was to pray that Jamie might not fail this girl. He knew instinctively that Henrietta Wentworth wanted only his silence then, and he left her alone under the lime tree. He felt curiously empty. She would go to Monmouth and they would be happy together, while he—he was even more aware of his own loneliness. He had no desire to take another mistress, but the gap left in his life by Cathy's going affected him profoundly.

As he walked away over the grass, he faced the fact that the only way out of this repression and unhappiness was hard work, and in the days that followed plunged himself into his duties with a vigour that surprised even the vigorous Duke. He had Monmouth, his work, his friends—and it was, it had to be, enough.

.   .   .   .   .

As a result of the interview with Henrietta he had expected Monmouth's gratitude, and as he saw them walking together in the gardens, riding in the home park, or dancing in the evenings, his last doubts were removed for Monmouth's whole attitude towards Lady Wentworth was one of respect and devotion.

'I thank God daily for her,' Monmouth said.

What Kit had not expected was Elizabeth's anger when, a week later, Henrietta Wentworth confided in her.

She sought him out and turned on him furiously.

'How could you?' she demanded. 'How could you go to Henrietta and induce her to sell her reputation for—for a duke's whim? For that is what she will do, she is so besotted over him, and I think it was despicable of you to do it. I thought you far too honourable ever to countenance such a thing!'

'Elizabeth!' he protested mildly. 'I did no more than give the Duke's message to Lady Wentworth.'

She laughed angrily. 'Oh, I know what you did. You made her think she would be different from all the others, but men are all the same, dukes or not. He will use her for a while and then——'

'Stop, child!' He caught her by the shoulders. 'It is time you grew up. All men are not the same, nor is any man the same all the time. I believe the Duke will put Lady Wentworth's welfare first, now and always.'

She twisted away from his grasp. 'And if he does—what is there for them but a dishonourable attachment? And she will be the one to suffer.'

'If she does, she will do it gladly. I think you do not understand what love is, my dear.'

'No, I don't,' she retorted, flatly, 'except that it turns men mad and makes fools of us women.'

He shrugged his shoulders and left it at that. She was very young and would no doubt learn by experience—all the more quickly for living at Whitehall.

He was not the only person who got wind of the newest gossip at court and disapproved of it. Philadelphia Wentworth, Henrietta's mother, came storming up to town and confronting her daughter, received a blunt confirmation of what the gossips said. Having cast her bonnet over the windmill, Henrietta was prepared to own it before the world.

Furious, Philadelphia swept her daughter away home to Toddington, in Bedfordshire, but Monmouth, in his usual headstrong fashion, pursued them both, turned his wiles on the elder Lady Wentworth and within a few hours of his arrival had won her over completely. She gave him a suite of rooms adjoining her daughter's and her blessing on them both. An emotional woman, she was as warm-hearted as Monmouth himself.

But for Henrietta and her lover their first happiness was shortlived.

The King had fallen ill with a tertian ague and the situation was extremely awkward. York, heir to the throne, was in Brussels; while Monmouth, idol of the people, was at his father's bedside. His friends made the most of this, stirring up trouble in the city, and Monmouth himself assumed the duties of the heir by informing the Lord Mayor of the King's progress.

Furious, the Duke of York returned. It was noticed that he and his nephew met very coldly.

Charles recovered and soon learned what had been going on during his illness. He sent for Monmouth and told him his ill-chosen friends had gone too far, even to inciting the mobs to scream abuse at York. In vain Monmouth protested he had had no part in this. Ten days later came the astounding news that he had been deprived of his command as Lord General and banished the Kingdom.

Stunned and incredulous, Kit's first reaction was a bitter anger against the King who had raised his son so high and then reproved him for the position in which he had placed him. It did not seem fair, either, that Monmouth should be blamed for a popularity he could no more help than he could help breathing. He wondered what the Duke would do, if the time had come to put into effect the plans so often discussed at the Green Ribbon Club, but Monmouth shook his head.

'No, Kit. I must go. I'll not break with my father.'

'If you must go, then I will go with you. I cannot stay here while you are so ill used.'

But again Monmouth shook his head. 'No. I am appointing commissioners to carry on my work as Master of the Horse, for I'm not deprived of that, and I want you to be one of them. You know how I like things done, and we haven't completed our military manual yet.'

Kit was pacing the Duke's bedroom, too angry and bewildered to think clearly. 'I'd rather come with you.'

'But I want you to stay.' Monmouth came across to him and held him by the shoulders. 'My dear Kit, it will not be for long. My father has promised that, and I don't want my work with the troops to do again when I return. I do ask you to stay.'

When Monmouth asked in that tone there was no denying him and Kit agreed, but it was a great deal more difficult than he had thought possible. His missed Monmouth every hour of every day, the houses in Bishopsgate and Soho Square, Hedge Lane and the Cockpit were empty without that vital presence, and he knew himself fretted into irritability because there was no Cathy to turn to for comfort and release.

He heard before long that the Duke was in Holland where he had called on William who received him warmly, seemingly welcoming this opportunity to flaunt his father-in-law whom he did not like. Monmouth also received a delighted welcome from his cousin Mary, though he wrote to Kit that she was changed, much subdued and missing Whitehall. Kit felt that with William for a husband this was hardly surprising. But it was clear from the Duke's letters that despite all the hospitality showered on him he was chafing to be home again. Deprived of the soldiering he loved it was small wonder he hated his exile.

It was a wretched autumn. Monmouth's disgrace seemed to cast a blight over the whole court, a blight which Charles attempted in vain to dispel by behaving as though his son did not exist.

Kit dined with Monmouth's friends and his own—the depressed Bab, the dying Rochester, and they had no more cheer to offer him than he them. It was Rupert alone, at this time, who comforted him.

'When his Majesty brings Monmouth home—as he will—keep him away from plots and politics. If you do not I fear you have enemies who will see you both ruined.'

Kit glanced at the hawk-like profile but it revealed nothing. He smiled a little. 'Your Highness was never known to run before your enemies. Would you give that advice to me?'

Rupert gave a most unprincely snort. 'Don't try to hoist me with my own petard, boy. You know what I mean. Neither of you is equipped to fight in that arena. Your enemies are.'

It was probably a compliment. Kit sighed. 'I know your Highness means me only well, but what can I do?'

'I know—where Monmouth goes, you go! Well, you're a pair of young fools who'd best heed my warning. I like young Monmouth but he's not the man for the game he tries to play.' The Prince saw the anxiety on the face opposite him and added more gently: 'My dear boy, do you think I don't understand that you want to set England to rights? I wanted to do the same once, but mine was the easier way—on the battlefield. I've spent most of my life around one throne or another and I know that intrigue can break a man the quicker. Keep out of it, boy.' His voice was suddenly harsh again, and he put a hand on Kit's shoulder, gripping it hard, before he repeated, 'Keep out of it.'

'If the Duke goes on, sir—I cannot keep out of it.'

Rupert stared at him and seemed about to say more, but then he smiled suddenly. 'I see. Well, if I cannot persuade you, at least come and tell me if you get into trouble.'

One night towards the end of November Kit was awakened by the pealing of bells. He was sleeping at the house in Bishopsgate which Monmouth had bought to be near his city friends and he lay listening to the bells, wondering why they should be ringing. Then he became aware of a disturbance downstairs, and flinging on a dressing-gown emerged into the passage to hear Jeremy's excited voice bidding someone enter.

'What is the matter, Jerry?' he called over the banisters, but before Jeremy could answer he heard another voice:

'I am the matter, Kit. Pray come down.'

For a moment he stared, unable to believe his eyes. A tall figure stood in the hall, brown hair hanging damply about his shoulders, and a black cloak hung over sober riding-clothes. Then he pelted down the stairs, hands outstretched, until they were seized in a firm grasp by the traveller.

'Is it all over, sir? Are you home for good?'

Monmouth glanced round the hall. 'We cannot talk here and I am famished. Hodge, raid the pantry for me, there's a good fellow.'

Jeremy, delighted, disappeared into the rear quarters and Kit followed the Duke into the library where he knelt by the hearth and blew up the embers of the fire with the bellows. Then he threw on two fresh logs.

'There, that will burn up.' He took Monmouth's cloak and hat and the Duke sat down, holding his cold hands to the blaze. Jeremy came in with a laden tray which he set before the Duke, but it was not until he had gone that Kit was able to turn to Monmouth. There was no need to voice the questions in his mind.

Monmouth picked up a chicken-leg and began to tear the meat from it with his teeth. 'I found I couldn't stand it any longer. I'd nothing to do. So I came back.'

Kit stared at him. The logs were burning brightly now and their light on the Duke's face revealed a mixture of defiance and anxiety.

'Without your father's permission?'

'Yes. But I'll write to him tomorrow and ask him to give me an audience. I'm sure he wants me back now—a little of my uncle's gloomy company goes a long way!'

'Perhaps, but to come without leave is likely to anger him again.'

The Duke wiped his fingers on a napkin provided by the thoughtful Jeremy. 'I shall win him over, if only I can see him. Perhaps Nell will put in a word. Pretty Mrs. Gwynne always had a soft spot for me.'

'Who has not?' Kit muttered under his breath. 'Curse you, Jamie, I've not found life very palatable since you left.'

Monmouth smiled. 'But then you are—you,' he remarked cryptically and yawned, but when Kit said he would have his room prepared, shook his head. 'Don't bother about that. I'll sleep with you tonight.'

Presently as he was undressing he glanced round the room and gave a little sigh. 'I can't live in exile, Kit—nor away from Henrietta. It's England or nowhere for me.'

He climbed into Kit's big four-poster bed. 'This is like old times, isn't it? When we were boys and I used to stay at Tolbrooke?'

'Sometimes I wish we were back there again.'

Monmouth grinned. 'Do you? I'd rather look forward. What will you wager that I'll be dancing at Whitehall by the end of the week?'

'Naught. I know you too well.' Kit leaned forward to blow out the candle but before he did so a thought struck him and he turned to look at the Duke who lay stretched full length, his hands clasped behind his head. 'When you came in I heard church bells. Why were they ringing?'

A strange expression came over Monmouth's face. 'Some of the people saw me riding into the city and spread the news. They rang the bells to greet me. If you had looked out of the window you would have seen a dozen bonfires lit in welcome.' He broke off, and his eyes filled with tears. 'Before God, Kit, I think their love will ruin me.'

.   .   .   .   .

Long after he was asleep Kit lay thinking of his last words. They had a prophetic ring, and he knew with certainty that the Duke of York would add this to the indictment he was piling up against his nephew.

As the days went by it seemed Monmouth was wrong for once, for he was not to dance at Whitehall for many a day. Charles told him in a short angry letter to withdraw immediately from England. Monmouth declined and said that though he might be deprived of all his offices, he would remain. Charles's answer to this was to take away all but his Mastership of the Horse, and, despite the entreaties of Nell Gwynne and others of Monmouth's friends, he refused to see his son.

Kit watched it all, sick at heart. Neither would give way an inch. Monmouth moved home to the Cockpit where his friends crowded to see him. The people shouted and sang his praises and the ballad-mongers extolled him.

> 'Young Jemmy is a lad
> Of royal birth and breeding,
> With every beauty clad,
> And every grace exceeding. . . .

Young Jemmy is a youth
Who thinks it no transgression
To stand up for the Truth,
And Protestant profession. . . .'

Charles, on the other hand, forbade his name to be mentioned at court. It seemed like stalemate until Monmouth's youngest son, Francis, lay dying. Charles gave him permission to remain at the Cockpit and after the boy's death did not order him away.

A few days later Nell Gwynne, maintaining that the Protestant Duke and the Protestant Whore should stick together, contrived a meeting between father and son, and the reconciliation was complete.

'Thank God,' Kit said, and went about his work with a lighter heart. But his rejoicing was short-lived. The Country party contrived to make too much noise and the story of the 'black box' became so popular and so accepted that York, dreaming of his vengeance, set to work on his brother, determined to lay the blame for the nation's troubles at his nephew's door.

At the end of April, on an evening when after a spring shower blackbirds were singing in the gardens, Kit was at the Cockpit, checking over some figures concerning the Duchess of Monmouth's Scottish rents. Monmouth was attending a meeting of the Privy Council and he had hoped for another hour's solitude in order to complete his work, but he had barely finished the first column when the door burst open.

Monmouth stood there, his eyes wild, his face so white that Kit rose, knocking over his inkstand but oblivious of the result.

The Duke slammed the door and set his back to it and the words poured from him in a torrent.

'He shamed me, there before them all! He read them a paper he had signed, and my uncle—my uncle stood staring at me, his damned cold eyes looking me over as if I were so much dirt.'

'Jamie! In heaven's name, who read what?' Kit had never seen him like this.

The Duke came over to the desk. He was trembling and scarcely able to control his voice. 'My father—he told the Council that he had never been married to anyone but the Queen—he told them, and the whole world beside, that I am bastard born.'

He sat down, and putting his head on to his clenched fists broke into a storm of angry tears.

.   .   .   .   .

In the summer Monmouth made a progress through the West Country, and Kit was among his company of gentlemen. The King's son was determined not to show to the outside world what his father's declaration had done to him and no one but Kit, and perhaps Henrietta Wentworth, had seen the hurt pride, the bitter humiliation.

It was at that time that Kit at last confided to Monmouth his doubts about his own birth, thinking it might show his understanding. Monmouth gave him a sad smile. 'My poor Kit, we did very ill, you and I, not to be born in the clear light of day.'

It was while they were staying at Longleat with the Duke's friend, the wealthy Tom-o-ten-thousand, that Kit received an urgent note from Lady Rochester. She said briefly that her husband was not expected to live more than a few days and had expressed a desire to see him. He went at once to Monmouth, asked for leave to go, and set off for Woodstock.

There Rochester lay in his great bed, his frail body supported by a mound of pillows. He smiled when he saw Kit and it was clear that though all physical strength was spent his spirit still burned as brightly.

'Kit! You're a good fellow to come all this way.'

He held out his hand and Kit took it, sitting down in the chair by the bed. 'My lord, I came the moment I had your summons. I am truly sorry to see you thus.'

'Oh,' the Earl gave a faint sigh. 'Don't let us talk about dying when it is inevitable. There are better things to speak of. Tell me what you have been doing.'

He seemed eager to hear and Kit complied.

'We've been on a progress through the Duke's West Country, and fine "duking days" they turned out to be! We were met outside Bath by more than two hundred people who took us into the city with all the bells pealing. The same thing happened at Bruton and Ilchester, everyone crying "God bless the Protestant Duke".'

'Dangerous!' Rochester commented. 'Where did you go next?'

'To Yeovil and there . . .' Kit paused. There *was* danger and he had seen it as clearly as Rochester did now. 'He touched a girl for the King's Evil and she was cured. I saw it myself.'

'Good God! Only the King or his heir can do that.' Rochester looked keenly at him. 'Be careful, and urge the Duke to be careful too, or you'll both end on a scaffold.'

Kit shrugged, endeavouring to laugh it off, but he knew it did not sound genuine. 'We are on a tide that can't be stopped. Once, a long time ago, I swore never to be involved in anything like this, but I am with him, come what may.'

Rochester sighed. 'I know it is no use asking you to be any different.' He leaned back against the pillows, too near death to hold for long to the urgencies of the world he was leaving. 'Did you know that Bishop Burnet is here? He is determined to help me to heaven when by rights I should go straight to hell.'

'You are going to God,' Kit said, gently, 'for I know how, of late, you have sought Him.'

Rochester turned his head a little to look out of the window at the billowing trees he loved. 'Yes, as He knows me, that is true.' For a little while he was silent, and then he turned back to Kit and smiled a little. 'You have a great gift for friendship. We all felt that.' His hand still lay in Kit's as though he had not the strength to move it. He looked desperately weary but there was peace in his face.

'You're a good fellow,' he said again, almost in a whisper. 'Pray for me.' His eyes closed and he seemed to sleep.

In the early hours of the following morning he was gone, peacefully, and a few days later Kit followed the funeral cortège through the bright summer countryside to Spelsbury, where he was to be laid beside his father. Standing with the mourners, the tenants from the Earl's estates, the villagers from Woodstock and Adderbury, Kit wept for the short wasted life and the friend whose vices had never dimmed his brilliant spirit.

.   .   .   .   .   .

In the months that followed he knew Rochester had been right to urge caution on him, but matters had got beyond him and he could only swim with the tide, praying that it was in the right direction.

The country was on the verge of civil war and the King had no course but to send his brother away again. In Parliament the

Exclusion Bill went triumphantly through the Commons but was thrown out of the Lords by a small majority. Halifax and Sunderland prudently went over to the King's side.

Furious with disappointment, driven to a frenzy by the pain of a diseased body, Shaftesbury tried to save his vanishing dream by whipping the Country party into a rising to banish York for good, and proclaim Monmouth heir to the throne.

'He's mad,' Monmouth said with conviction. 'Now is not the time.'

The King kept his head and with admirable coolness silenced Shaftesbury by dissolving Parliament.

In July he ordered the little Earl's arrest and had him committed to the Tower on a charge of high treason. Monmouth offered to stand bail for him, but it was refused. The Earl came to trial at the Old Bailey on the twenty-fourth of November and Kit was there to see it.

That evening, after Shaftesbury's hilarious acquittal that had sent London mad with joy, he was on duty at Whitehall and chanced to see the King in the Stone Gallery. Charles's face was pale and set and his eyes black with anger. He stopped when he saw Kit.

'Well, Christian, no doubt you and your wild friends are happy tonight. I wish to see none of you here, and when you speak to the Duke of Monmouth you may tell him that, as he offered to stand bail for an enemy of the Crown he need not expect the Crown to stand bail for him, should he ever require it.'

He stalked on, leaving Kit staring unhappily at his back. There was no healing this breach. In despair he went out to Windsor to see Prince Rupert.

He found the Prince in his laboratory with several gentlemen. Rupert took one look at his face and casually threw a chemical powder on the fire. The ensuing smell was so nauseating that his other visitors bade him a hasty farewell and departed.

Rupert grinned like a schoolboy. 'That never fails to get rid of them,' he remarked, and opened the window. 'What's to do, boy?'

Kit told him, pouring out all his anxiety for Monmouth.

'What should we do, sir? The Duke wants only what is good for England. A free Parliament, liberty of conscience, freedom from tyranny, the things you want too. Are we losing the fight because we want too much?'

Rupert began to pace the room. He was near sixty-two now and stooped a little so that his great height was diminished. 'I wish I could advise you, Christian. When I was young my blood was hot and I would have said "do this" or "do that". Maurice and I were eager to fight for England. He used to say——' He stopped abruptly and looked at Kit. 'That is strange. I have not spoken his name to anyone, not since I saw him drowned—more than thirty years ago.'

'He was your brother, was he not?' Kit asked gently. He saw the long furrows cleaving Rupert's face on either side from nose to chin deepen into unrelieved austerity.

'Yes, brother and friend and companion—my better self, I used to think.' The Prince stopped pacing and came to face Kit, drawing himself up to his full height, his hands on his shoulders.

'You put me in mind of him, Christian. Perhaps that is why——' he seemed to bite off the words. Then he went on: 'I can only say to you what I remember saying once to him. Be ruled by your own conscience—there is no surer guide. England will get her freedom in God's good time, and we can only pray that we have each in our own separate ways contributed a little towards it.'

Stirring words and Kit needed their astringent comfort when, shortly before Christmas, Charles deprived Monmouth of the last of his offices, the Mastership of the Horse.

With a stubborn lift to his chin Monmouth pulled a wry face. 'We'll have to start economizing. I'll be sadly out of pocket now.'

But Kit was too angry, too bewildered and unhappy, to see any humour in the situation. He immediately resigned his own commission and went a few days later to tell Rupert what he had done, only to find the Prince had fallen gravely ill.

He lay in his great four-poster, turning his head restlessly from side to side, for an old wound there was troubling him and it was clear that he was in a high fever. As soon as he saw Kit, however, he brushed aside the latter's anxious queries, asking instead for the latest news.

Kit told him, but his mind was no longer on his own problems. Death was reaching too close, taking too heavy a toll among his friends: first Mark, then Rochester and now Rupert, and it seemed to him unbearably poignant to see the strength draining from a man of such intense vigour and physical vitality.

Rupert, however, though aware he was not likely to recover, was conceding nothing to the last enemy.

'You have done what you thought best,' he told Kit. 'But I am

sorry, very sorry, that it had to come to this. Soldiering is a good
life for a man and it pleased me to see you become so excellent an
officer.'

Kit knelt by the bed. The Prince hated any show of sentiment,
but he could not forbear taking the familiar hand in his.

'Your Highness has always been so good to me. I wish there was
something I could do to repay you.'

'Tch!' Rupert pressed his hand feebly. 'You do not know it—but
you have already repaid me a hundredfold.' He looked intently at
Kit and there was a curious happiness in his face before he closed his
eyes. 'I am tired now, but come again tomorrow. There is something I would say to you.'

But when Kit came again on the morrow the great soldier was
already dead.

He stood by the bed and looked down at the hawk-like face, the
jutting forehead, the springing nose. Even in death Rupert looked
unassailable. It was hard to believe he was gone—his first master, his
mentor and of late years his friend—and gone with something
unsaid between them. He felt oddly certain that it would have been
something important.

Attending Rupert's magnificent funeral, even in his grief the
question remained at the back of his mind, a pinprick of unrest.

4

In the summer of 1683 he was called to Holland to settle a legal
difficulty that had arisen over the van Wyngarde property. He had
given Sophia a comfortable house on the estate and made adequate
provision for her, even though she had told him she had no desire
either to see or speak to him again, but she had become involved in
a quarrel with a neighbour over their boundaries and he had to go
and straighten it out himself.

The legal intricacies took some two months to settle, but at
last he was able to return to England. He rode straight to Whitehall,
reflecting that there was little joy to be found there now. The last
year had brought only grief and anxiety.

The Earl of Argyle had come to town earlier in the summer and
conferred with Monmouth. Everyone thought a rising imminent.
Monmouth was still in disgrace and, sick at heart, Kit carried on his

work as steward, endeavouring to make ends meet on the Duke's diminishing income.

Shaftesbury, sent into exile, was dead and the Country party governed now by a council of six: Monmouth, Grey, Essex, Hampden, Russell and Colonel Algernon Sidney. They were, Kit knew, very near to rebellion. He himself had withdrawn from the most intimate councils—he preferred to be the friend in the background, prepared to back Monmouth to the limit, but he would not, he said, take part in an outright act of rebellion against the King. Charles had been good to him and he never looked at his blue-enamelled watch without remembering that.

'Don't fear,' Monmouth had said. 'I'll not act against him—only for the Protestant succession.'

So matters drifted on with the council of six talking behind locked doors at night, Monmouth forbidden to come to Whitehall, and the Whigs and Tories, enjoying their new soubriquets, at each other's throats.

What end could there be? Kit wondered. He found out as soon as he rode into Whitehall.

He entered the courtyard of the Cockpit and almost at once heard his name called. It was Tom Bruce, hurrying across the cobbles towards him.

'Come to my lodgings,' he said, urgently. 'I must speak with you.'

Startled, Kit dismounted and it was in Bruce's tiny bedroom that he heard the horrifying news of the exposure of the Rye House Plot.

He listened until he thought he must be in the middle of some nightmare from which he would surely wake, and by the time it was finished he had his head in his hands.

'God in heaven! Tom, I can't—I won't believe it.'

'It's all true enough,' Bruce assured him wearily. He had been on the watch for Kit's return for days, determined to be the one to break it to him, to urge him to leave at once.

'Tell me again,' Kit said, in a low voice. 'Tell me again how it began. I must have it clear in my mind.'

'The first we heard of it was the arrest of Colonel Rumsey—you know the fellow, all talk and bluster. Before we realized what it was all about my lords Russell and Essex and Howard were locked in the Tower with Colonel Sidney. My lord Grey was sent for but he'd fled and Robert Ferguson as well.'

They would run, Kit thought, bitterly. It was what he would have expected of those two. 'And the Duke?'

'He was sent for, too, but he was—not at home. His coachman, Welsh, told me that his Grace heard the guards had come for him, and left his bed to make his way out over the roof. Arms and ammunition were found in Grey's house as well as lists of names. No doubt it will all come out at the trials.'

The trials! It was bad enough to think of Russell and the rest arraigned for high treason, but Jamie! Kit clenched his hands. 'What witnesses are there against them?'

'Plenty have been found, though God knows where from, to testify that a rising was planned—and worse!'

Kit looked up sharply. 'What is there that is worse?'

Bruce stared at his boots, an unhappy man torn between his great affection for Monmouth and his loyalty to the Crown and the Tory party.

'Well, it seems some of the hotheads planned to waylay the King's coach at the Rye House—you know the place, on the way back from Newmarket—and murder him and the Duke of York.'

'No!' Kit smashed his fist down on the table. 'That I'll not believe! Christ's death, it's the most damnable bloody lie I ever heard.'

'Calm yourself,' Bruce laid a restraining hand on his arm. 'No one who knows them believes that either Monmouth or Russell had a hand in that. Did you ever hear talk of such a plan?'

'No, I did not, but by God if I had . . .' Kit paused, struggling to grasp this awful catastrophe that had overtaken them all. Bruce could be trusted with his confidence. 'I do know there were men who wanted York, at least, out of the way. Monmouth never allowed such talk, of course. His plan was only to secure the Protestant succession.' He looked up at Bruce. 'Don't you see, Tom? No one was ever so right in his ideas as Monmouth is—nor so wrong in the methods and the men he uses. I always knew Grey and Ferguson were dangerous.'

Bruce sighed. 'Yes, I know. I don't wonder you're bitter.'

'Of course I'm bitter. These men will ruin James. He is easily swayed when his principles are appealed to, but he, and Russell too, are innocent of such a plot.'

'I believe you—but it's clear that your "great men" will come to trial, and I do implore you, Kit, to leave Whitehall at once and keep out of sight for a while.'

Kit stared at him. 'I? Why? I've done nothing.'

Bruce did not meet his look. 'Others of your party have said that but they are in the Tower all the same.'

For a moment Kit did not speak. 'Would it not be like a confession of guilt to run away?'

'There are times when discretion is the better part. Of what avail to add yourself to those already in custody? Mr. Secretary Jenkins is questioning everyone connected with Monmouth, and you have been the closest. Why give him the satisfaction of adding you to the list?'

Nor York, Kit thought, his mind made up. 'Very well, I'll go. I see it all now, this is the Duke of York's doing. Probably he invented the whole cursed plot. Lord Howard is his creature, and so is Sunderland. They betrayed us to him and he—he's waited years for this!'

Bruce got up and went to stand by the window. Two pages were playing tennis below and he watched them absently. 'He will be King one day and he will have my loyalty. I'm sorry, Kit. I'd give anything to see it any other way, but I don't believe his Majesty was married to Lucy Walter. He would have said so if it had been true—as it is he is loyal to his brother, sometimes I think against his own inclinations, and I in turn can only be loyal too. I am your friend and Monmouth's, but I am against you in this.'

Kit rose and gathered up his cloak. 'That's honest at any rate, and I'm grateful for your warning, Tom. God knows what will happen to us, but as He is my witness I never wanted any plotting. All I can do now is go to Monmouth.'

Bruce shot him a veiled look. 'You know where he is?'

'We both know.'

He turned and had his hand on the latch when there was a knock on the door. He opened it and outside saw two of the King's guards, both of whom he recognized. One stepped forward, his face dyed red.

'Captain van—Mr. van Wyngarde, I am ordered to conduct you immediately to Mr. Secretary Jenkins.'

Kit exchanged a quick glance with Bruce. Too late now for flight! He pressed Bruce's arm and followed them, they a good deal less at ease than he, down the passage and across a courtyard to the Secretary's lodgings.

Inside a small room Jenkins, one of his Majesty's secretaries of

State, was sitting at his desk and for a solid hour Kit faced a barrage of questioning.

When had he last seen the Duke? And Lord Russell and Mr. Hampden? Did he know Colonel Rumsey? Had he visited the Rye House? Did he know of the planned rising? Had he taken any part in the discussions of it? Did he know of the deeper assassination plot?

He answered yes and no, and no even more furiously to some questions, but nothing seemed to satisfy the Secretary who probed again and again, seemingly in the hope of trapping his victim into some revelation.

Kit answered him honestly, but the questions were of such a nature that he was beginning to lose his temper—a development that might well have led him first to rash remarks and then inevitably to the Tower—when the door opened and the King himself came in, followed by his brother.

'Well?' Charles queried in a hard voice, looking straight at the Secretary, who stood bowing.

'Nothing as yet, your Majesty, but——'

'Persevere, Mr. Secretary,' York broke in. 'By heaven, if I were in your shoes I would use other methods to loosen a tight tongue.'

'If you please, James——' Charles laid a restraining hand on his brother's sleeve. 'I know Mr. van Wyngarde, and I know he has nothing to hide except perhaps an excess of misplaced loyalty.'

'Your Majesty, permit me——' Kit broke in indignantly, but Charles held up his hand and glanced at Jenkins.

'I think no one but Lord Howard has been found to testify against Mr. van Wyngarde and his testimony amounts to no more than that Mr. van Wyngarde attended meetings he might have done better to avoid. There is therefore no case that I can see.' He turned from the desk and the deferential Jenkins. 'You may go, Christian.'

Before Kit could recover himself from this startling statement, York had swung round to face his brother.

'It is madness to let this man go. Why, we all know he stands as close to the Duke of Monmouth as anyone. In fact he probably knows where he is at this moment. I suggest your Majesty at least confines him until his case is examined.'

'No!' Charles seemed suddenly exasperated and at once Kit saw the wretched grief that lay beneath the cool exterior. 'No,

James. Have you forgotten how Mr. van Wyngarde served us in the past?'

'I have not,' James answered, stubbornly, 'but neither have I forgotten that he wore green ribbons in his hat and consorted with the founders of this bloody plot.'

'Your Highness implies my guilt,' Kit broke in angrily, 'but the men that I consorted with—my lord Russell and Mr. Hampden—are no more guilty of a plot to murder you than your most loyal servant. Nevertheless I am aware that your Highness has long regarded me with disfavour.'

'You?' York interrupted. 'I have not regarded you at all.'

'James!' Charles broke in sharply. He looked tired and strained. 'I want to hear no more of this. I tell you I must draw the line somewhere and I choose to draw it here. Go, Christian, but hold yourself available should you be required.'

He flicked his fingers in dismissal and as Kit withdrew, too shaken and angry to try to express any gratitude, he heard the King say almost inaudibly:

'Are you merciless, James? Will there not be bloodshed enough?'

.   .   .   .   .   .

Kit was away next morning before it was light. He had bespoken a closed carriage, driven by one of Monmouth's trusted men, and climbing in ordered the man to drive off. It was not until he had sunk back on the seat that he realized he was not alone.

'Elizabeth! What, in God's name . . .'

She was wearing a dark cloak with a hood that half hid her face. 'Please don't be angry with me. I wanted to talk to you. Lord Bruce told me what happened last night, but when I came to the Cockpit. Jeremy said you had retired because you had to be up early this morning. From that, and what Bruce said, I guessed the rest.'

'Perhaps you did,' he said, in some irritation, 'but that doesn't give you leave to come with me. I'll tell the coachman to take you back. He had no right to let you in.'

'He did not see me. Please, Kit.' She laid her hand on his arm. 'Let me come. The Duchess has given me leave to go home for a few days and Toddington is not far from Westfield, is it?'

'No,' he admitted reluctantly, 'but this is not a pleasure jaunt, you know. Monmouth is in very grave danger.'

'I know, and whatever comes Henrietta will face it with him. That's why I want to see her—there may be something I can do for her.'

'Yet you were angry with me once for urging the Duke's case with her!'

She glanced at him, and though her face was grave there was a faint gleam of amusement in her eyes. 'I was a child then and you rightly told me so. But I have lived long enough at Whitehall now to see why Henrietta chose to give up everything for the Duke. In fact I do not think I can go on attending the Duchess of Monmouth much longer. She is a fair mistress, but her wit is hard and, because Henrietta is my friend, she sometimes says things that . . .' she broke off.

'It cannot be easy for you,' he agreed, but for the moment he was not thinking of the Duchess, but of another matter which he should have broached before. An odd reluctance had held him back but now seemed the right moment.

'The last time I saw Isabel,' he began slowly, 'she asked me to speak with you, to tell you that your uncle, standing in your father's place, wishes to arrange a marriage for you. If you want to leave the Duchess, it might be a good time to consider it.'

She had flushed. 'I do not think so. There is no one I wish to marry.'

'Your uncle would help select a suitable husband for you. He spoke of Sedley's nephew who as I recall is a pleasant young man with a good fortune and——'

'I do not care what he has for I do not care for him,' she retorted. 'I do not wish to wed.'

'My child, you cannot remain for ever in attendance on some court lady. You need someone to care for you.'

'Fiddle!' She added, with sudden bitterness: 'I've seen what marriage can be like at court—more often than not a man loves his mistress more than his wife. Oh!' She put a hand to her mouth. 'You know I did not mean that unkindly towards the Duke. Perhaps that is just why——' She broke off. 'If I cannot have what Mark and Isabel had, then I will do without a husband.'

'You are hard on my sex,' he remarked wryly.

She did not meet his eyes but gazed out of the window. 'Oh no.' Her voice was cool again. 'It is just that I will not be given to the highest bidder.'

He said no more, but he wondered if she had not over-sanctified her brother's memory, if Mark's best qualities might not become the means of keeping her from happiness herself.

They drove in silence through Barnet and on to St. Albans where they stopped for a light meal, and it was late afternoon when at last they came to Toddington. Sunlight glinted on the fishponds surrounding the house and it occurred to Kit that here was a peace which might satisfy even the restless Monmouth.

A servant told them that Lady Wentworth and the Duke were in the gardens, so he led Elizabeth out through the stables and presently saw Henrietta sitting under a large oak tree, a book in her hand. Monmouth was lying full-length on the grass, his head in her lap. When he saw them coming he sprang up and hurried forward, more anxiety than pleasure in his greeting.

'Kit! How in heaven's name do you come here? Did you not get my letter? I sent Higgs to warn you not to return.'

Kit took his outstretched hands. 'No, sir. I must have left Holland before he arrived.' He bowed to Lady Wentworth, who was embracing Elizabeth, and then added hastily: 'But don't fear for me. I was sent for and questioned but the King himself spoke for me and I am in no danger of arrest.'

Monmouth let out a deep sigh of relief. 'Thank God for that. If any more of my friends, especially you, had been——' He bit his lip, glancing at Henrietta, and changed the subject. 'Is this not a beautiful place? I do believe the country fellow has the best of it.'

Kit glanced amusedly at Monmouth who was dressed in simple peasant clothes—a plain brown stuff waistcoat and breeches and a white shirt devoid of lace. He looked sunburned and very well.

'Your Highness has become positively bucolic,' he commented, and turned to Henrietta who was holding out her hand to him.

'I am so glad you have come,' she said, adding with almost painful eagerness: 'You can tell us what is happening in town. Is Lord Russell . . .'

Monmouth's burdens rested equally on her shoulders yet, Kit thought, she had bloomed during these years. Her face seemed to glow with her love as if it imparted health to her frail body, and in Monmouth's presence she had a vitality that was absent when he was absent. She lived his life and because of it the fate of the men in London had become her first anxiety.

'There is no fresh news,' he said gravely, and wished he could have wiped the fear from her face.

Monmouth had put his arm about her slender waist. 'My dearest,' he said, smiling but firm, 'we will not discuss serious matters until later. This is a pleasant reunion of old friends, so let us be gay for a little while.'

And gay they were that evening. Lady Philadelphia presided over supper but afterwards she retired and the four of them sat talking together, the Duke, ever boyish, on the floor and leaning against Henrietta's chair. No one mentioned the troubles in London.

Once Monmouth leaned forward and flicked Kit's hair.

'You've a streak of grey there. You ought to take to a periwig, ought he not, Mistress Elizabeth?'

She laughed. 'I doubt it would become him so well.'

'Thank you,' Kit made Monmouth a mock bow. 'That is an extravagance I dislike and therefore leave to my betters, your Highness.'

Monmouth grinned. 'Oh damn my Highness. When you look down your nose like that I know that, far from considering me your better, you are being confoundedly superior. It must be these clothes—what did you call me, bucolic? Where are your Whitehall manners?'

'This isn't Whitehall.' Kit smiled a little, watching Monmouth yawn and stretch. 'The evening would scarce have begun there.'

The Duke shook his head sadly. 'I know. I fear the rustic air is responsible, or else I am growing old. I go to bed early and I rise early—very plebeian!'

They went upstairs, still talking lightly together, and while Henrietta took Elizabeth to her room, he showed Kit to one next to his own suite. The moment the door was shut, however, all trace of his light smile vanished.

'Tell me quickly. What has happened?'

Kit sat down on the edge of the bed. 'They are all in the Tower awaiting trial. Lord Russell and Lord Essex will be the first. Howard has turned king's evidence and damning evidence it will be.'

Monmouth began to pace up and down, clasping and unclasping his hands, less concerned with the betrayer than the betrayed. 'If I could only do something to help them. I sent word to Russell that I would come in and give evidence on his behalf if it

would benefit him, but he wrote to me and said——' He broke off.
  'Yes?'

Monmouth's voice was unsteady. 'He said there was no hope for him and that it would not benefit him to have his friends die with him.'

'That was nobly generous, a generosity you must not waste.'

'I see what you mean—no more plots!'

'No!' Kit answered forcibly. 'Surely you can see now where it has led us? And in heaven's name, how did the Rye House idea and that damnable part of it go forward?'

'I've no notion. You know I told them I'd see them in hell before I'd allow harm to come to my father. God knows what possessed those few crazy fools to plot against my orders, but they've succeeded in ruining us all.' Monmouth sat down on the oak chest at the foot of the bed and stared down at his shoes. 'I believed we were doing right,' he said, half to himself. 'I want England for the Protestant faith, and I think I would die to save it. That was what I was striving for all along—only it all went wrong.'

Kit got up and went to the window. It was a clear night and the country silence seemed to enfold the house. It was deceptive, he thought, for there was no peace here.

At last he said wearily, 'You trusted the wrong men.' He turned back into the room. 'What now? What will you do?'

'Wait—which I ever found it hard to do—and see what happens in London. Later I will write to my father.'

The Duke relapsed into silence and Kit watched him with an almost intolerable pity—this dejected, remorse-stricken Monmouth was a stranger to him.

'At least you are here with Henrietta. Once I thought I was doing wrong in urging her to go to you, but now I'm glad I did.'

Monmouth smiled at him, a curious smile, half melancholy, half affectionate. 'Yes, you did it for me, against your principles.' He got up and stood before Kit, his arms folded on his chest. 'Ever since I have been here we have prayed God night and morning to know if He condemns our love, and we are certain it is not offensive to Him.' He put a hand to his head. 'I need His comfort now. When I think of Russell I feel I cannot bear to stay here, free and with her, while he——'

'I know, but he would wish it. He will count it a privilege to die for you—as we all would.'

'Don't!' Monmouth broke in. 'Kit, for pity's sake!' He managed to control himself and said, more calmly, 'God send I have not ruined your life also.'

'Now you are talking nonsense,' Kit answered stoutly 'I would not change an hour.'

To him that short time spent at Toddington seemed a snatched period of false happiness and when he and Elizabeth climbed regretfully into their coach he knew that he was returning to reality.

They drove away leaving Monmouth standing, tall and smiling, beside Henrietta's slight figure.

'They are so happy—yet so unhappy. Oh, Kit, where will it end?' Elizabeth burst into tears and he, though he took her hand and held it in his, could think of no answer that might comfort her.

In London he returned to his work and awaited developments. Russell was tried and sent to the block, suffering a horrible end due to a bungling executioner, and later, when Kit snatched a few more days at Toddington, he was shaken by the depth of Monmouth's vicarious suffering for this the wisest and best of his friends.

Colonel Algernon Sidney was also executed and Lord Essex committed suicide while in the Tower. Grey and Ferguson remained in freedom and long afterwards Kit had cause to wish they had not. It seemed that fate in allowing Russell to die and Grey to escape had already sealed Monmouth's doom.

Summer faded into autumn. At last, in November, after much careful correspondence, Monmouth returned to London and had an interview with his father. Charles told him he desired more than anything to forgive him but that first he must make his peace with the Duke of York. Monmouth swallowed his pride and confessed to have plotted against his uncle's right to the throne, but never, he firmly averred, to either his assassination or his father's. Charles forgave him with tears of joy in his eyes.

But York was not yet finished with his nephew. He demanded that he should sign a paper admitting the evidence compiled against the other conspirators, including Hampden who was still awaiting judgement. Monmouth vacillated from one side to another and then, on an impulse and with a desire to bring the whole horrible business to an end, signed one copy. Immediately he regretted it and implored the King to return it to him.

'It will hang Hampden,' he said, in an agony of self-reproach. 'I beg your Majesty to return it to me.'

'Don't be a fool,' Charles, who had also had enough, snapped irritably at his son. 'I told you it could not and it will not.'

Monmouth twisted his hands together. 'Then your Majesty need not keep it. I beg you, sir——'

'God's death!' Charles swore. 'I don't know what is the matter with you, Jamie. By rights you ought to be locked up yourself— and I might tell you that many a better man than you has only made peace by hanging his friends.'

Monmouth drew himself up. 'I've not yet learned to murder my friends to save my own skin.'

A dark flush crept up under the King's swarthy skin. 'You may go,' he said, in a voice stifled with rage. 'Go to the devil!'

For a few days longer the struggle held between them. Neither would give way an inch. Kit watched them in bitter despair. He would not advise Monmouth to yield because every principle told him that in this Monmouth was right and the King wrong.

Finally on the seventh of December Charles ordered his son into exile and for the second time Kit helped him to pack. For the second time he was to stay behind and conduct the Duke's domestic affairs. 'I shall need money,' Monmouth said wearily, 'and you administer my finances better than anyone else.'

But it was cold comfort within and it was bitterly cold outside also. The severest frost in living memory had settled on the country; the Thames was frozen solid and Londoners made merry, skating and sliding and holding a fair on the ice. Monmouth and Kit rode over London Bridge, muffled to the eyebrows, and watched the crowds on the ice below. No one observed them and once or twice the Duke gave a sigh that was more distressing than anything he might have said. He was bound for Holland and the Orange's court and hoped to find a house where Henrietta might join him.

On the wharf at Greenwich, in a biting east wind, he held out his hand. 'Well, Kit, we have had these farewells before and I have come back. Don't look so desperate. It will come right.'

Kit turned away and looked across the grey river where ice-floes were floating by. 'You don't believe it—not this time.'

'Nonsense,' Monmouth retorted, cheerfully, but his eyes were shadowed and he looked about the wharf and the clustering houses by the great palace as if he were seeing them for the last time. He took Kit's hand in a hard grip. 'Keep a good heart, old sober-sides.'

Afterwards Kit never knew how he kept himself from boarding the vessel that was to carry the Duke to Holland, the last ship to leave before the river froze right down to the sea. He rode back to Whitehall so deeply unhappy that he was past thought. Everything was buried under snow, each tree and shrub encrusted with frost, every pond and pump frozen. So, too, he thought, was his very soul.

5

Standing in the doorway of the great ballroom at Whitehall it occurred to Kit how many of the old faces had gone. Some habitués were still there, but among his own particular circle there were few. Bab had retired to Windsor to live out his eccentric bachelor life and Kit missed his salacious humour. Elizabeth too had gone for the moment. She had left the Duchess's service and presently travelled to Holland to stay awhile with Henrietta Wentworth in the little house Monmouth had rented.

'I hate to be going away from you,' she had said, 'but Henrietta wants me and perhaps before long you will come to Holland too.'

'Perhaps,' he had answered, and sometimes wondered why indeed he did not leave his two able clerks to carry on his work. He kept Monmouth's affairs in order, collected rents from the receivers and sent the Duke what monies he could, but they were dreary enough tasks only a little sweetened by the thought that he was doing what Monmouth wanted him to do, or was it by the ever-persistent hope that the Duke might any day ride into Whitehall?

Nearly a year had passed since Monmouth's departure and still there was no word of his recall. Letters came regularly from him. He had been warmly received at the Dutch court and was once again enjoying his cousin Mary's company—he had the better part, Kit thought wearily, and poured himself some wine.

Looking round the room now, he saw Richmond talking to old Lord Ailesbury, Bruce's father. Richmond was kind, but the barrier between them now that Monmouth was banished and York triumphant was the more pronounced.

He emptied his glass and reached for the decanter beside him. He was aware that for one who had always been abstemious he was drinking too much, but wine was the only solace left. It dimmed his senses, blurred the images in his mind, if only for a little while.

And he was fighting a strange personal conflict within himself. Only a few short years ago he had so much—Monmouth's daily companionship and a cause he believed in, a circle of intimate friends, and a mistress to pleasure his easy hours. All this was gone and in a desperate loneliness he walked the palace galleries and longed for the days that were gone. Was he, he wondered, paying for the pleasure he had taken so easily?

'You are too solemn these days, my dear boy. It seems you are earning your nickname.'

Kit started and turned to find the King standing beside him. Charles looked older and far from well, but he smiled and laid a hand on his arm in a more friendly gesture than he had shown for some time.

Kit bowed. 'Your Majesty must pardon me. I had forgot for the moment that I was at Whitehall.'

The smile left the King's face. 'Doubtless your thoughts were across the sea?'

'One cannot control one's thoughts, sir.'

For a moment Charles said nothing. Then he roused himself. 'Now I am doing the very thing for which I chided you. You should be dancing. Let me see if I can find you a partner. Now there's a handsome wench, not too young, not too old. Oddsfish, it is Lady Carrisford. Off with you, Christian.'

Kit followed the King's pointing finger. Yes, after all these years, it was she. 'Your Majesty will forgive me, but I seldom dance these days and——'

'I shall not,' the King interrupted. He was still looking across the room at his find. 'Lady Carrisford was widowed a year ago and this is her first appearance since then. She will be glad to see someone she used to know.' He turned to look cynically at Kit. 'God save us, why so hesitant? Go and dance.'

There was enough irritability in his voice to make Kit incline his head and walk across the room.

He knew she had seen him coming and she was smiling at him with the same warm look he remembered. The years had dealt kindly with Ann Ratcliffe; her figure was a little fuller, but her voluptuous beauty had taken maturity and enhanced it. She accepted his hand and entered the set with him, tilting her head to one side in a once familiar gesture.

'You have changed, Kit.'

'Have I? How?'

She laughed. 'You have grown older, but then so have I—only don't dare to say it! Thank God you have not become stout. I abhor fat men. But you look tired, my dear.'

'I work very hard.'

'How unfashionable. What do you do?'

'I administer the domestic affairs of the Duke and Duchess of Monmouth.'

'That can't be too easy a task.'

'No,' he said, abruptly, 'but it is the one I have chosen.' And he changed the subject by asking how she liked being back at Whitehall.

He left her to her next partner, but stood up with her again for the last corante. When it was over she stood fanning herself.

'I find all this very enjoyable, but wearying. When I first knew you, Kit, I could have danced all night. And so could you. Do you remember how we rode to Rotherhithe and I wore a suit of Michael's clothes?'

He laughed. 'I do indeed. You made a handsome boy.'

'Did I? But, I hope, a more handsome girl?'

He realized he had not laughed like this for months and somehow she made it impossible to remember old sores. 'You are very refreshing, Ann. Are you to be at court now?'

'Yes, I am to have a place about the Queen.' She shot him a sidelong glance. 'I hope that pleases you. Will you escort me to my apartments?'

In silence he held out his arm and as they walked slowly down the gallery it seemed to him that time had slipped a cog and they were back in the corridor at Merton College.

Presently she paused by a door, just as she had done before. 'This is my room. It has been very pleasant to see you again—dear Kit.' She put up her hand and touched his cheek lightly. 'And if you should not wish for sleep, you know now where I lodge.' She sent him a swift, half-mocking, half-inviting smile and went inside.

He paused, looking at the closed door, remembering how so long ago he had stood, an awkward nervous boy, before the door of her

room and she had spoken almost the same words. He had left that
boy far behind but as he walked away to a seat by a window and sat
looking out into the night, he realized that her invitation—for such
it was—had found him for once defenceless.

Had he met her again a year or two ago, he would have turned
her words lightly aside and gone on his way in peace, but now he
was lonely and unhappy and the iron control he had maintained
over himself since Cathy's departure had slipped a little. After all,
what did it matter? So little seemed to matter now. He got up and
went back to Ann's room.

She was waiting for him, her hair undone and loose about her
shoulders and wearing a wrap of blue velvet instead of her ball-
dress. When she saw his eyes sweep over her she smiled a little.

'So history repeats itself. Will you take a glass of wine this
time?'

He found her amusement infectious—he had forgotten this
side of her character. 'Thank you, I will.'

She poured out two glasses of wine. 'Lord, but you were hot
then, and so innocent.'

'I must have been somewhat of a bore.'

'Not that—but I think more interesting now.'

'Thank you,' he said again, and bowed ironically. Placing his
glass on the table he put his arm about her, tilted up her chin and
began to kiss her, slowly at first and then with a gathering passion,
until he felt all the loneliness and repression flowing from him in a
burning stream.

When he let her go, she looked up at him, her eyes wide and
warm. 'There must have been some pretty women at court these
years I have been gone.'

He picked up his glass again. 'Not at court, my dear. You
taught me a lesson there.'

'You never forgave?'

'I never forgot.'

'And now?'

'Now—I don't care.'

She tried to read his face but could discern nothing, and uncertain how to continue this duel in words, sat down on the bed
and leaned back against the pillows, prepared to employ tactics
she did understand. 'You are not very complimentary.'

'Am I not?' It amused him that she was using her familiar

charms, only now he could play the game her way. 'Then I will soon remedy that.'

He took off his coat and loosened the elaborate lace at his throat, aware of a curious sense of release; and as he sat down on the edge of the bed he knew that this way, for a little while, he would be free of the strain, the anxiety, the hope deferred, the hope dying that he had lived through in the last months. Looking down at Ann he saw her curved lips inviting him, her eyes large and luminous fixed on his, and putting aside the heavy velvet robe he laid his head between her breasts.

He felt her touch his hair lightly.

'Well, Kit, it seems that we have met again at a propitious moment. You must have been riding yourself on a hard rein.'

'Yes,' he said, almost inaudibly, and slid his arm about her, surprised at her perception. He was kissing her, again now, remembering how the touch of her mouth had sent the blood pounding through his young body all those years ago. That had been rapture —this, and he knew it, was no more than a momentary need as much for escape from himself as for Ann.

'What is it?' he heard her ask, her voice low and caressing. 'What is it that frets you so? There's nothing in the world worth a broken heart.'

He drew a long shuddering breath. He did not want to talk now, only to lose himself, but womanlike she would not let the subject be.

'My poor love, never tell me you are breaking it for our pretty Monmouth. Why, he's a bright enough spark at racing and dancing, but witless for all that, and a fool too if he thinks a harlot's bastard could sit on the throne of England.'

Somehow Kit found himself on his feet. He was trembling and heard his own voice shaking as he said: 'You will forgive me if I leave you now. The Duke is my friend and I'll not stay to hear him insulted.'

She laughed in genuine surprise. 'Surely you have not lived all these years at Whitehall and still kept your ideals. My foolish Kit!'

He snatched up his coat. 'I don't want your pity. I don't want anything from you.'

She laughed again, lounging against the pillows, but it was a less pleasant laugh now. 'You have changed your tune quickly enough.

Go, then, if you must be so high-minded. I'm glad that when I pinned my faith on a duke, I chose the brother not the bastard.'

He paused for one instant, staring down at her, seeing her for the sensual selfish woman she was. Perhaps she had set her cap at York once more. He did not know, did not very much care. Sick with revulsion against himself for having succumbed to a moment of sexual weakness, he wanted only to get away from her to solitude. He turned and followed by the sound of her mocking laughter hurried from the room, and away down the passage.

Rounding a corner blindly in the darkness he ran full tilt into the King.

Charles was clad in his dressing-gown and carrying a candle, for he was on his way back from the Duchess of Portsmouth's apartments. As Kit cannoned into him, he caught his arm and held the candle high to see who his assailant was.

'Christian! Have you forgotten my cousin Rupert's injunction never to run in the palace?' His eyes, bright with amusement, took in the rumpled shirt, the coat flung over one arm. 'Did she send you packing, eh?'

Kit caught his breath sharply. 'Sir, your pardon. If you would allow me to go——' He did not meet the King's eyes but he was aware of their scrutiny. When Charles spoke again it was without the bantering tone.

'There's more than that amiss here. Come, escort me back to my closet and we will drink some wine quietly together.'

There was such real kindliness in his tone that Kit found himself unable to escape and was propelled willy-nilly to the King's apartments. There Charles waved him to a chair while Chiffinch, tactful as ever, made up the fire and lit fresh candles.

Kit sat down, shaken by the strain of shackling both his passion and his revulsion, and though he did not know it his face was white. Charles watched him shrewdly and, when Chiffinch was gone, thrust a glass into his hand.

'Drink that, boy, and then tell me what happened.'

Kit hesitated, and then, aware that he was shivering, drank off the wine at one gulp. He had not entered this room since the evening twelve years ago when he had returned from Rome, and to be here again, with the King smiling kindly at him as he used, momentarily deprived him of speech.

'You were with Lady Carrisford, were you not?' Charles asked.

'I cannot think either that she refused to bed with you, or that if she had you would be so distressed. So it must have been something else.'

Kit glanced up, startled at the King's omniscient knowledge of all that went on in his palace. There was, as usual, no evading his penetration.

'She insulted the Duke of Monmouth,' he said flatly, and left it at that.

'God damn us all to hell!' Charles swore. 'That young viper! I thought at least in Holland he was out of the way. Put him out of your mind.'

'Does your Majesty really wish me to do that?'

'Yes, I do,' the King retorted truculently. He began to pace up and down the little room and a black spaniel climbed out of its basket to follow, sniffing at his heels. 'He's an ungrateful rogue and he'll lead even you into mischief.'

Kit watched the King unhappily, aware that Charles was ranting in order to hide other emotions; he seemed in a strange mood tonight, determined to be hard and cynical yet paradoxically warm and almost excited.

Presently he ceased his uneasy pacing and stood looking down at his visitor. 'I don't deceive you, do I?'

'No, your Majesty.'

The King sat down again in his big chair and crossed his feet on a stool. 'Was ever a boy as misguided as mine? And you, I suspect, have been fighting his battles tonight and for many a day.'

Kit bent his head, but there was nothing to say to this.

'Well? *Well?*' Charles snapped. 'Why haven't you gone after him instead of moping around my palace like a cursed Job's comforter?'

'For one thing, sir,' Kit met the angry gaze steadily, 'someone has to keep his affairs here in order and for another—I believe your Majesty will bring him home soon. Your Majesty must know he would do nothing to harm you and in all justice——'

'In all justice he ought to be in the Tower out of harm's way,' Charles broke in caustically, but almost at once he seemed to relax, a faint smile curving his mouth. 'But I'll not tease you further. He is to come home very soon.'

That short sentence, coming so unexpectedly after all the King had just said, sent the blood rushing to Kit's face. 'Your Majesty——'

'It is true. He was here a few weeks before Christmas, when you were at Tolbrooke.'

'He was *here*?'

'Yes, in this very room, but secretly. He brought that pale girl of his with him.' The King refilled Kit's glass and glanced at his astonished face. 'It is quite all right. He came at my order and I think he will try to make amends when he is home. You must restrain him from any further folly. Conspire with Lady Wentworth—she will keep him straight if any woman can.'

Kit drew a deep breath. It was as if a black fog had lifted. 'Sir, I don't know what to say except that this is what I have prayed for all these months. I'm sure the Duke wants to live at peace now. As for myself'—he looked up at the King—'I have never had a chance to thank you for what you did for me after the Rye House disclosures. But for your intervention I might well have died with the others.'

Charles got up and with great deliberation began to wind one of his clocks. 'I knew you had naught to do with that affair, nor Jamie—he may be a fool but he's not an assassin.' And he added, rather surprisingly, 'Sometimes I think it was my fault that he turned to plotting.'

'Yours, sir?'

'Yes. If I had not taken his offices from him he would have stayed content enough. I see now that he must have work to do and soldiering best of all, but I took away his occupation so he turned to politics—silly boy!' Charles stood swinging the key thoughtfully from its string. 'Well, by Easter we'll have him home to cheer us up, though for a moment it must remain â secret.'

Until the Duke of York is out of the way, Kit thought shrewdly and glanced at the King. Would he ever understand this man of strange conflictions—this man of charm and kindliness and genuine warmth, who was also a man of easy deceit and soft-spoken half-truths, who could play off son against brother and take his own pleasure at the same time? Did he plan now to acknowledge Monmouth his heir? Would he ever do it?

Kit did not know, but he had always been sure that Tom Ross had spoken the truth when he said he had seen Lucy Walter's marriage lines. He believed a marriage had taken place but in all probability one conducted in some clandestine manner, and for this reason Charles, in his wisdom and respect for the English crown and his Queen, would not own it. But it was legal for all that and Monmouth paid the price, suffering for the sins of his parents.

Still, he was to come home now and that was all that mattered for the moment. Kit went down on one knee and put the King's hand to his lips.

Charles smiled a little. 'Don't look so pleased, Christian, or the court will wonder what has occurred to make the Puritan so cavalier.'

'My friends, sir, know that my nickname is not entirely merited.'

Charles's eyelids flickered. 'We are none of us so good or so bad as people think.'

Outside in the corridor again, Kit stood leaning against the window-frame, looking out into the still clear night in speechless gratitude. He had completely forgotten Ann Ratcliffe and the scene that led to this nocturnal meeting with the King. When he did see her the next day he passed her without a backward glance.

.   .   .   .   .   .

He waited, but with a happy impatience now, for three more weeks. Day by day he attended the court, hoping for news, and then one morning as he stood aside in the Matted Gallery for the King to pass, Charles came over to him.

'Come and see me tomorrow morning,' he said in a low voice. 'I am going to send you on a mission that will be very much to your taste.'

He moved on with his companions, leaving Kit staring at his retreating back. There was no doubting what that mission would be—Charles was sending him to Holland to summon Monmouth home.

He snatched up his cloak and went out into the bright February morning. Only physical exercise could give rein to this joy, and fetching Chimera from the stables he went for a long, wild ride through the fields to Highgate village.

And in the morning as he walked through the palace gardens he saw that the first snowdrops were already flowering in the cold earth, a promise of spring and a resurgence of life that fitted exactly into his own mood.

Only as he entered the archway that led to the King's apartments did he see Chiffinch and stop abruptly at the sight of the keeper's face.

'Will! Is something wrong?'

Chiffinch paused only for a moment, his face ashen. 'His Majesty has been taken ill, very ill, not an hour since while he was being shaved. The doctors say—they believe it is the end.'

'God!' Kit put out a hand to steady himself against a pillar. 'Tell me, Will, did he say anything . . .'

But Chiffinch was gone across the garden where now the wind blew cold and spring seemed far away.

For four days the court waited, silent, anxious, moving about in restless groups, talking in hushed voices, while Charles suffered.

Kit waited, too, in a state of mental agony. Not only was he sorrowing for a man who had shown him constant kindness, but the thought that no one but himself knew of Charles's intention to recall Monmouth drove him nearly frantic. If Charles died—but it was unthinkable. He could not die, not now with Monmouth away in Holland while James of York was at his brother's bedside.

He hung about the galleries, hoping desperately for a summons, even a message, but it was soon obvious that whatever the King had planned to do for Monmouth he was too ill to do now. For long hours Kit sat with Bruce, listening to the latter's description of the torture inflicted on the dying man by his determined physicians.

'They won't let him rest or sleep,' Bruce said in fierce distress. 'They fill him up with their damned purges until he is too weak to move. I tell you, Kit, it is more than I can bear to watch him—and he is so patient.' He made no attempt to restrain his tears and it was soon more than Kit could bear to watch his uninhibited grief. His own nerves grew so frayed that he left Bruce and went out to walk alone in the deserted Privy Gardens.

On the third evening, coming back up the spiral stair, he encountered the King's brother. He was forced to stand aside and as the Duke came towards him their glances met. York paused and in that moment all pretence of courtesy and deference was lost in a naked revelation of what Kit had always known and York, for all his slowness, had sensed.

He stood now looking down at Kit, his mouth drawn into a thin line. 'I am surprised you are still here, Mr. van Wyngarde,' he said in a cold voice. 'Surely you cannot imagine the Duke of Monmouth is ever likely to return?'

'I do not waste my time in speculation,' Kit returned, with equal chilliness. 'I prefer to wait upon facts.'

A look of anger swept across the Duke's face. 'I never believed you innocent of the Rye House affair and I tell you now that if my brother dies you had best be gone.'

Kit made a slight bow but he managed to infuse it with an air of contempt. 'If his Majesty should not recover, which God forbid, I should have no desire to remain here.'

The Duke glared at him, but having, seemingly, no answer to this, walked on down the stairs.

At last, in the dawn of the sixth of February, Charles asked for the curtains to be drawn a little so that he might once more see the light of day. An hour later he was dead. The court dispersed, every man and woman weeping openly, and Kit left the Long Gallery for the last time, the heavy chime of Charles's death-knell tolling the ruin of his own hopes.

.   .   .   .   .   .

Harry Richmond, dressed in sombre black, was alone in the library of his Strand house when Kit came to say goodbye. He rose when his visitor was announced and held out his hand.

'I have been hoping you would come.'

Kit took the outstretched hand, shocked to see how grief had ravaged his cousin's face. 'He would not wish you to mourn him so, sir—indeed he would not.'

Richmond turned away to the window. 'We were boys together—a whole lifetime——' He broke off, but when he turned back he was outwardly calm. 'What are you going to do now?' And when Kit told him he was leaving England this night, Richmond nodded without surprise.

'You are going to Holland?'

'Yes, to Monmouth.' Kit came to stand beside him looking out into the garden. There were snowdrops here as there had been in the palace gardens when he went across them to see the King and receive his instructions to bring Monmouth home.

'Have you . . .' Richmond hesitated and then went on more firmly, 'have you seen the King?'

Kit stiffened. He had known this must come, yet still he wished

Richmond had not needed to say it. 'I have no King now. And I saw no one at Whitehall but the Duchess of Monmouth.'

He had gone to Anna this morning and handed over the keys of his desk and her money-chests.

She was at her dressing-table, stiff and cool, and he wondered what she felt at this moment with her husband far away in Holland and England now closed to him.

'You are going to his Grace?' she asked formally.

'Yes, madame.'

'I expected it.' She took the keys and sat fingering them. 'You may tell him the children are well.'

'And yourself, madame?'

She rose. 'Let us not dissemble, Mr. van Wyngarde. We have known each other too long for that. He and I have nothing in common but our children.'

He bowed, but he fancied he saw in her face the hint of a long-suppressed sorrow. When Monmouth charmed everyone, how should Anna have remained immune? He bent over her hand. 'Goodbye, madame. Pray make my farewells to the children.'

'You have been a good steward,' she said, in a voice quite devoid of its usual sharp tone. 'We shall miss you.'

He left her, aware of her defensive loneliness, but Anna could adapt herself to any circumstances and he did not pity her. She had always been on good terms with York and would no doubt make it her business to remain so, whatever her husband might do.

He became aware that Richmond had laid a hand on his shoulder.

'My dear boy! Is everything that has been to go for nothing? All of us who have been your friends—myself, Bruce, Bab May and a host of others—are we all forgotten?'

'None of you. But I must go to Monmouth now.'

Richmond gave a heavy sigh and returned to his chair by the fire. 'Yes, I knew you would go. It was but a selfish effort to keep you.'

Kit fumbled with the fastening of his cloak. 'You do not know what it costs me to say goodbye to you and Bruce, to Whitehall and Tolbrooke—so many years—but I would rather live in exile with Monmouth than endure again such months as these have been without him.'

He made an effort and came back to the hearth, master of himself once more. 'It is as we once said, you for the Catholic Duke, I for the Protestant.'

Richmond said, 'You will write, will you not?'

'Of course.' Kit took the outstretched hand and, unable to say more, hurried from the room.

Outside, Jeremy, who had refused to be dismissed, was waiting with the horses, and by nightfall they had reached the coast only to find the packet-boat forbidden to sail. King James had closed the ports.

Already he was afraid, Kit thought scornfully. Did he imagine that Monmouth was even now on his way home?

Leaving Jeremy at an inn with the baggage he went out, and after much bribery found a fisherman willing to take him across to Calais.

On the dawn tide the little boat slipped unobtrusively out to sea and Kit, wrapped in his cloak, watched the coastline disappear into the morning mist. It was more than twenty-three years since he had come to England and made it his home. He thought of those years, of the happiness and sorrow, of the friends made and the friends lost, of the King he had loved and never understood. They were all, now, in the past.

He was going back to Holland and already he felt an exile. Would he ever return to this green land, already half shrouded in mist? He did not know. At the moment he was only conscious of an overwhelming bitterness that Monmouth's restoration had been snatched away.

For what—so few nights ago—had he thanked God so joyfully?

BOOK FOUR

King James's Reckoning May–July, 1685

KIT wrote the date, Friday, the twenty-second day of May, in the year of our Lord 1685, at the top of the page in his small neat hand and began to draw up a list of figures.

It was almost impossible to see where the money had gone. Field pieces, pistols, breast plates, pikes and swords, match and powder had taken a considerable sum, but by far the largest expenditure was on the two ships and the heavy cost of chartering the *Helderenburgh*, a sturdy frigate.

He had been wrestling with these accounts for so long, determined to leave everything in order, that he had hardly had time to realize he was on the eve of the most hazardous venture upon which his life and everything he possessed was staked. At the moment he was only aware that he was very tired and closing his eyes for a moment he did not hear a light footfall behind him.

The Duke spoke over his shoulder. 'Your whole fortune, Kit! God send I can repay it one day.'

He sat up at once and shook his head. 'I don't want that for myself—only because it would mean success for you.'

Monmouth went over to the window and sprawled on the seat there. The sun was streaming in and in its light the lines of anxiety and strain, new to his face, were accentuated. 'Success! God alone knows what that would mean. I tell you, Kit, whatever they say to me I'll not go as a claimant to the throne. I'll go as the Protestant Duke or not at all.'

'Of course you are right. Has Ferguson been pressing you again?' Kit would have been better pleased had 'the Plotter' had no part in all this.

There was a heavy frown on Monmouth's face. 'Not in so many words, but it is in his mind all the same. Well, I have told him I'll not go otherwise and that must satisfy him. I can be as obstinate as he. Anyway, I count far more on my lord Sunderland's help.'

'Surely you don't still trust him, not after the Rye House affair?'

Monmouth's chin was set, seemingly to illustrate his obstinacy. 'He has given me his word.' He glanced at Kit, and changed the subject. 'By the way, did you know that my uncle's ambassador has been trying to get an order to prevent us sailing?'

'I heard rumours in the town this morning. Do you think——'

'Of course not,' the Duke interrupted, more cheerfully. 'William has no desire to stop me, in fact——' He broke off, obviously putting a thought from his mind. 'Well, I must see Jones on his way with my instructions. Please God he has a safe journey and then my friends in London will know where and when we shall land in England.'

When he had gone Kit finished the accounts and then began the task of sorting the Duke's papers.

It was difficult now to think back to that bleak day when in grief and bitterness at what seemed God's mockery he had seen the coast of England fade into the distance—for now it seemed He had, after all, a purpose for Monmouth and so for him too.

When he had arrived in Holland William had already broken to Monmouth the news of the King's death. At Bentinck's house he found the Duke, red-eyed and haggard, and Monmouth wept again as Kit told him of Charles's last hours. Whatever had gone wrong between them, his love for his father had remained unchanged.

Feeling it encumbent on him, Kit went the next day to the Huis ten Bosch to pay his respects. After a while William called him aside.

'So, van Wyngande, you are come back at last.' And not before time, his tone implied.

Bowing over his hand, Kit wondered what William's feelings were. If papist James allied himself to papist France, always threatening his borders, William might find his enemies increasing again. Was that why, although appearing to concede to his uncle James's wish that he should not give shelter to his cousin, he took no action against Monmouth?

Aware that William was waiting for him to speak Kit said: 'I must be honest and tell your Highness that I am only here for as long as it shall please the Duke of Monmouth to remain.'

He had expected the Prince to be angry, but William often did the unexpected and instead gave one of his rare brief laughs. 'Do you think I did not know that? Well, go your way. I'll not meddle.'

He kept his word. He wrote subtle letters to pacify his uncle and turned a blind eye to Monmouth's movements. He did not appear to have heard when Piet Daagen, gone very grey now but still constantly at the Prince's side, informed him that the Duke and Lady Wentworth had settled into a house at Gouda.

Kit and Elizabeth went with them. Monmouth himself had pressed Elizabeth to stay, for he felt Henrietta in need of her company and support.

So for a little while they were happy. 'I'll not make a bustle in the world again,' Monmouth said, and meant it. Living in simple domesticity with Henrietta he had found contentment at last.

Then his friends began to stir him. Argyle came from Scotland, urged on by David Hume, the Covenanter who had once defied Monmouth at Bothwell Bridge but who was so impressed by the Duke's generosity on that occasion that he now strenuously upheld him.

Hating popery, Scotland was for the most part eager for Monmouth. Hume asked him if he considered himself a lawful son of his father? Monmouth replied that he did but added that he would accept no position in the State but what the people thought fit to bestow on him. Hume liked this answer and the interview between Argyle and Monmouth, after a difficult start, went well enough. God was calling him to England, they told him. It was surely a great work, to preserve the country for the Protestant faith, a work no prince of England could refuse.

Monmouth hesitated, but such an appeal to him to whom that faith now meant so much could hardly fail. He would go, he said at last, but only as Protestant champion, no more. Hume smiled a secret smile and Argyle nodded wisely. So the venture was set on foot.

Money was the greatest need. Monmouth pawned his great 'George' and all the jewels he possessed. Henrietta gave him everything of value that she had and Kit, though for obvious reasons he would not touch the van Wyngarde property, put his own personal and not inconsiderable fortune into the funds, thankful that he had always been frugal.

Argyle was to organize Scotland and Monmouth to land in the West Country where his following was strongest. Promises came in plenty from the landed gentry, and my lords Delamere and Brandon were to assemble about London as many Horse as they could muster while Lord Macclesfield was to raise Cheshire. The ubiquitous Lord Grey arrived to lend his name and his person to the proceedings and Robert Ferguson began work on the necessary manifestos.

In the quiet of the house at Gouda Kit worked on the Duke's personal affairs, while Henrietta and Elizabeth stitched at the Duke's own standard until this morning, when it had been completed: a flag of deep green silk woven across in gold letters with the words 'Fear Nothing but God'.

When it was handed to him Monmouth had taken it reverently, caressing the heavy folds. Then he had given a deep sigh, and passing it to Kit, had gone alone to his room.

Perhaps only Kit and Henrietta knew of the doubts he suffered over the coming journey, only they knew how deeply three days ago he had regretted leaving the little house at Gouda and returning to The Hague.

Kit leaned his chin on his fists and stared out into the busy street. His own feelings were strangely mixed. He still distrusted Grey and Ferguson and he disliked Argyle, whom he suspected of using Monmouth to gain his own way in Scotland. Did the exiles who crowded round the Duke and urged on his rising care for him or for the cause?

A few perhaps—among them old Thomas Dare, a Taunton man of considerable standing in the West Country, Nathaniel Wade, a Bristol lawyer with whom Kit had struck up an immediate friendship, and Andrew Fletcher of Saltoun, their best cavalry officer—but to Kit they seemed pitifully few. Always less impetuous than Monmouth, he tried to persuade him to wait a little while—James of York given enough time would surely hang himself without their help—but the thing had gathered momentum and somehow they were in and committed before either felt it right.

Monmouth clung to the idea that God was calling him to a great work in England and if he believed it then Kit would uphold that belief. Now, either Monmouth would triumph and they would go home to Whitehall or York would triumph and they would both pay with their lives.

On this evening before they were to set off, he had no regrets, only, for Monmouth's sake, a wish that they could be as sure of their friends as they were of their enemies.

With a little sigh he got up to fetch the small bag in which the Duke wanted his personal papers packed, and it was then that Lady Wentworth came in.

She had been ill during the winter and still looked pale and even more fragile, but she was gaily dressed in primrose muslin and he knew she was making a gallant attempt to hide her failing health.

She crossed the room to stand by his desk. 'Are you not finished yet?' She picked up a quill, twisting it nervously between her fingers.

'Very nearly.' He turned to face her. 'Henrietta, may I say this—I have seen, as no one could fail to see, how complete your happiness with the Duke has been. So don't be afraid, nothing can take that from you.'

Her eyes filled but she shed no tears. 'You mean that if you fail, if he does not come back, at least I will have had that.'

'That was not what I meant,' he answered swiftly, 'though it is true. But he will come back, never fear.'

' "Fear nothing but God",' she murmured, half to herself. 'Ah, Kit, a woman has the harder part. You see, I know that if he succeeds it is not I who will share his triumph. That will be the Duchess's right.' She saw the expression on his face and added: 'Oh, do not mind for me. I do not.'

'No,' he said, 'for no one can be what you are to him.'

'I know that, too. That is why I sometimes feel it might be better if . . .' She stopped, the discipline of years holding her steady so that she was able to turn the conversation from herself. 'And what of you, Kit? What are your thoughts tonight?'

'For him, I don't need to tell you. For myself'—a melancholy look crossed his face—'unimportant. There is no one to be overly concerned about me.'

A door had closed and steps crossed the hall but as no one came in he went on, 'My affairs are in order and should anything befall me you have only to deliver to my attorney the papers in the box I am leaving behind.'

'Of course. Is there anything else you wish me to do?'

'No—except to care for Elizabeth which I know you will do.
He paused. 'You see her brother asked me before he died to watch
over her, so should—should things go against us, beg her to go home
to Westfield.'

'Of course,' Henrietta said again. She hesitated and then laid a
tentative hand on his arm, her eyes searching his face. 'But I wish
you would talk to her yourself, tell her what you wish her to do.
She is finding all this as hard to bear as I am.'

He was surprised. 'I know she has the cause deeply at heart, but
I should not have thought——'

Henrietta smiled a little. 'You have had too much to do to give
thought to anything else, but now she needs your comfort. She has
no one else.'

'That is true,' he admitted. 'Very well, I will talk to her if you
think I should.'

On the landing upstairs he saw that her door was ajar and hearing an odd muffled sound he pushed it further open. Elizabeth was
sitting on the bed, still in her outdoor cloak, and she was clinging
to one of the bedposts with the tears running wildly down her
face and a handkerchief stuffed against her mouth to stifle the
sobs.

At once he crossed the room and sat down beside her. 'Why,
child, what is it? We are not surely in so bad a case that you think
us lost already?'

She had stiffened as he came across to her but almost at once she
gave a stifled sob and flung her arms round his neck.

'Oh no, no—but when I came in I—I heard you say that there
would be no one to weep for you if—if——' she gave another sob.
'Do you think I would not weep for you?'

He was shaken, startled for the first time out of his preoccupation with Monmouth's affairs, and moved by the depth of
emotion in her voice. Withdrawing a little he sat very still, looking
at her, seeing the blue hood framing her face, the strands of fair
hair fallen loose, the wide tear-filled eyes fixed on his.

'You must not weep for me,' he said at last, and put his hands
on her shoulders. 'I chose my way a long while ago. I knew it
would be a lonely way and I knew what it would demand of me,
so do not waste your tears.'

She laid her cheek against his hand where it rested on her
shoulder. 'There is no other man in the world I would weep for.

Do you not know I have worshipped you ever since I was a little girl?'

He looked down at her in utter astonishment. 'My dear! I am a very unworthy subject for your worship. I am a great deal older than you and you should look for a younger man to love, one who will be able to give you a clean heart and an unsullied name.'

She sat up and wiped the tears from her face. 'You have both, and I have never wanted anyone else. Do you remember once, long ago, I said I would not marry until I found someone who could give me what Mark gave Isabel?'

'I remember.'

'But'—there was a tremulous smile on her lips—'as I grew up I began to understand that with you it would be like that, and if ever you wanted me I would come to you.'

'But you can't——' he began, aghast. 'You don't know what you are saying. Elizabeth, I cannot marry you. It—it would not be suitable. There is too much behind me.'

'Oh.' She gave a little sigh. 'You think I am so young and silly. But I knew about your lodgings in Axe Yard from the very beginning, and I knew too that you did not marry a long time ago because some woman hurt you. I heard Sir Harry say so to my father.'

He had recoiled, a flush on his cheeks, but impulsively she caught his hand and held it.

'Did you think I would mind about any of that? I have not lived so long at Whitehall without learning something about life. I would not expect any man to be a saint.'

He felt as if he were being swept away on a tide. 'It is too late, I have nothing to give you. The past has taken too much.'

'I would rather have half of you than nothing at all.'

'It would not be fair.' He knew his voice sounded harsh but this conversation was not going the way he intended, and he had to put an end to it even if he was cruel. He released his hand and walked away to the hearth.

'Elizabeth, you must understand this. I am not the man for you —nor even the man you think I am. Even if I were I am bound upon a venture which may well end in ruin or death.' He heard her catch her breath, but he had to go on. 'If we succeed—and please God we may—my life will be as always at the Duke's disposal.'

'I know that,' she said, in a small voice. 'He comes first with

you. Only I thought—but if you do not care for me in that
way——'

'It is not that I do not care,' he interrupted firmly. 'Ever since
you were a child I have cared what happened to you, that is why I
know it is best for you to seek a husband more your own age.
Believe me, my dear, you will find some younger man whom you
can love far more than you think you love me.'

'No.' She shook her head. 'I shall not marry now.' She spoke
quietly and without any undue pathos, so that turning round he
saw that she meant it. Two tears began to run slowly down her
cheeks.

He came back across the room and knelt beside her. 'That would
be a pity. My child, think! You do not want me, only the image of
me that you have built up. My past has not been free from license
and selfish desire and——'

'I do not care about your past.' She put out a hand and touched
his hair. 'I have been very forward, I suppose, to speak as I have,
but—I have loved you for so long that I could not bear that you
should go without knowing it.'

He did not know what to say. He had not expected, nor deserved, love like this. Gently he put his hands about her waist. He
could feel her trembling and the young warmth of her body. She
was very much alone in the world, as he was, and for all her in-
dependent spirit curiously defenceless. If she needed him so much,
why could he not take her into his care? Would it not, a small voice
suggested, atone a little for the things of which he was ashamed?

'My sweet,' he lifted his hand sand took her face between
them, 'if you truly want me, if you will take a man who is not
worthy of you, then I shall be honoured if you will wed me.'

The joy on her face, transforming it into radiant beauty, filled
him with shame—the old familiar shame that had haunted him for
so long—his own feelings were so much less open and straightforward. She was young and innocent and ardent while he—he had
known too much. But there was no turning back now.

'If I come alive through this,' he said, in a low voice, 'we can
be wed as soon as I can come back for you.'

'Oh! You have to go so soon!' She clung to him, her face
hidden against his shoulder. 'Kit, stay with me tonight—then at
least we will have something to remember.'

'No,' he said, and held her from him. 'No, I have used other women like that. If I should not return I would have you—untouched.'

The colour rose in her face. 'Do you imagine I want that? I do not think I shall be truly alive until I carry your child in my body.'

He seemed in her words to hear an echo of Cathy's voice, and gentleness, engendered by a deep humility, came into his own. 'Not yet, not yet. With you—I must do what I know to be right.'

Could she understand what he felt? He could not explain about his own particular devil that he had fought for so many years, could not tell her of that most intimate struggle.

Slowly she raised her head and looked at him. 'I know. It must be right this time, and then the past can be truly put away. I should not have asked.'

Miraculously she had understood—perhaps indeed she understood him as no other woman had ever done before, and he stood up, drawing her into his arms.

'You will never have cause to regret this,' he said, very low. 'I swear to you upon my honour, upon Mark's memory, that I will endeavour for the rest of my life to make you happy.'

But much later, lying on his bed, with Jeremy snoring softly on the pallet at his feet, he felt the old uncertainty of himself come back. Was he acting unfairly in taking her youth and her love when he had so little to give in return? He thought of her with affection, and for her understanding he had a deep gratitude, but where— where was the rapture he had once known, where was the lost inarticulate joy of his youth?

.   .   .   .   .

In the morning, dressed as common soldiers in buff coats and long thigh-boots, he and Monmouth with Jeremy and one other servant left The Hague.

They had eaten an early breakfast with Henrietta and Elizabeth —a betrothal breakfast, Monmouth called it, smiling warmly at Kit and Elizabeth—but nothing could detract from the farewells that had to be said. Monmouth parted with Henrietta in the privacy of their little parlour while in the hall Kit took Elizabeth into his arms. He had put his hat on the back of his head at the usual Monmouth cock, but Elizabeth, standing on tiptoe, tilted it forward.

'Not today,' she said. 'Neither of you must be recognized today until you reach your ship.'

Her mouth was trembling but she managed to smile, and her courage touched him to the heart. She was to be his wife, this girl, this child Elizabeth who clung to him so desperately, and in that moment of parting he saw at last that he would find in caring for her an escape from himself and his own self-probing. He closed his arms about her and bending his head kissed her for the first time as a lover. It had become, suddenly, very hard to go.

As they rode away down the street, bright in the morning sunlight, Monmouth said, 'Henrietta told me that the ministers here are going to pray in church today for the captain of a ship and all aboard that they may come safe to port.'

Kit thought of their frigate, their two fly-boats, their eighty-two men.

'We shall have need of their prayers,' he said.

2

At the very outset the weather turned against them, causing a fatal delay. They were a week reaching the *Helderenburgh* in the Texel and it was another ten days before, in the dawn of a summer morning, they dropped anchor off the Dorset town of Lyme.

Monmouth was asleep under a quilt on the deck when Kit went to wake him. He scrambled up instantly and together they stood by the rail watching the land materialize out of the mist—white cliffs, green-topped, distant woods hazy in the early light, the little town clustering in a hollow.

England, Kit thought, and remembered that day twenty-four years ago when he had first arrived here and experienced the strange sensation of coming home to a land he had never seen.

He turned to look at Monmouth, guessing at the emotion that must possess him, too, and saw the Duke's eyes glisten with unshed tears.

All that day people gathered on the beaches to watch the strange ships lying off-shore. They flew no colours and the gunports were closed but Kit guessed that many people must already suspect the Duke was on board. What sort of welcome would they get?

'A good one,' Nathanial Wade said confidently. He was to be

in command of the Foot, a dependable upright man who knew his West Countrymen.

He was right, for shortly after eight o'clock that evening when their landing-boats were pulling inshore to the west of the Cobb, those in the forefront of the crowded beaches recognized the man sitting in the bow of the leading boat and at once raised the old cry of the 'duking days'.

'A Monmouth! A Monmouth! Blessed be God, Monmouth is come!'

It echoed along the beach and as men threw their hats in the air for sheer joy Monmouth sat still, listening. Turning to Kit, he said in a low voice meant for him alone, 'God send me worthy of these people, for I fear in myself I am not.'

It was a moment's human shrinking from a task too large, too overwhelming, but then as the boat grounded on the shore he stepped out, his head erect, grave and firm of purpose.

When all the men were disembarked he called for silence and knelt on the sand, waiting until they had followed his example. Then, in a voice that carried clearly in the still evening air, he thanked God for their safe journey across the sea and asked a blessing on their enterprise.

He rose and, drawing his sword, lifted it so that the evening sun caught the blade in a flash of red fire, as though it was already red with blood. A good or bad omen? Kit wondered, and, resolutely drawing his own, followed Monmouth as he led his little army of eighty-two men up the style-path towards the town.

He marched alone in front of his colours, that banner of deep green woven by loving fingers, and every step of the way men joined him so that by the time they entered the town their number had increased more than four times. People flocked to greet them, lining the road and pressing so close on the Duke that he could scarcely pass through them.

And all the way the cry followed him: 'Monmouth is come. Blessed be God! Monmouth is come.'

．　　　．　　　．　　　．　　　．

At first, hope ran high. Their reception in Lyme made them all feel that men had eagerly awaited their coming and within days England and Scotland too would be in arms, for James of Monmouth.

'I'll walk to Whitehall with no more than a switch in my hand,' Monmouth said confidently.

With the Duke, Grey, Wade and Fletcher, Kit lodged at the George Inn in Coombe Street, but his bed there saw little of him. All the first night he had assisted Wade in landing their four precious cannon and supervising the bestowing of arms and ammunition with Anthony Buyse, their master gunner. He also took charge of their money-chests, pitifully empty until reimbursed by £400 which Monmouth took from the Customs house in exchange for a promissory note to be honoured when he had succeeded.

In the morning his standard was set up in a field outside the town and there Ferguson, in his fervent ringing tones, read aloud his declaration. Its opening phrases were reasoned and well-planned.

'The declaration of James, Duke of Monmouth . . . now in arms for the Protestant religion . . . to preserve the people from violence and oppression . . . and proclaim war against James, Duke of York, a popish usurper of the Crown. . . .'

But it went on to accuse York of starting the great fire in London, of organizing every popish plot, and of the murder of Algernon Sidney and Lord Russell as well as that of his late Majesty whom the declaration said he had poisoned.

When Kit had first read it, he had thrown it down in disgust. 'You know my feelings towards your uncle,' he told Monmouth, 'and God knows I think him capable of much, but let us at least be reasonably honest. I don't believe he had anything to do with the fire, nor that he poisoned your father.'

'Neither do I,' Monmouth agreed cheerfully. 'I've not had time to study the document too closely, but Ferguson knows what he's about in these matters. You must admit my uncle doesn't hesitate to blacken my character.'

Kit shook his head. It was quite customary to hurl abuse at one's enemies without much regard for truth, but he guessed, shrewdly enough, that this document would do them more harm than good for it would antagonize men who would believe Monmouth countenanced the lies it told. No one else, however, appeared to share his doubts and men hurried forward to enrol in the new army.

Monmouth stood by his standard wearing a new suit of royal purple, the Star of the Garter on his left breast; he looked his handsome best with a gracious greeting for each man and an acknowledgement for the cheering that broke out every now and again.

His officers stood a little apart.

'We'll have five thousand men in a few days,' Grey said confidently.

Kit looked round the field at the ever-increasing numbers, men arriving as the word spread to outlying villages, men in smocks, men with bill-hooks, young blades in search of adventure, soberer citizens in the dress of merchants and clerks. 'I wish to God we had arms enough for them,' he said.

Grey laughed. 'Upon my soul, van Wyngarde, you are pessimistic. Arms will come with more men.'

'There is a deal of difference between being a pessimist and being a realist,' Kit pointed out, and went over to talk to Wade. He thought Grey took the whole affair far too lightly and aboard ship had already had one strong difference of opinion with him concerning the best use of cavalry, but for Monmouth's sake he was not going to quarrel with him. One quarrel, however, was to rob them at once of two of their best men.

Old Thomas Dare had gone out foraging and returning with a welcome addition of forty good horses had appropriated the best of these for himself. Fletcher, as second-in-command to Grey, took Dare's fine horse, claiming that his need was the greater. A somewhat rough and plain-spoken countryman, Dare protested volubly, threatened Fletcher with his riding switch and called him a young jackanapes.

Nerves were tense and Fletcher, being a proud Scot, lost his temper. He drew his pistol and fired point-blank at Dare. The old man fell, a bullet through his head, and his son, half beside himself with grief and rage, would have torn Fletcher from his horse had not Kit and Wade held him back.

'I'll have justice,' he shouted. 'Your Highness must give me justice! That devil murdered my father.'

Monmouth, pale and shaken, stood looking helplessly from one to the other and then, seeing nothing else to be done, ordered Fletcher aboard the *Helderenburgh* to await his pleasure.

Realizing what he had done Fletcher fell on his knees before Monmouth and burst into tears. 'God forgive me, and your Highness too,' he cried, 'for I'll never forgive myself.' It was true, for though he went safely aboard the *Helderenburgh*, his remorse went with him and stayed to embitter the rest of his life.

'We needed him desperately,' Monmouth said later to Kit, 'but I had to send him away. Dare was much loved in these parts and I must not make enemies here.'

'You did what had to be done,' Kit said, but he too felt the loss of Dare and Fletcher to be a major disaster.

'You must take Fletcher's place,' the Duke told him. 'You're more experienced with cavalry than anyone else now.'

Kit nodded but he did not relish the prospect of being second-in-command to a man he neither liked nor trusted.

The forming of the army had begun. By Saturday their numbers had increased to 1000 Foot and 150 Horse. They turned Lyme into a garrison town, arranging quarters for their men to be paid in full as long as funds held out, though many eager citizens offered them free lodgings.

Monmouth's orders were read daily, orders against plunder, against stealing, swearing and loose behaviour. His were to be Protestant soldiers, dedicated to their cause, and no mere collection of mercenaries.

'A fine Puritan army for you, eh, van Wyngarde?' Grey queried, smiling, but there was a mocking note in his voice and Kit told Wade caustically that it would be a miracle if he got through the campaign without yielding to the desire to wipe that smile off Grey's face.

Nevertheless he set to work under his commander with a good grace and laboured to instil the simple principles of cavalry fighting into these country fellows on their plough-horses, thankful for the leaven of a few country gentlemen used to hard riding. Given a month, he thought, they could make an army out of these eager recruits, but neither the Duke of Albemarle, now at Exeter, nor Jack Churchill, on his way from London with the advance of the King's army, were likely to allow them peace in which to train their troops.

In the meantime Monmouth's personal organization was bringing excellent results and a discipline, astonishing in so raw an army, was rapidly ridding it of its amateurish appearance. Grey left much of the cavalry work in Kit's hands and the latter chose a young Minehead attorney, Paul Jakeman, for his captain-lieutenant. Jakeman was strong, sturdy and afire with eagerness to serve; he also had the ability to grasp his orders quickly and carry them out without question, so that between him and his commander there was soon an understanding that made Kit's task a good deal easier.

On Saturday evening a week later Monmouth decided it was time to test out his men and he ordered a party of picked Horse and Foot to beat up the quarters of the Devon Militia, some eight miles away. Grey elected to take his own squadron on this excursion, and on the following afternoon, as Kit and Monmouth awaited news of them, they heard the thunder of cavalry and hurrying out to the main road saw Grey and his troop in full galloping retreat.

'Wade's dead,' Grey cried, his face white beneath smirches of powder, 'and the Foot cut to pieces!'

Monmouth gave him one glance and then swung himself into the saddle. 'Kit, come with me.'

They gathered a body of fresh Horse, as many as they could find, and set off at breakneck speed but near Charmouth met Wade himself and all but a few of his men.

The Colonel was dirty and sweat-stained but cheerful enough. He saluted Monmouth and reported not only beating up the enemy as ordered but taking a dozen prisoners and, most important, capturing thirty horses.

'I thank you, Colonel,' Monmouth said warmly and then, after a slight hesitation, asked in a low voice, 'Did my lord Grey run?'

Wade looked uncomfortable, but he was a plain man given to speaking the truth. 'Yes, sir, he did.'

Monmouth said nothing more and together they returned to Lyme, but that night, in the privacy of his bedroom and alone with Kit, he burst out: 'Was ever a man as cheated as I? I thought Grey would be a rock to depend on.'

'I did not,' Kit answered grimly.

Monmouth was roving restlessly up and down the room. 'But we cannot do without him, he's the only man of any standing that we have. Pray God he has learned his lesson.'

'Amen to that,' Kit said without confidence.

Little of the promised help was reaching them. None of the nobility, so eagerly expected, had shown any sign of supporting them, and there was no report of risings elsewhere. Kit's anger grew. Where were all their old friends with whom they had hunted and dined? Where were the men who had so eagerly fêted the Duke in the old 'duking days' and made easy promises they now chose to forget?

He went to bed at midnight, tired and depressed after a chilly supper with Grey who was alternatively aggressive or busy making easy excuses for his failure. At two in the morning, however, Jeremy roused him from a bare two hours of exhausted sleep to attend officers' call and dressing hastily he went down to the parlour. There Monmouth told them all that Albemarle refused his offer of a place and was marching against them.

Their army was not yet ready to fight such superior forces and it was imperative to move to a better-fortified town. In an hour the drums were beating and soon the army was on the march, 3000 strong now, but oddly assorted, lacking uniforms and arms, some even lacking good shoes, but all possessing a devotion to their leader and his cause which was, Kit thought, some compensation for the missing arms and powder.

Two hours later they came upon some of the Devon and Somerset Militia. These outnumbered them by more than 1000, but as Monmouth charged with the cavalry into the town of Axminster the Militia bolted, more than half of the Somersetshires coming over to the Duke's side. They were more than welcome, well trained and neat in their red coats, and Kit, by a smart piece of field-work, appropriated a number for his own regiment, leaving them in the charge of a grinning and appreciative Captain Jakeman.

Flushed with his first taste of success Monmouth rode into Taunton the next afternoon. The streets were lined with wildly cheering crowds, every window open and filled with eager faces; flowers were strewn everywhere to make a carpet for his feet and while women gazed in undisguised adoration at their 'brave and lovely hero', the men decorated their hats with Monmouth's green emblem and flung them in the air for him.

Kit, riding Chimera beside Lord Grey and directly behind the Duke, was almost deafened by the cheers. Nothing, even in the journeys of '80 and '82, had equalled this. For a brief joyous moment he saw success before them. Looking at Monmouth's straight back and bare head, the long curls of his periwig lying gracefully on his shoulders, he felt his love for the Duke rise so strongly that tears burned his eyes. It was a moment for love and triumph, for hope and courage, and it was the last they were to have.

That night they slept at a certain Captain Hucker's house, a man loyal and experienced who was welcome to their ranks. In the morning as they came out of the house another procession awaited them, a procession vastly different to that of the town dignitaries who had attended them yesterday for it was composed of little girls, led by their schoolmistress who carried a naked sword in one hand and a Bible in the other.

As the Duke stepped out into the sunlight she swept him a low curtsey and presented him with the Bible, declaring he had come to defend its truths.

Monmouth took it, a warm flush suffusing his brown cheeks. For a moment he stood in silence, holding it reverently. Then he said, 'Madam, I will defend these truths, and if need be seal them with my blood.'

Sunlight fell on the shining faces and smoothly brushed hair of the little girls as they stood watching in their homespun dresses and white caps, and, as Monmouth beckoned them forward that he might give each a kiss, the first child, Mary Mead, handed him a small green flag with a coronet stitched in gold and beneath it the letters 'J.R.'

Kit glanced swiftly at Monmouth. He saw the Duke stare at the letters and then without a word take the flag and little Mary up on to his saddle-bow. He called to his officers to do the same and Kit, beckoning to a shy little maid, lifted her up before him.

' What is your name, child?'

'Eliza Simpson, sir.' She dived into her apron pocket. 'I have made a flag too, though the stitches are not very well done. Will it please you to have it?'

He took the green square with its clumsy gold stitching and looked down at her. She reminded him of the young Elizabeth and impulsively he put his lips against her hair.

'It will please me very much, Eliza,' he said and tucked it into his coat pocket.

.   .   .   .   .

'You must do it, sir,' Grey said. As usual he was leaning casually against the fireplace, his manner easy and smooth.

Ferguson, his thin body tense, added his own fierce urging: 'Highness, it is the only way. All men here know you for their King. It is only a matter of proclaiming you.'

'And many noble gentlemen doubtless hold back because they think you desire only a Commonwealth,' Wade put in, ignoring a sour look from Colonel Venner who was a stout republican. 'Our scythemen are all very well, good stout fellows that they are, but we need men of standing in our ranks, men who might come to serve a king.'

From his place at the head of the table Monmouth shook his head with equal determination. 'No, gentlemen, no. I thank you for your confidence in me but I will not take that title unless it is given me by Parliament and the nation.'

'The nation is ready to give it to you,' Ferguson said. 'Has not today shown your Highness that?'

Listening to the interchange, Kit glanced at the Duke's face and saw the uncertainty, the doubt, registered there. Well might he doubt—it was a decision Kit himself would not have liked to face. He agreed primarily with Monmouth, but he was also sure that more men would come in if he were proclaimed. Given wise councillors, like Halifax, many would realize Monmouth could make a good king.

Grey came over to the table. 'Has it occurred to you, sir,' he inquired softly, 'that if—if we should fail, those who follow you might be saved if they could say they served a king *de facto?*'

Monmouth stiffened. There was dead silence now in Captain Hucker's dining-room, some of the officers shifting uneasily in their seats. No one had liked to say this, to hint at failure, but every man knew it to be a possibility and saw the cogency of Grey's remark.

Monmouth was silent too, his thoughts, transparent to Kit, chasing across his face. Only such an appeal to his generosity, his humanity, could have swayed him at this moment; and only Grey, Kit thought angrily, would have used that approach to make Monmouth do something he felt instinctively he should not do.

But the Duke was thinking now not of himself but of his army of ill-armed, half-trained, devoted soldiers, men prepared to die for him. Was there anything too hard to do in return for that?

'So be it,' he said gravely, and ignoring their move towards him, the phrases of lóyalty half-spoken, went alone to his room and closed the door.

It was done in the morning, by Taunton Market Cross:

> 'We therefore do recognize and proclaim the high and mighty Prince James, Duke of Monmouth, our lawful and rightful sovereign, by the name of James the Second, by the grace of God King of England, Scotland, France and Ireland, Defender of the Faith. . . .'

At the same moment, though none of them knew it, in St. George's Chapel at Windsor he was being degraded from the Order of the Garter and his banner, so nobly hung, kicked out of the chapel and into a ditch by the officers-at-arms.

It was not until late that night that Kit saw him alone. Monmouth called him across the passage as they were retiring and at once he came to the new King and knelt, putting Monmouth's fingers to his lips. He had done this only once before, long ago on that Sunday morning after they had attended service in St. Martin's and he had accepted the Duke's legitimacy.

'Your Majesty,' he said, in a low voice, 'I pledge you my sword and my service for as long as I shall live.'

Monmouth stood still in a surprise that was so genuine that it was touchingly modest. Then he pulled his hand away and laid it on his shoulder.

'Why, Kit, old sobersides, what is this? Who shall I ever be to you but Jamie?'

Kit smiled, but he remained on his knee. 'You are my sovereign lord and I have the honour to be your friend. God save your Majesty.'

A flicker of unusually bitter humour crossed Monmouth's face. 'I pray He will, for I'm very sure my supporters elsewhere won't.' Then he bent over Kit, making an effort to banish the disappointment, the depression brought on by lack of encouraging news. 'But I'll not have you kneel to me. God knows I did not seek to be King and I'll not be so when we are alone, though'—his smile came back—'if it pleases God to take me to Whitehall, I'll have no subject dearer to me than you.'

Kit rose and began to help him undress as he used to do in the old days when they travelled together, all the while talking

cheerfully of the morning's ceremony and the enthusiasm for 'King
Monmouth'.

He was King indeed here—but Kit knew now that he would
need far more than a switch in his hand if he was ever to be King in
Whitehall.

3

'Argyle has failed!' Monmouth, standing at the head of his
assembled council of war, raised a grey face and put down the letter
with a trembling hand. 'His army has been defeated and the Earl
himself captured.' He looked dazedly round the table. 'Gentlemen,
we are utterly abandoned and alone.'

A horrified silence greeted his words. The table was littered
with maps and papers, lists and reports that now seemed only so
much waste paper. Of what use to plan a march north into Cheshire
or east towards London if none there would support them? The
blow, added to their other misfortunes, killed stone-dead any last
lingering hope Kit had.

In exactly one week since the proclamation at Taunton everything had gone wrong.

Men had come in willingly enough but they were all of the
commoner sort, unarmed and untrained, and there was no money
for arms, no time for training. All Monmouth could do was to
order every scythe to be brought in and riveted to a pole to make a
crude weapon, and be thankful that the countryside and its people
provided enough food for them all.

At Bridgwater they had received a wildly enthusiastic welcome,
the Mayor proclaiming Monmouth at the Market Cross, and their
army rose to 6000 men, but as they marched on towards Glastonbury the weather, hitherto dry and warm, broke. The army
struggled on through pouring rain that turned the roads into
morasses of mud; men's shoes wore thin, the baggage-waggons
got stuck, and the cannon had to be hauled free of cloying mud.

The plan, an excellent one, was to take and hold Bristol, a good
port and the most important city in England after the capital. The
Duke of Beaufort was holding it but without too many men, and
Monmouth surmised correctly that being a Puritan city many of the
citizens would be willing to join him. His army skirmished with

Albemarle's men and came off well before they reached Keynsham where the Royalists had broken down the bridge. They drove out some enemy troops and repaired the bridge without difficulty, but here news came in that Lord Delamere had been captured and that there would now be no rising in Cheshire.

It was obvious that none of their London friends were able to help and furthermore report reached them that the Royalist commander-in-chief, Lord Feversham, was a bare seven miles away with the bulk of the King's army. Scouts brought in the news that Bristol was more strongly held than they supposed and, with Albemarle converging on them from the south-west, the plan for taking the city was abandoned. Later—and too late—they learned that their scouts had been mistaken and that Bristol might have fallen without much difficulty. It was one more bitter pill to be swallowed.

A terrible melancholy settled on Monmouth. He sat in his chair at headquarters, staring blankly before him, hardly managing to answer his officers' requests for their orders.

'Let us go on, sir,' Wade had said briskly, his courage undiminished. He was a soldier of the Cromwellian school and refused to be dismayed by reverses. 'The way to Gloucester is open to us, and beyond it the Midlands where we have many friends.'

'We have no friends,' Lord Grey said moodily, and Kit, torn by his own overwhelming compassion for their unhappy King, bade his lordship in a low angry tone to say nothing if he could not say anything constructive. Their relationship was by this time strained almost to breaking-point.

Dejectedly, unable to bring himself to take Wade's sensible advice, Monmouth ordered his little army to retreat.

'Must we go back, sir?' Young Jakeman asked Kit. 'Surely we can do some good here?'

He voiced the feelings of two-thirds of the army and it was in unhappy silence that the men tramped wearily away through the windswept night, away from Bristol and what might have been the scene of their triumph.

Kit rode at the head of the cavalry. He and Grey had done what they could with these raw horsemen and since that first disgraceful affair at Charmouth had kept better control over them, but he knew only too well the quality of Feversham's troops that they would soon have to face. Desertions had begun now, and through that long, miserable night the ranks thinned, many shadows slipping away into the darkness. They were for the most part simple fellows who had done their best but now, seeing the rain about to ruin the harvest, went home to salvage what they could.

Now they were at Frome and it seemed, with this news of Argyle's capture, at the end of their tether.

Colonel Venner spoke up from his place at the end of the table. 'Your Majesty, we can all see that despite your valiant leadership and the efforts of every man here, our task has become a hopeless one. None of the expected support has materialized and, though we have good men coming daily to our standard, others leave us and we have no arms left and no money. The Usurper's forces have all they need and their men are seasoned soldiers. It is futile to go on. If we retire now across the sea every man in the west here can take advantage of the offer of pardon if he gives himself up. We who came over with you and are exempted can wait in exile for a better opportunity. A more favourable time will come and for the moment you will avoid the useless shedding of blood.'

It was a reasoned, sensible argument and one likely to appeal to Monmouth. He wavered, a hand to his chin, his eyes restless and unhappy, but before he could speak Grey sprang to his feet.

'That would be a base thing to do, and never to be forgiven by your Majesty's followers. Why, no man in the west would acclaim you again if you deserted your army now.'

At the word 'deserted' Monmouth flushed. He glanced at Grey who, unrepentant, met his stare with one equally truculent, before he turned to Wade. 'And you, Colonel, what do you think we should do?'

Wade hesitated. 'Sir—it is my opinion that we are too far in to go back. And our men have shown that they can fight. Who knows but in battle we who have right on our side may yet defeat our enemies?'

Monmouth nodded. 'And you, Colonel van Wyngarde?'

Kit looked up, full of pity and desperately sorry for what he had to say. 'I agree with Colonel Venner. If we go on we will destroy our cause and lose many lives that might otherwise be saved.' He saw the hurt, the miserable doubt on Monmouth's face. But he had to be honest.

'I'm surprised at you, Colonel,' Grey said scornfully. 'I should have thought a man who fought at Bothwell Bridge would have been willing to see the business through.'

Kit felt the blood rush to his face and half rose in his seat. 'Is your lordship calling me craven?'

Grey shrugged. 'You must be the judge of that. When the rest of us are willing to go on, you and Colonel Venner——'

'Gentleman!' Monmouth banged on the table, shaken out of his despair into a despairing anger. 'Gentlemen, our cause will indeed be destroyed if we quarrel among ourselves. As my honour seems to be at stake over this I will stick by my army. We will go on.'

Grey nodded. 'Nobly said, sir. We may yet come off well.' He seemed oddly satisfied.

Outside in the passage Kit stood barring his way. He had lost his temper and only for Monmouth's sake had throttled it at the council table. 'If your lordship pleases. Our lives are not our own at this moment, but when this campaign is over we will settle our difference. I'll be damned if any man calls me coward and does not pay for it.'

Grey looked at his irate second-in-command and then laughed in his usual mocking manner. 'You are too quick to take offence, Colonel, but if we come through I'll meet you when and where you please. If not—why, papist James will doubtless settle it for us.'

They were casual words, but Kit was to remember them afterwards and wonder just how loyal Grey had been to their cause.

Later, requested to wait upon Monmouth, he went to his room and found him sitting on the bed, his head in his hands.

Stricken, Kit sat down beside him. 'Sir, forgive me. I had to say what I thought and I do believe it would be better to go.'

'And live to fight another day?' Monmouth raised a wan face and smiled faintly. 'I am not angry, Kit, I know you too well for that. You are probably right and God knows I would give much to go back—to her—but I was set upon my honour and you near enough called coward. What else could I do?'

'Naught,' Kit said. 'We go on.'

Quite suddenly Monmouth began to shiver, his teeth chattering uncontrollably. Kit fetched him a glass of wine, but to his surprise the shivering went on. Monmouth's face was ashen and all at once the flood-tide of his pent-up feelings broke out of control. Half sobbing in acute distress he was gasping out all his resentment, all his disappointment in his friends, in the failure of his well-laid plans, in the wretched twists of fate that had stripped him at last of all illusions.

Shaken by this collapse Kit could do not more than hold his hands firmly, letting him find relief in words, for what could he say to comfort such desolation?

This enterprise, though conducted brilliantly from a military standpoint, demanded in every other way a man with an iron hand, an iron purpose—an Oliver Cromwell perhaps. Monmouth was not such a man—he was too sensitive, too humane, too easily influenced and the long strain of trying to be other than he was had beaten down his morale and shattered his nerves to this breaking-point. God knew, Kit thought bitterly, there was cause enough. Nevertheless he braced himself.

'We are not lost yet,' he said, with quiet intensity. 'While you live we are not lost. I've faith in you and so have our brave boys with their scythes and bill-hooks.'

Slowly the shivering subsided. Monmouth drank the wine and sitting up straightened the lace at his throat.

'Thank you, Kit.' He rose and set his hat on his head in a pathetic attempt at jauntiness. 'Come, let us go down to supper.'

They walked downstairs together and to Kit's admiration he gave no sign of the emotional storm he had just suffered. Having made up his mind to go on he discussed calmly with his officers the best plan to adopt and it was agreed that they should march towards Warminster where some promised Horse awaited them.

Only, as they parted that night, Monmouth said, 'I doubt I could have faced this, Kit, without you beside me.'

Sad words, yet Kit went to bed much comforted.

They marched in the morning, but hearing that Feversham was barring their way swung westwards and so came to Wells. Their stay here was cheered by the capture of some enemy arms and money-chests, but Feversham was hard on their trail and they marched on through the pouring rain to Glastonbury and thence to Bridgwater where Monmouth planned to rest the men and get the arms dried out. He ordered supplies to be assembled there, for Bridgwater had always been loyal, but the lack of success that had sent him back brought out a deputation to beg him to go elsewhere lest the enemy storm and burn the town. Some of the older citizens clearly remembered the burning it had suffered forty years ago in the Civil War.

'I shall do as I think best,' Monmouth told them, in a rare burst of temper, and sent them packing. He had now decided to follow his old plan to go up into Gloucestershire and on to the Midlands to rouse his friends there. If they saw him in person, he told Kit with pathetic hope, they would surely rise.

This plan, however, was changed when a local man named Godfrey reported that Feversham and the whole Royalist army was encamped at Westonzoyland, not more than three miles away. Hastily Monmouth, calling to Kit to come with him, climbed to the parapet of St. Mary's church tower to view them with his perspective glass.

Presently he said, 'They're all there—our dragoons and guards, see!' He passed Kit the glass. 'If we had them with us now I'd be sure of victory.'

The same thought was in both their minds. They had fought with those soldiers and knew them to be far superior to their own raw troops.

Monmouth turned away. 'Officers' call in ten minutes,' was all he said.

When they were assembled in the church below he laid two plans before them, either to break away entirely and march north, or to attack the enemy by night and gain a victory by surprise.

'I'm for the latter, your Majesty,' Wade said. 'We must fight sooner or later. The men are eager for it and to postpone it will only lose us time and the advantage.'

Venner agreed, Grey nodded, and Kit, feeling the time had indeed come for the inevitable battle, added his vote. Seeing them unanimous, a new confidence seemed to possess their general. He expounded a plan, brilliant in its conception, whereby Godfrey, who knew every inch of Sedgemoor where the enemy lay, should guide them across the marshland. He could show them how to avoid the ditches that could so easily spell disaster to a marching army and, by encircling the enemy position, by-pass the Royalist artillery and thus bring the army up to attack where the heavy guns so laboriously brought from London could do no damage.

Listening to Monmouth expounding this plan Kit felt a resurgence of hope. It had a chance of success even though the odds were against them, and for some reason he remembered their first fight together in Holland and how he had seen then that Monmouth was a general born. This campaign, if it had done nothing else, had shown that he could create and handle an army.

When the plan had been thoroughly discussed and understood the officers went to service and received the Sacrament. Kit knelt beside Monmouth and for a little while allowed his thoughts to leave the present tense moment. He thought instead of Elizabeth, so far away and waiting for him, praying for him.

He knew now that he wanted her love, that he wanted her, and so to come alive out of this battle had become a desperate need— but still and always Monmouth's need came first and if that need demanded his life he would give it, gladly.

Turning his head a little he glanced at his King's face. Monmouth was gazing at the east window, hands clasped beneath his chin, and Kit was shocked to see in sharp relief how he had aged in the last weeks. His face had become thin, the lines of strain heavily marked; there were purple shadows beneath the weary brown eyes and he bore an expression of such profound sadness that Kit could scarcely bear to see it.

As the chalice was held out to him, Monmouth seemed to hesitate for a fraction of a second before he partook of it, and an intuition, born of long years of shared thought, brought to Kit's mind the words that were passing through Monmouth's.

'If it be possible, let this cup pass from me.'

Now his prayer was all for Monmouth, yet even as he prayed for victory, there was a deeper, unvoiced plea that the outcome, whatever it was, might take that look of strained misery from Monmouth's face.

.   .   .   .   .   .

They were to march at eleven o'clock and an hour beforehand Kit was dressing in buff coat, steel back and breastplates, gauntlets and wide-brimmed felt hat, with long boots reaching to his thighs. As if Jeremy sensed that this was to be the fight of his master's life, he fussed over the dressing, taking extra care with the strapping of his sword-belt.

When he was ready Kit glanced at him, now methodically folding away his cast-off clothes.

'Jerry, I've something to say to you. If the fight should go against us tonight I want you to get away as fast as you can and make your way to Tolbrooke. I don't want you taken so don't look for me. Is that plain?'

Jeremy's stolid face betrayed nothing. 'Plain enough, sir, but with your permission I've engaged to push a pike with the Green boys tonight. You'll recall, sir, that I practised with that weapon when we were in Holland.'

Kit smiled. 'Lord, Jerry, you are a secret fellow. Why didn't you tell me you wanted to fight?'

Jeremy blushed. 'I thought you might say I ought to stay with baggage, sir, me not being a fighting man as you might think.'

Kit came across the room and laid both hands on his shoulders. 'The King needs every man this night so I'll not say you nay, only if we are defeated remember what I said. Get home, somehow, and Sir Harry will care for you.'

'Very good, sir,' Jeremy answered phlegmatically and continued to pack away his master's things. Not until this was done did he go out to his place with the Green regiment, nor did he mention that he had no intention, in the event of defeat, of abandoning his master.

Kit in the meantime went to Monmouth's room where he found a servant kneeling on the floor and buckling on the King's spurs. As soon as it was done he bowed himself out and they were alone.

'Well, Kit?' Monmouth smiled faintly. 'Did you want to see me about anything in particular?'

'No, sir, only—I wish I could be with your Life Guard tonight.'

Monmouth picked up his notebooks and stuffed them into an inner pocket of his scarlet coat. 'You are needed with your own men—you know I've doubts about our cavalry, raw as it is, and I'm relying on you to hold them. My good fellows will look after me.'

'I know, but . . .' Kit turned away to the window to watch the forty-odd volunteers who formed King Monmouth's bodyguard saddling up in the courtyard below. They were lodged as before in what remained of the castle, and in the field beyond he could see the troops assembling, the drums beating a steady rhythm. In the evening light they made a good array, the standards fluttering bravely in the breeze, but he knew how pitifully those proudly held scythes compared to muskets and good swords.

Monmouth came to stand beside him. 'We've faced too much together to fear this, Kit. If it should bring a parting—but there is no need of words between us. God keep you and bring you through safe.'

Kit found himself unable to speak—there was so much to say and none of it could be put into mere words. Instead he went down on one knee and put Monmouth's hand to his lips. Then, together, they went out to the field.

Here Kit inspected his own troops, passing through the ranks with a word for each man, and finally drawing rein by his captain-lieutenant who asked if he might carry his colours into battle.

'Hold them fast,' Kit said. He had chosen a white banner embroidered with a gold cross and the words 'For God, King and People'. 'We want our boys to see them as they go in and the moon will soon be up.'

In silence they marched, a silence so deep that only the sound of hooves and the jangle of harness broke it. It said much, Kit thought, for the discipline of this army that no man spoke during that long night trek out of Bridgwater and along the Bristol road. After a while they turned right into Bradney Lane, muddy from the recent rain, and then along Marsh Lane, completely out-flanking the enemy camp.

When at last they came out on to the open moor a halt was called, and the officers joined Monmouth for their final orders. The password, he said, was to be 'Soho' and Kit wondered if he was thinking of his abandoned house there and the old happy days.

The Horse were to cross the Bussex rine, a ditch about twenty feet wide and normally fairly dry but running with water now because of the rains, by the upper plungeon, a bridge left virtually unguarded, so Godfrey said, because the enemy had no inkling they might come in that way. They were to fall on the enemy Foot who would be unprepared and unable to form into any sort of order. Wade's Foot would follow up in support, tackling the enemy gun-emplacements before the guns could be turned or the Horse had time to saddle up and assemble. It was well worked out, simple and deadly, and the officers listened in inspired silence, every man recognizing it as a masterly plan and, given reasonable luck, bound to succeed.

The cavalry now took the van with Monmouth and Grey leading while Kit brought up the second regiment. Still in utter silence they followed Godfrey who found his way unerringly through the marshland to the ford over the Black Ditch, and the army filed in safety over it. Kit crossed ahead of his men, the water swirling about Chimera's hooves, as they slipped a little on the wet stones.

and then up on dry land again he watched his men cross with a nod of encouragement for Jakeman, who filed the troops over with a regular sweep of his arm. A good soldier, Kit thought, as Jakeman pulled up beside him, the colours flapping over his head.

But there was yet another ford to cross and in the darkness and the ground fog that had risen, Godfrey missed it.

A halt was called. The men waited in silence, the horses champed and stirred restlessly on the marshy ground. There was a curious charged atmosphere running along the ranks now, nerves were tense and hardly able to bear the silence and the waiting, yet they maintained both silence and stillness and Kit felt a rising pride in these untried lads who were behaving like seasoned soldiers.

Presently, after a half hour that seemed an eternity Godfrey returned, signalling to the General that he had found the ford. Monmouth raised his hand and the Horse moved slowly forward to defile across the last barrier between them and the Bussex rine behind which the enemy lay encamped.

We've done it! Kit thought in triumph. They were within a few hundred yards of the enemy guards and they none the wiser.

Then, startlingly, a single pistol-shot rang out into the night.

'God!' Kit caught at Chimera's reins, soothing him as he plunged. 'Who fired that shot?'

No one knew. Not one sound came from the ranks, no one seemed to have moved, but someone, somewhere, had betrayed them, whether accidentally or on purpose.

Almost at once the enemy drums began to beat, trumpets sounded out and Monmouth rode furiously to the cavalry, his face dark with anger and disappointment.

'Lord Grey, take the Horse in over the plungeon!'

He swung round and galloping back to the Foot flung himself to the ground, placing himself at their head as he ordered the columns to swing into line.

Grey was shouting to the cavalry officers to form their men into open order, the very move over which he and Kit had argued so strenuously aboard the *Helderenburgh*, and his second-in-command obeyed reluctantly. This was no time to argue but Kit was sure it was a mistake. He was soon proved to be right.

They rode forward in the darkness, following Godfrey towards the plungeon but Grey with his long line not only lost Godfrey but missed the plungeon. Kit, cursing his lordship to hell, went on

without any knowledge of where Godfrey was. He hated this
manœuvring over ground he had not seen even in daylight, but
by sheer good fortune he ran on to the bridge. Already now the
enemy, forewarned, were assembling. It was about two o'clock and
the moon had risen so that in its light he could make out bodies of
men on the move. Gunfire had begun from their own guns,
desultory at first but gathering method and strength as the minutes
went by. As swiftly as possible he got his men, some 300 of them,
over the plungeon and, left on his own, formed them into the close
order he knew to be wisest. Where Grey was he no longer knew nor
cared and it was useless to look for him. What mattered now was to
take some sort of attack into the enemy camp and retrieve at least
part of their lost advantage.

With the men formed he shouted the order to move forward
and with drawn sword led them over the rough ground. A challenge
rang out eerily through the night.

'Who are you for?'

'The King,' Kit shouted back.

'Which King?'

'King Monmouth and God with him!' He flung the words
triumphantly into the darkness. 'Come on, lads. Forward for King
Monmouth.'

He heard them thunder after him, yelling their battle-cry, and
felt again the curious battle-fervour rising in himself.

The Royal Blues were the company they encountered. These
had been hurried to the bridge and Kit's men rode straight into
them, hoping to over-run them, but they had taken a good position
and were holding it firmly. Kit charged them twice and at last,
sensing a yielding in the ranks, was drawing his men off for a final
assault when a scout rode up from the rear.

'Lord Grey has fled, sir. The Horse are broke!'

Kit swung his horse's head round in a fury.

'God damn him to hell,' he swore, and at that moment would
have cheerfully shot his lordship had he encountered him.

'What shall we do, sir?' Jakeman asked anxiously.

It was almost impossible to assess the situation. The Royal Blues
were re-forming and he had either to attack them again, quickly, or
draw off. In the flashes of fire he saw, however, that the Foot now
held the centre unaided and that it would be best to reinforce them.

'We'll flank the enemy, attacking the centre,' he called out to his officers and in good order they drew the men off, following his lead along the rine towards the main part of the field.

Here, as he thought, the Foot led by Wade and Monmouth himself were holding firm and fighting like veterans. He charged into the mêlée, taking some enemy horse in the flank. It was a good move and should have dislodged them from their own flanking attack, but in the darkness and confusion he misjudged their numbers and failed to see a second body of Horse behind him.

Before he realized what had happened he and his men were hemmed in on three sides. There was nothing to do but stick close together and hold the enemy as long as they could, and even in the stress of this he was conscious of an elated pride in the courage of his troopers who, in the face of these odds, stood firm and fought. But gradually the ranks thinned.

A sword cut laid open his left forearm but he scarcely heeded it and had dispatched some half-dozen enemy cavalrymen when a bullet struck Chimera in the head. The animal went down, pitching him to the ground.

For a moment he lay stunned, surrounded by plunging hooves. Then, aware that by some miracle he had not had his head kicked in, he felt hands pulling at his.

'Up, sir, up!' It was young Jakeman, his face streaked with sweat, agonized in his fear for his commander. It changed rapidly to relief as Kit scrambled to his feet. 'Here, sir, take my horse.'

The animal, terrified in the confusion, reared wildly and plunged away; Jakeman yelled to another trooper to give the Colonel his horse, but the men were by now too excited, too confused to listen.

'Get back,' Kit shouted, knowing they had no chance in this on foot. 'Get back!' But even as he turned he saw an enemy horseman plunge forward and drive his sword with deadly accuracy into Jakeman's throat.

There was no time for grief, except to be conscious of the fact that he owed the dead boy his life, and sword in hand he beat his way through the muddle of men and horses towards the rear, searching all the time for a fresh mount. But it was too late to rally what were left of his men. Some were already in flight and the rest cut to pieces. There was nothing more he could do here and in a desperate anger at his helplessness he began to make his way to the right where the Foot still held.

The air was full of smoke, its acrid smell mingling with the stench of blood; the field had become hideous, a nightmare of gunfire, of injured men screaming in their pain, of maddened horses; but he plunged on, beating off an enemy soldier who came at him with a sabre and killing another who swung the butt of a musket at his head.

Then, miraculously, he came upon a last reserve of the Yellow regiment and, joining up with them, went on towards the centre. He asked a lieutenant where their musketeers were and why their own guns were silent now.

The young man's face was grim. 'When the Horse bolted the drivers of our waggons thought the right wing lost too and drove off with all our ammunition. There's none to be had.'

Was there no end to the havoc Grey's presence seemed to spread? Kit wondered. How were they to hold the enemy without powder? And had Wade held the right? Where was their master gunner? Where, above all, was Monmouth?

Certain now that he would not come alive off this field he marched with the Yellow regiment. All their lives would end here, he thought.

Then, to add to his horror, as they came up to the rear of their own Foot two of the battalions on the left gave way before the Royalist dragoons and in the space of a few minutes had broken utterly and were fleeing the field. At the same time, far away on the right, the last of Monmouth's gunners had been beaten from their posts and were fleeing after their comrades.

For one moment the Yellow regiment wavered.

'My God!' Kit swung round, raising his sword. 'Come on, come on! Will you desert your King now?'

He went off at a jog-trot and with an answering shout they followed him in where they were most needed, to try to stem a flood of enemy infantry who were advancing inexorably along the front. And there, in the grey light of approaching dawn, he saw Monmouth, bearing a half-pike and fighting like a madman at the head of his own regiment of Foot. At least, thank God, he still lived. But the Royalist cavalry were converging on them now on both flanks and if they stayed where they were they would be surrounded so that not one of them would come out alive.

In terrible fear for Monmouth, but a fear that in no way impaired his judgement, he pushed his way through the thinning ranks to where Monmouth had been. There was no sign of him now.

Kit went cold and sick. Where was he—oh God, where was he? He beat his way forward, shaking with the need, physical and emotional, to find Monmouth, if only to die with him.

A moment later he saw him, moved a little to the rear and on to a piece of rising ground to review the situation with Buyse. Trembling with relief Kit plunged forward and sprang up the hillock.

'Thank God you're safe!' The words broke from him. 'What has happened on the right?'

'Kit! They are all fled or cut down except the men Wade still holds.' Monmouth was dirty and dishevelled but he was unhurt. 'What happened on your wing?'

'We held as long as we could, but without Lord Grey . . .'

Monmouth's face was suffused with anger. 'By God, I swear I'll hang him for his cowardice. Is there anything we can do now?'

'Little enough. You have fought to the utmost but the Horse are gone and your Foot almost all killed or fled.' He would have given his soul to have brought different tidings.

Monmouth gave one last despairing look round, the whole of the field visible in the light of the rising sun. 'We could have won, we could have won! If the Horse had held . . .'

At that moment Grey himself rode up. 'All is lost,' he cried out. 'We must shift for ourselves.'

At the sight of him Kit, furious and exhausted, lost the last rags of his temper. 'You miserable bloody coward! I wonder you dare to come back.'

Monmouth caught his arm. 'Stop, Kit—there's no time for that now.'

'My men got lost and ran into the enemy guns,' Grey retorted, with astonishing blandness, 'so of course the poor fellows fled. I couldn't hold them. I came back to warn you. Come, your Majesty, you owe it to those who believe in you to save yourself.'

Monmouth wavered, glancing uncertainly at Kit. 'What is for the best?'

Kit said stoutly, 'If you choose to stay we will fight it out.'

'Buyse?'

The Dutchman looked grave. 'I'll do as your Majesty directs, but I see nothing to be gained by staying.'

'For God's sake!' Grey broke in, 'Hurry, or we'll not get away at all. There's naught to do here. Your Majesty must think of your own life.'

And yours, Kit thought, raging. No one but Grey could be so thick-skinned and careless of the men they would leave behind, but he too must think now of Monmouth's life. Of what use to throw it needlessly away? He caught at the reins of the King's horse, held a few yards away by a trooper.

Monmouth met his look and then without another word began to fling off his armour. He vaulted into the saddle, and Kit, seizing the reins of a riderless horse, sprang up himself, throwing away his own breastplate as he did so.

He took one last look at the grim spectacle the field of battle now presented, and, fightingt he desire to go back, to do something to aid the last of their men, to look for Jerry, turned and followed Monmouth, Buyse and Grey into the morning mist that surrounded the Polden hills. But some deep passionate instinct told him that it would have been better if they had stayed to die on this blood-soaked moor.

·   ·   ·   ·   ·

There was a strong smell of moss and cow-dung in his nostrils when Kit awoke. He was conscious first of a ravening hunger but there was nothing left to eat and he lay for a little while longer, his eyes closed, for even after a few hours of sleep he was still utterly exhausted. He was wearing a shepherd's coat and a two-day growth of beard, and his left arm was wrapped in a dirty bloodstained piece of cambric torn from his shirt.

Since that dreadful moment of flight two dawns ago he seemed to have lived through a nightmare. The four of them had fled first to Chedzoy where they found fresh horses and presently Buyse left them, determined to make his way to Bristol while Grey—always, Kit thought, Monmouth's evil genius—urged them to go towards the New Forest where there were friends who would help them find a ship to take them across the sea.

'As my father did,' Monmouth said, wearily.

They found a guide to lead them through the hidden, less-frequented paths of the forest and went on their way on foot when their exhausted horses could bear them no further. As an added precaution they exchanged clothes with some cottagers and into the pocket of his dirty shepherd's coat Kit put all he had left of his personal possessions, a small flask of brandy and his watch, wrapped in Eliza Simpson's little green flag.

Throughout that summer day they fled on through the silent forest. They had no more than a little bread to eat, though one cottager gave them some milk, and they seldom spoke, saving their breath and their energies for the desperate bid for freedom.

Kit could scarcely bring himself to look at Grey, seeing in him the author of two-thirds of their misfortune, but neither his anger against Grey, nor his grief for the men left behind on Sedgemoor was uppermost in his mind now, for nothing mattered but Monmouth and getting him to the coast and back to Henrietta. She, he thought, was the only one who could take the torment from her lover's mind.

Kit watched him stumbling along, utterly broken now in spirit. Occasionally that strange shivering would seize him again and Kit knew that last night he had not slept but had lain wide-eyed, staring into the moonlight.

'Try to rest,' Kit had said, his own aching pity a physical pain within him.

'I cannot sleep,' Monmouth had answered, and Kit knew he was living again the destruction of his army, seeing his Life Guard slaughtered to a man, his soldiers cut down around him. For a man of Monmouth's temperament it was enough to induce a remorse that was almost beyond bearing.

In the afternoon Grey and their guide had gone on ahead and never returned. It seemed more than likely that they had been taken and the hunt for Monmouth would consequently be on in this area.

Kit was alone with him now and they had pressed on together, not stopping for food or drink, until, in the early hours of this morning, they had turned into this field to pluck a few raw peas and beans for food. Now they lay in a damp ditch where they had fallen exhausted beneath the shelter of a great ash tree, both so deadly weary that sleep would no longer be denied.

He stirred and sat up, looking around him. Monmouth was still deep in the sleep he so desperately needed, but he was so changed from the man who had stood in royal purple by his standard at Lyme, so gaunt and hollow-cheeked, that Kit closed his eyes again and pressed his palms against the lids.

Oh God, what were they going to do?

Without food they could not go on and they dared not enter even a farmyard, much less a village. He remembered then that last night he had seen a cow in the next field. His flask was empty now of brandy for he had made Monmouth drink the last of it yesterday, but he might be able to fill it with a little milk.

He got up, brushing the dead leaves and twigs from his hair, and, as Monmouth still did not stir, made his way along by the hedge. When he reached the gate he saw the cow still grazing peacefully and climbing over approached the animal, hoping her udder was full. He had never milked a cow before but he had seen it done at Tolbrooke and thought it looked easy enough. It was not, however, as simple as he imagined. The cow, very properly, objected to such amateur handling and lowed indignantly, casting baleful looks in his direction. Kneeling beside her he discovered it was almost impossible to direct the stream of milk into the neck of his flask—and suddenly he was seized with an irrational fury against this stupid animal; against the dirt and the hunger and thirst he and Monmouth now suffered; against the fate that had dealt them blow after blow, bringing them at last to this naked hour.

For a moment, in impotent rage and despair, he leaned his head against the warm body of the cow. Then, because his thirst was, just then, stronger than anything else he decided to crouch down and try to direct the milk into his mouth. This worked a little better and presently, freely spattered but with his thirst at least slaked for the time being, he crawled out from under the mildly indignant cow. Monmouth would have to come and drink the same way, he decided.

He was wiping his face on his sleeve when some instinct made him turn and look up the slope of the field.

It was then that he saw, over the far hedge, the heads and shoulders of a troop of soldiers, spread out and apparently beating the field and the bracken around it.

His body went stiff with shock. Flinging away the flask he began to run, bent low to keep below the level of the hedge. Monmouth had not moved and it did not seem possible that he could reach him in time. He flung himself over the gate and ran on, his legs threatening to buckle under him, his chest heaving, a cold sweat on his forehead.

Two men climbed over the bank by the ash tree and stood there, calling and gesticulating.

He hurled himself forward. 'Jamie! Jamie!' He was shouting in his agony. 'Oh God! Oh God!'

He had a brief glimpse of Monmouth struggling to his feet and standing between his captors, dazed and bewildered, as a dozen more soldiers poured over the bank.

Kit never knew what struck him then, but a trooper, beating the hedgerow, heard his frantic cries. Leaping the bank the man swung up his musket and caught the fugitive a hard blow with the butt on the side of his head.

He went down without a sound into the ditch below.

4

Sir Harry Richmond, crossing the Privy Gardens on his way from the royal apartments, had his head bowed and his eyes on the ground so that he did not notice Lord Bruce approaching until the latter caught his arm.

'Sir Harry! Have you seen his Majesty?'

'Yes.' Richmond saw that Bruce was pale and his eyes red-rimmed. 'Yes, I have seen him. It is all right.'

Bruce let out a deep sigh. 'Thank God at least for that. Did you know——' he paused, turning his head away as if he did not wish Richmond to see his face as he spoke, 'did you know that his Majesty saw the Duke of Monmouth yesterday?'

'Yes,' Richmond said again. He had had enough of this whole wretched business and, loyal as he was to the King, and much as he rejoiced to see his religion in open practice, he did not think after it was all over that he would come to Whitehall again. King James's cruelty in admitting his nephew to his presence seemed to him utterly cold and calculated to extract the last ounce of torment and humiliation from one broken enough, surely, to satisfy even his vengeance. No sovereign ever, by long accepted custom, allowed a condemned man to see his face unless it was for the purpose of receiving a pardon, and for this ungenerous act Richmond thought he was not likely to forgive the King—who had never had any intention of pardoning his nephew—nor my lord Sunderland who laughed off the mere idea that he had ever promised help to Monmouth, and who made sure that the entire court knew how the King's nephew had knelt to beg for life.

He saw now that his companion, too, though he would not admit it, felt the injustice of it. 'Did you see the Duke?' he asked.

Bruce nodded. 'When he was brought up the Privy Stairs.' And then he burst out, 'I wish to God I had not for the look on his face will haunt me till I die.'

He turned and hurried away across the gardens and Richmond watched him sadly, knowing the depth of his love for Monmouth.

Out in the street his carriage was waiting and half an hour later it was rumbling down Tower Hill; he caught a glimpse of sunlight on the river before it turned into the main gate and came to a halt at the Byward Tower. There he presented his permit and presently the Lieutenant himself came out. They were slightly acquainted.

'Good afternoon, Sir Harry. If you will follow me I will take you to the prisoner.'

He led Richmond on through the gateway of the Bloody Tower and round by his own garden to the Beauchamp Tower.

'How is he?' Richmond broke the silence. 'I think you know he is related to me.'

'Yes, indeed, and I am very sorry for the situation he is in. We had a surgeon attend to the wounds on his arm and on his head. Both are healing but I am afraid you will find him very low in spirit.'

Richmond nodded. He had expected that.

At the entrance the Lieutenant paused. 'You will understand, sir, that I am not permitted to do much for my prisoners nor allow them to meet, but at this last hour if Mr. van Wyngarde wishes to send a verbal message'—he glanced up towards the Bell Tower, its round turret rising above the roof of his own lodgings—'I will repeat it faithfully.'

'Thank you,' Richmond said, warmly. He too looked up at the tower, his heart heavy with pity for the man caged there. 'I know my cousin will appreciate that.'

They went out of the sunlight into the darkness of the doorway and up the narrow spiral stair which seemed chill and dank after the warmth outside, setting an even greater chill on Richmond's spirit.

At the top of the stairs they heard voices and walked in upon an unfortunate scene.

'Rumour has it he crawled on his knees to the King,' a rough voice was saying. 'Weeping for his life! I don't know if it is true, mind, but I had it from a fellow who knows one of the King's Guards and he heard——'

The Lieutenant strode into the room. The gaoler, in the act of laying a tray of food on the table, stopped speaking when he saw the Lieutenant and looked distinctly uncomfortable, escaping thankfully when the latter jerked his head angrily towards the door.

Richmond stood aside to let him go and then looked round the room. The only furniture was a narrow truckle bed, a stool and a table; the stone hearth was empty and the stone walls bare.

On the far side, his back to the wall, stood Kit. In one glance Richmond took in the dirty crumpled shepherd's coat, the bandages round his left arm and head, but the shock came from the white pinched face and the expression on it.

'I'll have your gaoler changed for one less garrulous, Mr. van Wyngarde,' the Lieutenant was saying, rather stiffly. 'See, I have brought someone to call upon you.'

He saw his prisoner turn and focus his distraught gaze on the visitor and then went out, leaving them alone together.

For a long time neither spoke. Richmond was so horrified at the change in Kit's appearance that he stood speechless by the door. But at length he crossed the room and took his arm.

'Come, my dear boy, sit down and eat a little. It will do you good.'

Kit sat down obediently but he pushed away the food. 'I cannot eat.' He looked up fleetingly at his cousin. 'It was good of you to come.' Then he lowered his eyes and lapsed into silence.

Richmond stood beside him, perplexed. He had been prepared for much but not for this apathy. He poured some brandy from his flask into a mug, but Kit did not seem to notice it. Yet it was he who broke the silence.

'They have taken away my watch.'

Slightly bewildered, Richmond repeated, 'Your watch?'

'Yes. The one King Charles gave me. I would like it back, at least until . . .' His fingers toyed with the handle of his mug but he did not attempt to drink.

Overwhelmed with compassion for him to whom in utter defeat this small loss now seemed so large, Richmond promised to try to regain it. Kit inclined his head but he said nothing further and Richmond wondered what he could say to rouse him, for rouse him he must if Kit was to understand fully what he had come here to tell him. Inadvertently he said the very thing that was needed.

'The Duke has been asking after you. He was concerned about that wound on your head.' He saw Kit's face quiver and come alive again.

'I would have taken worse than that to save him. I would to God I had died before I let them take him. Every night I dream I am running up that field, not able to reach him in time. . . .' He clasped his hands together to still their trembling. Then he added, almost irrelevantly, 'He caught a cold lying in that cursed ditch.'

He broke off again, his hands pressed to his mouth. He could not tell Richmond of that nightmare drive to London which had followed their capture—the three of them, Monmouth, Grey and himself, travelling in a coach with Lord Lumley whose troops had taken them and who escorted them to London. Their captor occupied the first part of the journey in telling them of the liquidation of their army and that Colonel Kirke, a man renowned for his cruelty, was in charge of searching out the rebels that had fled. Grey, who had been taken the day before, seemed undiminished and did not share the horror that Monmouth and Kit suffered while thinking of their fleeing, defeated soldiers at the mercy of Kirke's 'Lambs'. He talked cheerfully to Lumley of horses and dogs and sport.

Kit had watched him with incredulity. Even loathing Grey as he did he could not believe what looked obvious—that Grey had allowed himself to be taken, and, in return for a promise of his own safety, had betrayed their whereabouts. Could even Grey do such a thing? Yet if he had not why should he be so unconcerned?

Once Monmouth asked for a fresh kerchief because his cold was so heavy and Grey remarked blandly that no doubt his uncle would soon find a cure for that. His callousness was more than Kit felt called upon to bear. He had flung himself at Grey, his fingers at the latter's throat. Lumley called the guards and for the rest of the journey Kit had been forced to ride outside the carriage, his arms pinioned and his feet tied beneath the horse's belly, cursing himself that he had forfeited by his temper the last precious hours when he might be with Monmouth. Nothing could have added more to the anguish of that journey.

He must not think of it. Slowly he turned his head and looked fully at Richmond, seeing for the first time some of his own wretchedness communicated there.

'I'm sorry the gaoler told you what he did,' Richmond said. 'It was not wholly true. The Duke did indeed kneel to the King to ask for life but so would any man as broken and exhausted as he was.'

'He did it for her.' He had thought often of Henrietta these last few days. Then, realizing what Richmond had said, hope rose—so suddenly that a flush filled his face. 'But if the King'—he brought out the word with difficulty—'if the King saw him then surely it was to save him from——'

'No,' Richmond interrupted. He could not look at Kit. 'No.'

Kit felt himself trembling again and held on to the edge of the table to steady himself. 'You mean that he—Great God, no one else could have done so damnable a thing!'

Richmond sat down on the edge of the bed. 'We'll not talk of that. But I can tell you that whatever the Duke has suffered he has overcome now. The Lieutenant says that since he has known there is no hope he has come into a calm and fearless frame of mind that has astonished everyone who has seen him.'

'Thank God.' Kit put a hand over his eyes but, after a moment, removed it and seized his cousin's arm in a fierce grip. 'When—when is it to be?'

'Tomorrow, before noon.'

A shudder, uncontrollable, ran through his body but he did not move from his seat. 'And when for me? I would have preferred the axe but I suppose as a commoner I cannot hope for other than Tyburn tree.'

Richmond winced at the indifference to life and leaned forward earnestly. 'You are not to die. That is what I have come to tell you.' He saw only stunned disbelief and went on: 'It is true. Your life is to be spared, for which I thank God.'

Watching the face opposite as the meaning of his words penetrated the benumbed brain he saw a strange expression follow. It was not relief, and certainly not thankfulness, but rather fear as if something wholly undesired had now to be faced.

Richmond was profoundly shocked. 'Do you understand what I am saying?' he asked gently. 'King James has been merciful to you. . . .'

At the word 'merciful' Kit sat up, stiff with suppressed emotion. 'He—merciful to me? You must be deluded. James of York knows

I hate him and he hates me for what I am to—my King. He warned me once that he would not spare me when King Charles was dead.'

'Kit, I beg you—think what you are saying.'

'What do you want me to say? I expected death and no one can do worse to me. I don't want mercy.'

'You have it,' Richmond said deliberately, 'whether you want it or not.'

'Why should he spare me? He knows I will never acknowledge him King.'

'Perhaps. Nevertheless he has commanded me to tell you that you are to be released tomorrow afternoon on condition that you are gone from the country within twenty-four hours. There is also'—he hesitated—'a fine of ten thousand pounds.'

Kit leaned his head on one hand and began to laugh, a helpless laughter without amusement. 'Trust York to make the most of it —but I'll not pay such a sum. Even if I would I haven't got it.'

'I have paid two-thirds of it, which was as much as I could lay hands on,' Richmond said in a low voice, 'and his Majesty has graciously allowed you three months to raise the rest, in Holland or wherever you choose to go. I have myself offered surety for your promise to do so.'

Kit raised his head and looked across at his cousin. He saw how lined his face had become and how tired he looked.

'No,' he said sharply, 'I'll not have that. I could never repay such a debt. And anyway—I do not wish to go. For twenty-four years I have served King Charles and then King Monmouth. I have been very happy. Now there is nothing left and I would rather die with my sovereign lord.'

'The choice is not yours, and even if it were—life is not so mean a thing it can be thrown away lightly.'

'Lightly! What should I do with my life, then?'

'Is there not someone in Holland who is waiting for your return?'

Kit jerked his head up. 'What can you know of that?'

'Elizabeth wrote to me and told me what had passed between you. She wanted me to let her know if things went badly for you. Go back to her, my boy, and together you will find that life is still worth something.'

Kit thought of the little house at Gouda, of the evening before he had left, of the feel of her arms about his neck. What was it she had said? 'I would rather have half of you than nothing at all.' But now it would have to be nothing.

'I can't,' he said almost inaudibly. 'Everything I had went into our venture. It would be better for her if I were to end it here.'

'She would not think so.'

Kit felt an inexplicable revulsion rise in him. 'I cannot think of that now.' His head was beginning to ache, the wound where the musket-butt had split open his temple throbbing unbearably, but there was something he must resolve, something he had to understand while he could still think clearly. 'You have not told me why I am not to die. There cannot be any doubt of my complicity.'

Richmond got up again, too restless to stay still. Outside he could hear the relief guard marching across the courtyard and it was growing cooler, for the sun had nearly set. 'I asked his Majesty for your life and he yielded to my plea.'

Kit watched him as he walked to the window. 'There are always those to plead for the condemned,' he pointed out. 'There must have been some further reason.' And, as Richmond did not answer, he went on: 'I thought so. I think I am entitled to know it, sir.'

It seemed a long time before Richmond spoke. 'There is a reason, yes, and you shall know it. To make it clear I shall have to tell you an old story, one which started before you were born. But first, tell me, did it ever occur to you that you are not very like the van Wyngardes who usually run so true to form?'

It was so unexpected a question that Kit hesitated from sheer astonishment. 'How strange that you should ask that. My aunt Sophia once said—but what connection can it have with my pardon?'

'I will tell you, but first tell me what your aunt said.'

Beyond caring now about that twelve-year-old hurt, he explained as briefly as he could. And then, raising his head, he saw the expression on Richmond's face.

'You know! Great God, you know!' He half rose but as a sudden faintness turned him giddy he sank back again.

Richmond made him drink some brandy. 'Yes,' he said quietly. 'I have always known.'

The spirit, taken on an empty stomach, ran through Kit like fire. 'Tell me,' he said hoarsely, 'for God's sake, *tell me*.'

Richmond sat down again. 'First of all I must have your solemn word that you will never divulge one word of what I am about to reveal.'

'I swear it.' If Richmond wanted his promise he should have it, but he wished he would get on with it.

'It began a long time ago, during the civil wars. Do you remember I once told you how Tolbrooke was besieged? What I did not tell you was that during that siege, apart from my own household and my troops, two other people were in the house—your mother and our cousin, Hendrik van Wyngarde. He had come over, as young men will, to try his fighting skill in a war not his own.'

Richmond was finding the telling of this story even harder than he had expected, and he began to pace about the cell. 'Well, the news of our predicament reached Prince Rupert's ears. He was not many miles away with his cavalry and as soon as he heard of our danger he set off at once to relieve us.' He smiled. 'You know what sort of fighting man his Highness was! He stormed up the drive like an avenging fury and drove out the Roundheads. He stayed with us while we re-fortified the house. They were'—he paused— 'a few days of snatched pleasure in the midst of war. Hendrik, Margaret, myself, Rupert and his three officers supped and danced each night as if there were no war outside the walls. It was foolish perhaps and created a situation where men think a night's happiness worth the next day's sorrow. Women, too . . .'

Kit looked up. He was beginning, by some sixth sense, to guess where this story was leading. 'Go on,' he said, tensely.

'After four days Rupert rode off and I was ordered to hold the house until we had certain news that the Parliament soldiers were cleared from the district. As it happened, some six weeks later we had very different news. A report reached us that Rupert had been killed and his men slain or captured.' Richmond paused again. His face was grey in the shadowed light. 'Your mother nearly went out of her mind with grief. By that time she had told me she was pregnant and I thought it best to send her away to Holland while it was still possible, to our Dutch cousins. Hendrik offered to take her, and on the way, in Paris, she married him.'

Kit put a hand to his head. 'Then what—what am I to understand from that?'

There was a moment of quiet in the cell, that curious moment that precedes revelation. Richmond's voice, when he spoke, was so low that it barely broke the stillness.

'That your father, Kit, was his Highness Prince Rupert.'

There was no stillness any more. The room swayed about him. Kit felt the colour drain from his face and then flood painfully back.

'Rupert? *Rupert?* It's not possible.'

'It is true.'

He got up and went blindly to the window. He could not hold this knowledge, could not accept it. Yet Richmond would not deceive him, not over a thing like this.

And then memories of Rupert rushed upon him: Rupert's height and strength, his bark of laughter, his swift anger, his austerity that was often softened by unexpected acts of kindness, his justice and above all his integrity. This man, this Prince, Rupert whom he had served and grown to love, had been his father!

He put both hands before his face. What matter if he were a bastard? He had had more than twelve years to get used to the idea—it was the ignorance of his paternity that had so galled him. Now he knew, and the knowledge more than compensated for all he had endured before. If only he had known before, if only Rupert had told him, what happiness might they not have had together? Yet Rupert had wanted to tell him something before he died. Could it have been this? He was sure of it now.

Richmond's voice, behind him, broke the silence. 'Will you hear the rest?'

He did not turn round. This moment was too intimate to share, even with Richmond, but he said, 'Yes, yes, go on.'

'By then the war was nearly over. The Roundheads had often put out the story that they had taken Rupert, and I learned soon enough that once again rumour lied and Rupert was alive. As you can imagine I was shaken to think what this would mean to your poor mother, but it was too late to do anything about it and anyway I had my hands full. The King's forces were defeated at Naseby, and Tolbrooke besieged again. As you know I surrendered it to General Fairfax and he granted us safe passage to any place of our choosing. I took my men to Hereford, to the King, but there I was wounded in a skirmish and by the time I was on my feet again Oxford was surrendered and the King in the hands of his enemies.'

Richmond's voice reflected the strain he was under, but he forced himself to go on. 'As soon as I could I went to Holland and saw Hendrik. He was a good man, Kit. He had known, when they left me, of Margaret's condition, and thinking Rupert dead married her to save her good name and give one to her child. You were not three when she died and he was determined to do all he could for you. You see, he loved your mother and he loved you as his own son—perhaps all the more because, in the light of what you told me, he must have known he would have none.'

Kit rested his head against the stone wall. 'And what of—my father?'

'He went to sea for a long while and I did not see him again until King Charles was restored. I was an exile, without money, without much hope, and it was not possible for me to get in touch with him before. By this time Hendrik was dead and the truth died with him.

I did not speak—I had promised both him and your mother never to do so—but as soon as Rupert came to England I told him the whole story.'

Richmond sat down by the table. 'I think he loved your mother deeply for those few brief days, and he was very distressed to learn of the suffering he had caused her. Much as he would have liked to acknowledge you, he said he would not sully her name by doing so, nor bring scandal on the Dutch family among whom you were growing up.

You may think we cheated the van Wyngardes by keeping the truth from them, but we both believed it would hurt them more to know it. Nevertheless with Hendrik dead, the Prince wanted to do what he could for you and that was why I came to fetch you.'

Kit swung round. 'But why did he not tell me? Once Hendrik and my mother were dead . . .'

'Don't you understand? We could not know you were to have any inkling that you were not a van Wyngarde. The Prince wanted you to be free to live your own life.'

'But never to tell me, never to——' Kit broke off. He remembered, sharply, that he had done the same thing. He had let Cathy go, had not tried to find her, nor acknowledge his child that he longed to see, because he thought that child would be better off in a lowly but legitimate home. What right had he, with his past, to reproach Rupert? There was indeed no reproach in him, only a deep affection, a profound relief that doubt was gone for ever.

Richmond's voice broke into his thoughts. 'Kit, tell me—tell me you do not hate me for keeping this secret from you, nor your father for doing what he believed to be right.'

'Hate you?' Kit came across the room and sat down beside Richmond on the bed. For a moment the present, the dark shadow that hung over him, was forgotten. 'Hate you for bringing me to England and all that I have loved here? How could I? And I cannot begin to tell you what it means to me to know the truth at last. As for my father——' he hesitated, unable to put what he felt into plain words, 'I think you must know what he was to me. Now—even more.'

Richmond gave a sigh of relief. 'Thank God. You are very like him, Kit.'

'Am I? I should not have thought so.'

'You have your mother's fair colouring, but look in the mirror and you will see your father's obstinate chin. You have his temperament too. To almost everything I have watched you react as a son of Rupert might. At times it was almost uncanny. From him you get your love of soldiering, your preference for the simple life, your single-mindedness, even'—Richmond smiled a little—'your temper! I think, particularly towards the end of his life, he was very proud of you.'

Kit leaned against the wall. He was beginning to grasp this new knowledge, to be glad of it, but Richmond's last words brought him back to his situation.

'I am pleased to think I gave him pleasure, but I think I must thank God he is not alive to see where I am today.'

'He would have understood why you did all that you did,' Richmond answered, gently. 'He was glad of your friendship for Monmouth because he always felt King Charles raised his son too high for his own good. Monmouth was one of the reasons why he never spoke concerning you. And now you owe him your life.'

'My life? I don't understand.'

'It is because you are his son that King James is letting you go. He thought more highly of his cousin Rupert than of any man alive and it is for Rupert's sake that he is sparing you. Perhaps a little, too, because you are very dear to me and I am of his faith and loyal to him. It is nobly generous of him, Kit.'

Kit said nothing. He could not, even in return for his life, be grateful to King James, nor think him generous.

The present was back with him now, bearing down upon him. 'If I must go'—he could hardly bring out the words. 'May I not go early tomorrow, before——'

'I'm afraid not. The streets will be impassable.'

'The streets——' Kit clasped his arms tightly across his chest, for he was trembling again. 'Do you—do you remember Lord Russell and how he died? I keep thinking of him and how . . .'

Richmond fetched the brandy. 'Take some more of this. It will steady you.' He held it out and watched Kit drink, his hands shaking so that the mug clattered against his teeth.

'Thank you,' he said, at length. 'I am all right now. The worst part is not being able to see him.'

'I know. But the Lieutenant is an acquaintance of mine and he has said he will take the Duke a verbal message if you wish it.'

Kit looked round the room, his mind frantically searching for words to express a lifetime shared, companionship, trust, endeavour, all the long years that had gone before.

'Oh God, what can I say?' he muttered, half to himself, and then the words came, summoned by his desperate need.

'Tell him—tell him I would rather not have lived than not have been his friend.'

    ·   ·   ·   ·   ·

After Richmond had gone he sat still and sleepless by the window. He could no longer think clearly. His mind was too stunned by all that Richmond had told him—yet coming when it did it made less impact than it might otherwise have done.

Now there was nothing but the morning before him and beyond it a timeless abyss without meaning. It crept on inexorably while he waited—his mind, his body, all his being poised in one sensation of waiting. It had neither past nor future, but held him in a prison stronger than the stone walls that surrounded him.

But during the long night odd thoughts came to him; thoughts of his father and his mother—the father he had known and yet not known, and the mother he could not remember. He thought of their brief love, that must have been overwhelming to sweep the rock-like Rupert off his feet. But he had been young then, a great soldier with half England at his feet. Dimly, he sensed that when this night was over he would think much of his father, see him anew in the light of this discovered relationship.

It was strange that the bend sinister should lie across his life as it had lain so long over Monmouth's—and with sudden curious joy he realized that Stuart blood flowed through his veins as it did through Monmouth's. He wished he could tell Jamie—but Jamie would soon be where there was nothing hidden.

He dropped his head into his hands. He could not, must not, think of that; and, to turn his mind from it, tried to conjure up the past. It seemed, in the darkness of this tortured night, to be more real than anything else.

He remembered going to Paris with Monmouth and watching him dance with Minette, both of them fully endowed with Stuart grace, he remembered Monmouth being installed as Captain of the King's Guard, riding a magnificent horse, magnificent himself. He remembered a hundred light-hearted evenings spent with Bab and Rochester, Mark and Jack Churchill, Tom Bruce and Kit Monk. He remembered Monmouth dancing with Henrietta Wentworth in the Calisto ballet hardly aware of her existence; Monmouth at Toddington aware of little else; Monmouth at the Cockpit, at Whitehall, Soho Square, Hedge Lane. He did not think of the political machinations that had swamped them of late years. He did not want to remember Monmouth torn by his desire to do right, persuaded by unscrupulous men into mistaken actions, influenced by those who sought only to use him and lacking the necessary ruthlessness to be their master. He thought instead of a Christmas at Saxmundhan; a horse-race at Wallasey that Monmouth had won; a banquet at Longleat with Tom-o'ten-thousand. Surely it could not be ending tomorrow with no more than half their lives lived?

Drained at last of emotion, bereft of thought, incapable even of prayer, he still sat on by the window. Slowly the stars faded and the sunrise came in full summer glory, flooding the east with colour. But the weather was breaking up and heavy rain-clouds scudded up from the west until the sky was overcast.

Down in the courtyard men began to hurry about their business, soldiers going to and fro, and on a wall below a cat stretched and began to wash itself.

A guard brought his breakfast. It was a different man from the

one the Lieutenant had dismissed last night, but he scarcely noticed
him, merely telling him to take the food away.

'Och, sir,' a soft Scots voice said. 'Will ye no' tak a sup o'
coffee. It will hearten ye.'

Kit turned and saw that the man was one who had once served
in the Dragoons at Bothwell Bridge. It was oddly comforting to
see a familiar face. 'Give me the coffee then, but take the rest
away.'

The man brought him the mug and then, picking up the tray,
went to the door where he stood shifting uncertainly from one foot
to the other.

'I'm terrible sorry,' he said gruffly and then, opening the door,
added: 'They'll be coming by yon window.'

The door closed behind him, leaving Kit staring at it as the full
meaning of his words dawned.

He would see Monmouth again—he would see him once more
as he passed to his death.

Hastily he took the mug, gulping down the hot coffee. It put a
little warmth into him, a little strength into his limbs. He went to
sit again by the window.

Shortly before ten o'clock a strong guard was drawn up below
by the Lieutenant's garden, a line of steel to ensure that death was
not cheated. Then from a door across the garden the Lieutenant
emerged, followed by several clergy and a small posse of soldiers
bringing up the rear. It took a few seconds for Kit to realize that the
tall man walking in their midst was Monmouth.

The escort came on steadily up the slope and Kit, his fingers
twisted round the bars of his window, saw Monmouth walking
with them as unconcernedly as if among friends. He was wearing
a grey suit with black trimmings and a richly curled periwig; on
this he had set a black hat at the Monmouth cock and trimmed
with green ribbon. As he walked he turned once and spoke to Dr.
Tenison, his parish priest from St. Martin-in-the-Fields, whom he
had requested to have with him.

And Kit, watching from his window, saw that this was indeed
not the Monmouth from whose side he had been taken two days
ago, this was not the broken tormented man with whom he had
fled through the New Forest. This was the old Monmouth: handsome, debonair, grave yet smiling a little. He looked calm and
strangely happy.

Kit sat as if turned to stone. Surely he would look up, must look up. But Monmouth was walking with his eyes fixed straight ahead and there were only about a dozen yards to go before he reached the waiting coach.

Kit clutched at the bars. Dear God, he must look up, he must!

And then, as if in answer to that desperate prayer, Monmouth turned his head and glanced at the windows above him. He saw Kit instantly and stopped. For a long moment they looked at each other. Then Monmouth smiled—his familiar smile full of warmth and courage and affection—and in that instant all that Kit had ever done or suffered for him was repaid in full.

Before he realized what was happening, the procession had moved on and Monmouth disappeared into the coach. A moment later it was driven away and Kit slid to his knees by the window, still gripping the bars, certain somewhere in his anguish that if he let go he would also lose command of himself.

Then—how long after he did not know—a faint sound reached him, growing gradually louder until at last he recognized it for the once-familiar cry from a thousand London throats: 'A Monmouth! A Monmouth!' Not as it had once been cried, but with a sad, lingering note.

Then silence fell, a silence that lasted more than an hour, though he had no sensation of time, until at length another sound rose. And he knew it to be, unmistakably, the long slow groan of those same thousands.

He got to his feet and stood swaying. Consciousness, mercifully, was leaving him now. He made no effort to cling to it, but slid thankfully into darkness.

Outside the rain began to fall heavily.

.   .   .   .   .   .

He came back to consciousness, a long while after, to find Richmond bending over him and holding a flask of brandy to his lips. With the revitalizing spirit memory came back, sharply, and with memory the full flood-tide of grief.

Richmond sat down on the bed, his arm about Kit's shoulders, his own hand holding the brandy flask none too steadily.

'Come, drink this.'

Gradually the racking sobs quietened, the trembling ceased, and Kit sat up, drawing long, gasping breaths.

'Thank you. I am sorry. I think I have been mad, or in hell, these last hours.'

'I know,' his cousin answered compassionately. 'I've brought you some clean clothes. Would you like to change before we leave?'

Kit nodded and, getting dazedly to his feet, went over to the basin and washed the tears from his face. With that one shattering breakdown the tension had been released and now he felt only overwhelming weariness. And that a part of his life was over.

He changed, throwing off the shepherd's coat and blessedly aware of the comfort of fresh linen. It made him feel better to be wearing one of his own coats again. It was dark green, his favourite colour, and he remembered having left it at Richmond's town house.

'I don't know what happened to my baggage,' he said, as he slid his feet into the long boots Richmond had brought. 'I suppose it provided plunder for one of Kirke's "Lambs". There is no Jerry to care for my possessions now,' he added sadly. 'God knows what happened to him, poor fellow.'

Richmond smiled. 'I've some good news for you. Jerry is safe.' He saw a spark of warmth come into the pale face.

'Thank God. Where is he?'

'Outside in the carriage. I found him hiding in my garden last night. He escaped from Sedgemoor and made his way here when he learned you and the Duke were taken. I've managed to get the necessary permit for him to go with you.'

Kit gave a tired sigh. 'He ought not to come. I shall be a poor man and have to live by my sword.' But there was comfort in the thought that Jerry would take from him all the wearisome need to cope with the necessities of life.

When he had finished his toilet Richmond said, 'I've something for you,' and brought from his pocket the familiar enamelled watch.

Kit took it and looked at it lying in his palm, the yellow sprigs gay against the blue background. He remembered the day the King had given it to him—it seemed in another life—and his hand closed over it. It was something left to keep. He wondered what had happened to Eliza's little green flag in which it had been wrapped—poor Eliza, after all her careful work it was lost, as so much else was lost.

Richmond spoke again. 'And I have a gift for you.' He had purposely returned the watch first. 'The Duke sent you this—with his love.'

It was a small leather case, fitted with several combs and bearing Monmouth's arms, and Kit recognized it at once. He himself had given it to the Duke, years ago, and Monmouth had always carried it. That he had sent it back now was balm, the first easing of insupportable grief. His fingers gripped it convulsively and then, without another word, he put it into his pocket with the watch.

Richmond picked up his hat. 'There is one more thing. Would you—would you like to see him? I have the necessary permit.'

Kit caught his breath, but he had himself well in hand again. 'Is he—as he was?'

'Yes. There is nothing you need fear to see.'

They went out together, Kit turning his back thankfully on the cell that had seen his near-madness. Outside the air was cool and fresh, for the rain had cleared away the dust and heat of the last few days. He drew deep breaths of it and looking up saw that the rain-clouds had gone. It would be a clear starlit evening. He remembered walking once with Monmouth under the stars at Tolbrooke, when they were little more than boys, and Monmouth had pointed out the Great Bear.

But he must not remember, not think of these things—one day perhaps he would be able to think of them, cherish them, but not yet.

Up a staircase and out on to a narrow battlement—he found himself walking along it quite calmly to a small door that led into the circular room at the top of the Bell Tower. There was a man on guard there—though none was needed now. He glanced at Richmond's paper and opened the door, but Richmond stood back and Kit, after only a moment's hesitation, entered alone, the door closing behind him.

There was nothing inside but the long bier in the centre, covered with a black velvet pall. Across the foot of it fell a shaft of the late afternoon sunlight.

Monmouth lay with his head on a pillow, a small piece of white lawn drawn up close under his chin. When Kit realized what this implied the room went black about him and he thought he would faint. But then he saw that he need not have feared to come for the Duke looked only as if he was gently sleeping. His eyes were half closed, the heavy lids only partially drawn down and the finely shaped lips resting naturally together. There was nothing to indicate suffering, little to indicate death.

The dizziness passed. He came slowly forward and knelt, his hands folded on the pall.

They were beaten, he and Jamie. They had been born nameless into a world where names counted, and it had taken from them even what they had. Yet in death Monmouth had found a vindication; for his face, feature by feature, so resembled that of his grandfather, the Martyr King, that no one could doubt any longer that he was a Stuart. He might be a king, as Kit truly believed him, or a king's bastard as the world thought, but it was no longer important.

If they had succeeded, if Monmouth had been at Whitehall instead of here in this lonely, high-arched cell, would he have been happy? Even had Kit ever believed it, he knew now he would not, for there would have been no place Monmouth would have deemed fitting for Henrietta Wentworth and he would never again have been happy away from her.

So for her, love remained and for Kit, friendship. Monmouth had only gone ahead of them, untouched by age, deeply loved by all who knew him and worshipped by his people in the west, who had faced death for and with him, and who thought the sacrifice worth while.

With no conscious effort on his part, comfort came to Kit then. To be here alone with Jamie was all that was needed, for the manner of his dying, his courage and his faith, verified by that quiet peace on his face, washed away all past evil, all failure, all sin and weakness and folly.

He remembered how he had prayed in St. Mary's church in Bridgwater that the strain and misery might be taken from Monmouth's face. God had answered that prayer, and there was no need for anything but gratitude that Jamie had borne his suffering and was now come out of it.

He heard the door open behind him and Richmond's voice:

'It is late, Kit. We must go if we are to reach Harwich by noon tomorrow. Are you ready to leave?'

He rose from his knees and, bending forward, kissed the cold forehead, taking one long last look at the still face.

'Yes,' he answered. 'I am ready.'

Holland—July, 1685

KIT slid his head back against the window-frame and a long shuddering sigh escaped him. It was as though all his former life had passed before him so vividly that he came back to this little turret room with an effort.

Dusk had fallen now and there was a scent of honeysuckle in the air; in the garden below roses were in full bloom and there was a patch of marigolds that seemed to glow in the evening light. Above him the first star hung low in the sky and the tranquil beauty of the night moved him the more because he had thought he was beyond response to anything.

He had clung, on the journey from England, to the calm that had entered his soul as he knelt by Monmouth's bier, but it was inevitable that grief should return. He had been prepared for that, and for loneliness, yet, in the face of the utter and solitary desolation that confronted him now, his courage wavered.

He dared not think of what was happening in England, of the butchery in the west, of the fate of all his friends. Only Grey, he thought, with the old bitterness, was likely to escape the net and worm himself back into favour—yet not even he, by the wildest stretch of the imagination, could guess at the truth, that his lordship would be dancing again at Whitehall before Christmas.

For the rest of them it was death, transportation or exile, and for himself an austere and loveless service in the army of the Netherlands.

This morning he had attended the Prince of Orange at the palace and asked for a place in his army.

William had given him one of his usual long, discomposing stares, betraying nothing of his own feelings concerning the failure of his cousin Monmouth's expedition.

'You have suffered, van Wyngarde,' he said, at last. 'Well, that breeds better men than mere ease, and whatever misunderstanding there was between us is in the past. You shall have a commission in my own regiment.'

Kit was grateful—though William, besides needing experienced officers, was probably only too glad to annoy his father-in-law by employing a man James had banished. Still, whatever the reason, he had what he wanted and he was grateful, but he wondered why he alone of so many remained to live on with a bitter longing for the old, remembered faces.

The aching loss, the nightmare knowledge he now had of the bungling of Monmouth's dying, all had to be borne; had to be lived with day and night—but he did not know how long such a life would be tenable and he wished, not for the first time, that he had followed that instinctive urge and stayed to die on Sedgemoor.

There was only one refuge from such thoughts and bowing his head he began to pray for Monmouth's soul in the golden words of Jeremy Taylor, words that the Duke himself had loved.

'. . . gather him to his fathers . . . grant he may never sleep in death eternal but have his part in the first resurrection . . . receive his soul returning to Thee.'

It was the last, the only thing he could do for him.

Presently in the silence he heard the sound of hooves on the cobbles below, and guessed it was Jerry returning, but he stayed a moment longer, taking a last look at the garden and the newly risen moon. How was it that beauty could be so painful?

Then he heard steps outside and the door opened.

'I'm coming, Jerry,' he said, wearily, and turned—to see Elizabeth standing before him.

Her familiar long blue cloak hung from the shoulders of her riding-dress and her cheeks were flushed as if she had ridden hard.

He could not move. Her arrival was so unexpected that he could not think what to say. He had planned to see her when he had schooled himself into a state of mind where he could tell her that she must not marry a homeless, nameless, penniless man. He was burned out, marked by all that he had endured and no fit bridegroom for a young and lovely girl, but before he could speak she had fallen on her knees beside him and put her arms about him.

'You have come back,' she was repeating, over and over again, half-crying. 'You have come back to me.' She put her lips to his forehead. 'But you have been hurt. Oh, my dear, what have they done to you?'

He had stiffened instinctively. 'You—you heard what happened?'

'Yesterday. General Bentinck rode out to tell us.' She gave an involuntary shudder. 'I thought I should never see you again.'

'And Henrietta? How has she borne it?'

'With courage; indeed I never knew anyone so brave. But she is very ill, she was ill long before you left, only she would not let the Duke know it. She is to go home soon and I do not think she will stay long behind him.'

'She is fortunate,' he said, very low. Then, resolutely, he drew back a little. 'Elizabeth, I wish you had not come.'

She knelt without moving at his feet. 'Why do you wish that?'

He stared beyond her into the shadows, not daring to look at her face in the moonlight, for there was that in it for which his deepest need cried out.

'I can't marry you,' he said harshly. 'You must go home with Henrietta.'

Still she did not move. 'Why cannot you marry me?'

'Don't you understand? I have nothing left. I am penniless and in debt. I don't even own the name I bear.'

'I know all that,' she broke in gently. 'Did you think I should mind?'

'You know?' He turned back to her in astonishment. 'How can you know?'

'Sir Harry wrote to me, and Jeremy brought me the letter not an hour since. Sir Harry knew you would say all this, that you would make out the blackest case for yourself, and he thought I should understand beforehand. He told me your father was an honourable man, a soldier in the civil wars, and only unfortunate circumstances led to your birth out of wedlock.'

'How it came about does not alter the fact. Don't you see, child? Now—I am not what I was. You cannot marry a man without a name, without substance.'

'As to that, take what name you will and I shall be proud to share it. And I have a little money so between us we shall manage.'

'No.' He twisted his head restlessly. Why would she not accept that it was impossible and so take temptation from him? 'You must go home.'

She looked up at him, a faint smile in her eyes. 'You told me once that I would understand one day what love was and what men and women would do for it. Now that I know, you must not blame me if I will not let it go.'

'Elizabeth! For God's sake——' He did not think he could bear much more of this.

She reached up and took both his hands in hers. 'I am not going to leave you. You cannot make me go unless you can tell me that you do not need me now—as you never did before. Can you say that?'

He tried to speak, tried to say the words that would send her from him, but the denial would not come. He could only sit staring at her in stricken silence.

'Then we will talk no more of my going.' But she had known as soon as she entered the room that this was not the man who asked her to wed him only a few short weeks ago. He was utterly changed, and this Kit would need her love far more than the other. It would be a strange, sad marriage at first, perhaps, but she knew that love, born of his need, would come and with it a release from sorrow, and in the end happiness.

She held his hands tightly against her breast and said in a low voice: 'Do you think I don't know what hell you have endured? But I will make you well again. My dear, my love, I will make you well again.'

For one moment longer he held back. But somewhere at the back of his tired mind he sensed a ragged gleam of hope, the first faint indication that life might, after all, hold something for him.

'Elizabeth,' he said, 'Elizabeth . . .' and reached out for her, not with his prisoned hands but with all that he was. For if there was an ending, if there was death, there must also be a beginning again, a resurrection.

Releasing his hands, he took her face between them. In the moonlight he saw there were tears in her eyes but no more fear.